MW01206156

MURDER
AT
FIRST LIGHT

---

a Modern Midwife Mystery

Christine Knapp

To Edward Thomas
Tá tú stardust, tá tú órga

To Beth
Is tusa an spéir a choinníonn na réaltai

"Midwives know that birth is not only about making babies. Birth is about making mothers—strong, competent, capable mothers who trust themselves and know their inner strength."
—Barbara Roth Katzman

CHAPTER ONE

Midwife means with woman.

Ah, September! It's the time of year when the days are still long and the sun still shines brightly, but the tourists are gone, the school buses are rolling, and the seaside town of Langford itself seems to let out a comfortable sigh.

I felt a sense of nervous anticipation, however, as I took in both the harbor and the hospital grounds. I also was going back to school. A few months ago, I had agreed to a dual appointment between Rosemont College, a small, highly-ranked institution with an excellent nursing program, and Creighton Memorial. I would continue as a midwife at the hospital for half the week, and then teach the obstetrics module to the nursing students at Rosemont and provide gynecological care to the faculty and staff the rest of the week. How would this work out? Was I up to the challenge? Would I regret being the pioneer for this new partnership between the hospital and the college?

Looking at my watch, I realized I better focus solely on my midwife role today and get a move on.

As I picked up my pace from the staff parking lot to the main entrance, I saw a red minivan with flashing lights speed towards the emergency entrance. As it passed, I realized that the driver was gesturing frantically to me.

Martin! The driver was Martin Long, whose wife Sienna was a patient in the midwifery practice. What was going on?

I ran to catch up, accidentally dropping my large burgundy tote along the way. From the corner of my eye, I spied my apple rolling down the drive. Oh well, so much for a healthy snack.

I caught up to the minivan, which Martin had already parked outside the ED, leaving the driver's door open and the ignition running. Since I didn't see him anywhere, I assumed Martin had disappeared beyond the hospital's revolving glass doors, looking for help. Sliding open the van's back door, I saw a wild-eyed Sienna in a semi-sitting position, desperately clutching at the back seat.

"He's coming!" she said through gritted teeth.

Hoping Martin had put the van in *park*, I climbed in. I recalled as much as I could about Sienna's history as I squeezed into the back seat, trying to find room for both of us. I knew this was her second baby and that she was full-term, but that was about it. Her long, curly black hair was clipped on top of her head, and she wore a blue gingham cotton nightgown along with what looked like Martin's well-worn hiking boots.

"Maeve, help me," she gasped.

"I got you, Sienna," I said in what I hoped was a calm, reassuring tone. At the same time, I pulled a rolled-up yellow beach towel from the rear seat and placed it under her.

"Okay, Sienna, blow out now, try not to push. I can see your baby's hair."

"I have to push!"

As was typical with many precipitous births, Sienna was reacting to her body's cues and the sensations that were directing her to have her baby now! I better be ready.

Guiding the baby's head as it rapidly emerged, I helped the baby be born. Suddenly, the back seat was full of a crying newborn, copious amounts of amniotic fluid, Sienna, and me.

I settled the little boy on Sienna's chest and, pulling off my navy cardigan, covered them both.

"My beautiful Roman," Sienna cried. "Is he okay, Maeve?"

"He looks and sounds wonderful."

As I said this, I saw Sienna's umbilical cord lengthen, indicating that her afterbirth had separated.

"Sienna, I'm going to deliver your placenta."

"Do I need to do anything?" she asked distractedly while stroking Roman's face. Now that the baby was here, her attention was on him, not herself.

"No. Just relax, Sienna. You'll feel the afterbirth passing," I responded, holding the umbilical cord taut.

I needed just one thing. Looking about, I spotted a very old, dented metal beach pail on the floor. It was perfect. As the placenta gently slipped out, I placed it in the makeshift container.

"Hurry, hurry," I heard Martin bellow as he led a group of Creighton Memorial's first-rate emergency department staff to the van.

One of the ED attendings, who was the first to reach us, said, "Looks like they called the midwife already." As she spoke, she handed me tools to clamp and cut the umbilical cord.

"You have a lovely little boy, Martin," I said, giving him a wide smile to hopefully allay his fears.

"Wow, oh wow," was all he could say initially. Then, once he awkwardly maneuvered his lanky frame to lean over the front seat, he broke into a wide grin as he gazed at Sienna and Roman. A look of pure relief crossed his face and he added, "Thank goodness I got us here in time."

"Let's move Sienna and Roman to a more comfortable place so you can see them," I said.

I picked up Roman, still wrapped in my sweater, and wiggled out of the car. MJ, one of the seasoned emergency room RNs, took the baby from me. She exchanged my cardigan for a hospital-issue baby blanket and placed Roman in a wheeled bassinet. MJ eyed me as she held up my heavily soiled garment in her gloved hands and said, "I saw this sweater on the Gap site, but I never really thought of wearing it for backseat births. You are a trendsetter."

"Funny woman," I laughed. Looking around, though, I realized that I was indeed leaving a mess in my wake.

"Use our staff lounge to clean up. I'll get you some scrubs. Is that your tote on the curb?" she asked, gesturing towards my now deflated bag.

"Yes, I dropped it when I saw the car pull in."

MJ placed a warm hospital blanket around my shoulders. "Go ahead. I'll get everything for you."

I watched the team settle Sienna on a stretcher and then turned to get myself together.

"Hey, Maeve," MJ called out. I whirled around. She gave me a thumbs-up as she grinned widely.

I smiled and nodded my thanks as I made my way inside.

Creighton Memorial Hospital was indeed my home away from home. I still remember arriving for my midwifery interview years ago. The long row of imposing red brick buildings and immaculate lawns made me think I had arrived at a bucolic New England college campus. I soon realized that although the façade looked like it was from olden days, the interior housed state-of-the-art facilities. On top of this, an excellent reputation for providing care and a progressive management team had top doctors-in-training from Boston rotate through the various departments. They came to get a feel for the private practice sector under the tutelage of the outstanding medical staff. This, in turn, fostered a seamless relationship with the Boston academic medical community, which benefitted both patients and staff.

The town also played a significant role in the development of the hospital. The wealthier citizens of Langford generously endowed the impeccable grounds, first-class personnel, and outstanding patient programs.

That's not to say that everything had been sweetness and light during my time here. In my early tenure, things at the top of the OB department had been a bit rocky, you could say. At present, however, Creighton Memorial was on an even keel.

After letting my midwife colleagues know that I would be a bit detained, I took a long, warm shower. My mind drifted to my little family as the water flowed over me. My eldest daughter, Rowan Margaret, was sixteen months old, and Sloane Genevieve was eight months. My youngest had been born with as much drama as Roman had just been, and I was forever indebted to the Creighton staff for their superior care. Both girls were thriving, and Will, my husband, and I had made them the center of our world. Of course, our pack also included Fenway, our fiercely protective dachshund. Currently, our lives were happy and full. Looking back on our fertility struggles, I never imagined we'd be so blessed.

Now, though, I needed to get moving, so I turned off the shower and stepped out to towel off and dry my hair. As I did, I saw that a set of red scrubs had been left for me by MJ. It occurred to me that wearing red would mark me as part of the Emergency Department staff for the day, since each unit at Creighton Memorial wore different color scrubs and navy blue was worn in OB. Although I was partial to the navy blue ones, as I dressed and looked in the mirror, I decided that I rather liked red for a change.

The hairdryer was professional grade and worked its magic quickly, which wasn't surprising since it had been selected by someone knowledgeable about such things. At Creighton Memorial, every women's staff bathroom was outfitted with hairdryers, various lotions, and other accoutrements of a five-star bed and breakfast, courtesy of the hospital's Women's League. Perhaps a little sexist, but also a welcome touch for female staff who worked long hours each day providing the excellent care the hospital was known for.

Finishing up, I saw my tote and a steaming cup of coffee on a side table in the main lounge. Again, I could detect MJ's helpful hand.

Dressed and ready, I stepped into the ED, which was relatively quiet. MJ and another staff member were standing in front of one of the bays.

"Maeve, this is Jeremy, one of our finest nurses. Jeremy, this is Maeve, Creighton's intrepid midwife."

I smiled and nodded at the trim, tall man. In typical ED fashion, he had a beeper attached to his scrub pants, his phone in his top pocket, and a pen attached to his hospital ID lanyard.

"He's a beautiful baby. I must say we don't often see them mere minutes after their arrival," Jeremy said, raising both eyebrows.

"Strong work, Maeve," MJ said, giving me a fist bump.

Coming up to the bay, I saw Sienna and Martin cooing at Roman.

"Hello, Maeve," Sienna called out.

Martin turned toward me as I stepped into the curtain opening. "We can't thank you enough. What would we have done without you?"

"Sienna did it all," I countered. "I'm happy I got to be with her."

One of the senior residents stepped forward and asked me to look at the notes he had entered on the hospital computer system. He had described Sienna's arrival and wrote up his post-birth findings. Sienna's placenta appeared to be intact, and she had no lacerations. Her vital signs were within normal limits, and her bleeding was minimal.

The delivery section was blank, and I quickly perused Sienna's prenatal chart to double-check her labs. Then I added the birth details, and finally signed off on her record.

Turning to Sienna, I asked about the onset of labor.

"All day yesterday, I felt slightly off but had only a few irregular contractions. I went to bed early and was up and down during the night. But, you know, the third trimester is often like that. I got up at 5:00 a.m. and took a shower. That's when I started having a few strong contractions. I was about to call the midwife line when my water suddenly broke, and I had a powerful cramp. My mother is staying with us, so Martin woke her up, and we decided to drive straight to Creighton Memorial. We figured that we would call on the way. Carl, our first baby, only took five hours of labor, and at my last office visit the midwife told me to call and come right in with regular contractions. We thought we would make it in time, but Roman just couldn't wait." She threw her hands up in mock exasperation.

"I drove as fast as I could," Martin added, almost apologetically.

"I dropped the phone under the car seat, so I couldn't call," Sienna said, letting out a little giggle.

"Well, the three of you did just fine," I told them. "You handled it like a pro, Sienna. Martin, your timing was impeccable. It was great teamwork. Now let me see that beautiful boy." I picked up Roman, now looking cozy in a tee shirt, diaper, and blue and pink striped baby blanket instead of my cardigan.

"Roman looks very official now," I said as I adjusted his covering.

"I'll buy you a new sweater, Maeve," Sienna said, deep frown lines crinkling her brow.

"That old thing. Please, it was past its time. I am thrilled it was used for such a good cause."

Then I pulled the curtain shut to examine Roman and give Sienna one last check. Both passed with flying colors, and I discussed the next steps with Sienna, who was about to be admitted to the postpartum unit. After bidding the family goodbye, I grabbed my tote and coffee and went to say thanks to MJ and the staff.

At the main desk, the Beach Boys' song "Kokomo" began to play as six staff members started singing and swaying to the beat. They sang in unison about Aruba and Jamaica while one of the techs gently swung the freshly sterilized metal beach pail adorned with tall palm trees.

"Gee Maeve, you may have started a new trend in placental basins," MJ observed.

Shaking my head, I burst out laughing. Hospital peeps—you could not beat them. They were my second family.

"You're one of us now wearing those red scrubs," the curly-haired ED security guard chimed in. Giving me a big smile, he continued, "You can be our on-call midwife for door-to-door service."

"Just think if they'd had a golf club bag or a picnic basket in the car," MJ contemplated.

Still laughing, I waved goodbye and headed off to Labor and Delivery to begin my day once again.

Was there ever a typical day in the midwifery profession? Squeezing my six-foot frame into the back seat of a car for an emergency birth with no equipment was a first for me, but, as Melville wrote, "Midwifery should be taught in the same course with fencing and boxing, riding and rowing."

CHAPTER TWO

———

Certified nurse midwives are licensed to practice in all fifty US states, the District of Columbia, Puerto Rico, Guam, American Samoa, and the US Virgin Islands.

By the time I arrived at Labor and Delivery, the entire staff had heard all the details of Roman's birth. As in most hospitals, the Creighton Memorial hotline was alive and well.

"I see you've changed sides, Maeve," Maddie, the chief nurse midwife, said, greeting me in the midwife call room.

"Red does become me." I laughed as I put a hand on my hip and twirled around to give her a full view.

"I heard you did a great job in very—well, tight circumstances. Good thing it was the car's rear seat and not the front with your height," she said with a chuckle.

Maddie and her wife, Joy, had four young children. Joy had been treated for breast cancer in the past, but luckily, there was no evidence of the disease at present. It was great to see Maddie's sense of humor return along with Joy's progress.

"How does your week look?" Maddie added, sorting through a stack of papers. "I was thinking of having a department meeting on Thursday at 4:00 p.m. Will that fit your schedule?"

"The academic calendar hasn't formally started yet, so Thursday afternoon is fine." I nodded. "I don't need to be home until six."

"Terrific," she said, scribbling a note.

Maddie then looked up at me and studied my face.

"What?" I asked, holding my hands up.

"Come on, Maeve. It's me. Getting cold feet about Rosemont?"

Maddie and I had been friends for so long that she could easily pick up my mood, even if I thought I was hiding it well.

"Oh, Maddie, I want to represent midwives in the best light possible. Am I suited to the academic life?"

"Maeve, you will be fabulous. The students need a currently practicing clinician to teach them. Remember, the entire staff will support you."

Maddie was always so positive, but I was well aware that the jury was still out.

My dual position had been created by Dr. Daphne Saunders, the dynamic, newly-installed president of Rosemont. She was a transplant from the UK who firmly supported midwifery care. In her eyes, the appointment of a midwife to the faculty was a double win for the college. She thought adding dedicated on-site health care for women staff would be a great perk. Dr. Saunders also believed that having a midwife teaching obstetric care would enhance both the educational experience and the visibility and status of midwifery.

For my part, I had found her charming and inspirational during our initial meeting. I was excited if a bit apprehensive about this new aspect of my career. Really, though, how fortunate was I? I could continue midwifery at Creighton Memorial while also participating in college faculty life.

Leaving Maddie after receiving a hearty pep talk, I went to check on my current patients. The day passed quickly, in no small part because I was the target of many seaside-themed jokes and more Beach Boys tunes. But at the end of my shift, as I went to the locker room to change, I realized I had no sweater for the ride home. The wind was brisk today, and I wished I had my warm wool sweater. Oh well, my commute was quick, and there was always the seat heater in my car for warmth.

Approaching the wooden bench in front of my locker, I saw a large white paper bag with the hospital gift shop logo and a *Happy Birthday* balloon. A small card attached to the bag read, *To our favorite lifeguard...the L&D Crew.*

Opening the bag, I unwrapped a white sweatshirt decorated with a colorful beach scene, complete with gold glitter for sand. On the back, *Lifeguard Maeve* was written in red, puffy paint, and all the staff had signed their names underneath.

They were the best, I thought, as I changed out of my scrubs and happily put on my new top. I would wear it with pride.

As I pulled up to Primrose Cottage, I found myself smiling broadly. Our home was a converted carriage house that Will's grandmother had gifted him, along with an acre of land, for his twenty-fifth birthday. She was affectionately called Grand and lived in Seacrest, an oceanfront manse on the adjoining six acres.

Tonight, Will and his crew were catering a private engagement party at the Isabella Stewart Gardner Museum, so I knew he'd be home late. A Thyme for All Seasons, Will's business, had grown into a successful food service company with an associated café.

Our competing schedules would have caused a time crunch after our prior nanny had departed for sunny San Diego. I had no concerns now, though, because I knew our daughters were in good hands. We had found an equally skilled nanny, Kate, courtesy of my mother's intervention. Mom had sent word to relatives and friends near and far to help us find the nanny of our dreams. Twenty years old, Kate was spending a few years in the States before returning home to Galway to study law. She was the eldest of four, loved children, and had quickly become part of our family.

I had taken a three-month leave after Sloane's birth, and Kate had started with us a few weeks before I went back to Creighton. Despite my opening day jitters, I knew that the dual appointment with Rosemont was better for this period of my life because it would reduce my call time by half.

As I entered the foyer, I heard Kate's delightful brogue as she talked to Rowan and Sloane.

"Well, I see you are enjoying my shepherd's pie, Rowan, and you love the mash, Sloane. Ah, yes, Fenway. Don't you worry. You'll get a wee bit with your kibble."

Rowan and Sloane were seated side by side in highchairs next to the large oak dining table. Fenway was pacing between them, desperately waiting for food to drop. Kate sat on a high-backed stool, spoon-feeding Sloane. Appetizing aromas filled the air, and I saw that Kate had steamed apples for dessert. Besides her childcare skills, she was an accomplished cook.

"Mama," Rowan cried when she saw me at the doorway, her coppery curls framing her face. Fenway let out a loud, welcoming bark, and Sloane reached her arms out to me.

"Well, look at you," Kate said, taking note of my new top. "Welcome home. What a jumper! Where did you get that?"

In typical Irish fashion, Kate referred to sweaters and pullovers as jumpers.

I kissed the girls and gave Fenway a pat. "It's a long story. The labor and delivery staff made it for me."

"I can't wait to hear it. I must say it's quite unique," Kate said, laughing.

Kate was five feet eight inches tall and slim with chin-length chestnut brown hair. Her deep navy eyes and long lashes lit up her alabaster complexion. Intelligent, determined, and with an outgoing personality, she was a delight to be around. Mom had indeed found us an exceptional nanny.

Kate had started late today due to Will's schedule, so she helped me with bath time and bedtime and insisted on giving me a hand with kitchen cleanup.

It was great that she was so flexible with her hours. Will so loved his morning playtime with his daughters. While we did the dishes, I told her about my day, and she listened with rapt attention.

"Now I understand the arty jumper."

We both laughed. "Arty is one word for it. How is the nanny group doing? You said it was getting larger."

Kate and her best friend Bridget, who also hailed from Ireland, though from Athlone, had started an informal friend group for international nannies. At last count, it had swelled to ten.

"Two new nannies have joined. They're both from Sweden and will be nice additions."

She paused for a moment. "It's such a fun group. Most of us signed up with the same agency."

"It must be great to discover a new country together."

"It is. We plan trips on our days off. We go to museums, Newbury Street, Haymarket, or just ride the T and explore neighborhoods. Most of the nannies who live out room together."

She was pensive for a moment before she continued. "You know, there's been a fair influx of nannies from Bloomsby College to the area. You've probably heard of that school. It's in England, and all the royals get their nannies there. For them, nannying is a lifelong career. They often stay with families for years."

"I've read about it. Their graduates are in very high demand. In fact, my husband had a wonderful nanny from there whom he dearly loved."

"Rightly so. They are the crème de la crème." She bent to put away the pot she'd been drying. "Our nanny group extended an offer to join us for a dinner or a pint, but they have turned down every invitation so far. They're all live-in nannies, so maybe they are too busy. Who knows?"

"Perhaps they will come around in time. I'm sure they are great, but I hope you know that Will and I think you're amazing, Kate." I handed her the last dish and dried my hands.

"Ha, thank you, Maeve. I'm so happy I landed with your family. Nannying suits me for now, but I want to study law eventually."

"I know, and we are so thankful you took a small break. What about Bridget?"

"Bridie is enjoying herself. She was placed with a great family, too. She writes stories all the time and is thinking of applying to a special literature program at Trinity. Our other friend Fiona is struggling a bit. She is with a fancy family in that Mariner Heights development. She always needs to miss our outings because her employers change their plans so often. The missus is a tough taskmaster."

I could tell Kate was still holding something back. Hopefully, my silent presence would give her room to speak. I followed her to the hallway as she started to gather her things.

"Oh, Maeve, that foolish woman accused Fiona of both stealing a bracelet and having an affair with her husband. It's total nonsense, of course. The husband even said it's not true and the 'stolen' bracelet was found in the woman's purse. I don't know how long Fiona will last in that house."

"Wow, that's awful, Kate. Can Fiona get a different placement?"

"She wants to stay and work things out. She's so distraught, she can't see another way."

Kate shook her head briskly as if to clear her thoughts, gathered her coat, and continued, "Well, I'm off now, Maeve. I'm meeting Bridie for a pint at the Bluestone Pub. I'll see you first thing in the morning so you can get an early row in before work."

Kate knew I loved rowing. I had competed at the University of Massachusetts in Amherst and now regularly used my single shell, *Suaimhneas*, on the bay. The name was Irish for serenity. I had found a robust rowing community at the Regatta Club.

With Kate gone, I checked on the girls once more. Seeing them sound asleep, I packed my tote for tomorrow and curled up with Fenway on the couch to read the latest Deborah Crombie mystery and wait for Will. I was distracted by imagining poor Fiona trying to provide childcare under such trying circumstances and by my new work worries. Hopefully, tomorrow's row would bring some serenity to my life.

CHAPTER THREE

———

Certified nurse midwives have been licensed in Massachusetts since 1977.

Flat water! It was a rower's dream. The sun was rising, the air held a slight chill, the water was still and gleaming, and I was flying across Langford Bay. Rowing here was otherworldly, especially in the early morning. On the shore, both rustic cottages and large mansions built by shipbuilders of old stood silently as the brightening morning brought them into view.

At the bend, I passed First Light Lighthouse, a Langford landmark since its construction in 1816. The structure's tall white exterior and bright red cupola were visible for miles, and I used it as a marker every time I rowed. It was two thousand meters to First Light and two thousand meters back. Some days it seemed insurmountable, but today it felt too short.

As I glided by, I took in First Light's majesty. What had it seen over its two centuries? How many sailors had it saved? I was sure it had extraordinary stories to tell.

Although I didn't want to stop, I was cognizant of the time, so I began to swing wide to turn *Suaimhneas* back toward the Regatta Club. After the row, I would need a shower before heading to my busy day at Creighton Memorial.

As the shell turned, I saw joggers on the Bay Trail. That was typical because it was a route many people used to run, cycle, or skate. A few of the very physically fit ran up the two hundred steps inside First Light as part of their routine.

Cruising past it, I noticed several people had stopped running and were frantically waving and shouting. It also looked like someone was on the ground. What was happening? Did they need medical personnel?

Since I was so close, I turned my boat around again and quickly rowed to shore. As *Suaimhneas* closed on the jetty, I pulled my oars in, letting the shell drift. When the water was shallow enough, I stepped out and pulled *Suaimhneas* up on the beach. Then, I trekked carefully over the rocky shore to the lighthouse in my stocking feet since my rowing shoes, like those of all rowers, were firmly attached to the inside of the boat. Still, even though my socks were thick and I was very cautious, I could feel sharp surfaces with each step up the slope.

As I approached the grassy lawn in front of First Light, I saw a woman administering CPR to a middle-aged man who was clad in a long-sleeved white tee and black running tights.

"Has someone called 911?" I inquired while taking a long look at the fallen jogger.

"They're en route," a worried-looking, dark-skinned woman replied. She sported a fitted jacket of fuchsia nylon with *Ride Like a Girl* printed across the chest. She was closely watching a tall blonde doing chest compressions.

"If you need a break, I'm here, Sadie," she said.

Sadie nodded that she understood, her long braid bobbing with each push on the man's chest.

Looking over the victim, I saw that his face, as well as his fingernails and hands, had a distinct bluish cast that indicated he was oxygen deficient. How long had he been like this, I wondered.

"Did you see him go down?" I asked the female cyclist.

"I did. We always stop at First Light if it's a nice day. We saw him stumble out of the lighthouse door and collapse as we approached. Sadie is a respiratory therapist, so when she found he had no heartbeat, she started CPR immediately."

Both of us looked up as sirens heralded the arrival of the ambulance team, followed by a Langford police cruiser driven by my brother Patrick. Well, there was no place for me to hide. Six feet tall, front and center, here I was. Emergencies always seemed to find me, much to Pat's chagrin. The paramedics ran to us and immediately took over from the tiring Sadie. Within minutes, they had the victim packed up and began racing toward Creighton Memorial as the group watched them leave. When they were gone, the two officers from the cruiser started taking names and asking questions.

"Morning, Maeve. Were you out for a pre-work row?" Patrick, or rather Deputy Chief Patrick O'Reilly, one of Langford's finest, asked me.

"Good morning, Pat. And yes. I was on the water and didn't see what happened. But when I saw the excitement I came ashore to see if I could help."

In the past, I always seemed to show up at Pat's crime scenes by some twist of fate. But this time, it wasn't a crime scene. This poor guy undoubtedly had a cardiac event. I mean, running for miles and then going full speed up and down First Light stairs was a true cardiac stress test.

"It doesn't look like foul play this time," I pointed out. "Plus, you can see I'm merely an innocent bystander."

Patrick shrugged but kept his tight smile firmly in place. Then he turned and joined the other officer. Listening in, I overheard someone say the man's name was Theo Archer, and he was training for an Ironman competition.

I wanted to stay and learn as much as possible, but a glance at my watch told me I needed to get going. I waved goodbye to Patrick, got back in my shell, and began my row back to the Regatta Club.

After a quick shower, I called Will on the way to Creighton Memorial.

"Hi, honey, how's your day so far?" I asked.

"Good. I'm checking out a new goat cheese farmer in Western Mass today. It's a long ride, but I hear her product is first-rate. How was your row?"

"It was fine, but some guy collapsed after running the stairs at First Light," I said, noticing my hands were tightly gripping the wheel.

"Gosh, Maeve, were you there? Is he all right? Are you okay?"

"I'm fine. I didn't see him collapse. I rowed in to help, but the emergency crew got there quickly." I stretched my fingers out and loosened my grasp.

"What a morning."

"Well, I'm used to dealing with medical emergencies, but having an event occur outside a healthcare setting always presents challenges."

After reassuring Will once again, I signed off.

As I pulled into my usual parking space and gathered my belongings, "Lean on Me," sung by Bill Withers, pealed from my phone.

It was Meg. My older sister was a world-class real estate agent and sibling. Meg could be arrogant and snippy, but she always puts her family first. She was both my harshest critic and my fiercest protector.

"Hey, Meg."

"Busy morning, Maeve?"

"Well, I rowed and—"

"And just happened to come across a dead body. Do you have some special death radar I don't know about?"

"A dead body? What?"

"Dead as a doornail. Shelley heard from her sister that a DOA from First Light was brought into the Creighton Memorial ED."

Shelley was Meg's longtime house manager and was part of a large, prominent Portuguese family. They had lived in Langford for generations and always knew the latest happenings.

"Her sister is a jogger and said a female rower stopped to help. Early morning, woman rowing on the bay, and a dead body. Hmmm…now who else could it be but my baby sister, the young Jane Marple?"

"How did Shelley's sister find out the man died?"

"Apparently, the guy's brother, Jeremy Archer, is an RN in the Creighton Memorial ED. The victim was part of a runner's group and the brother called the leader to let him know what happened. After that, the word was out."

Small towns held no secrets for long.

"Oh, no," I exclaimed. "I just met the brother yesterday in the ED. That's awful. Imagine seeing a family member come into the emergency department in that condition."

"Terrible," Meg agreed. "The victim's name was Theo Archer. He retired early after he sold a large software company."

"Hey, Meg. I'm late. I need to run. Talk to you later. Love you."

"Go, save lives. Try to stay out of trouble. Love you."

As I walked down the corridor, I once again thought of how fragile life can be. It could change in an instant. Poor

Jeremy! My hand closed around my locket that held photos of my pack as I sent up a silent prayer for protection.

CHAPTER FOUR

———

As of 2024, there were approximately 14,000 certified nurse midwives in the United States.

My schedule was fully booked, and the morning passed swiftly. Jayda, the stellar ambulatory RN, had written *Itching/34weeks* on a sticky note and attached it to my notepad for my final patient. She never missed a beat and always kept our sessions running on time.

Geena Sheehan was a primigravida, a woman pregnant for the first time, whom I had met a few times before. The Creighton Memorial midwifery group tried to have our patients rotate among all the midwives so they would be familiar with whoever was on call at the time of their birth. Geena had a glowing olive complexion, and her jet-black hair was pulled into a low ponytail.

"Hi, Geena. I know we've met before."

"Hello, Maida. It's nice to see you again."

My Irish name was a mystery to many. It was often misspelled or mispronounced. I usually let it go, but I always had a list of rhyming verses ready.

Like Dave with an *M.*

Like cave with an *M.*

Like brave with an *M.*

But today, I would be Maida.

"How are you doing? Jayda says you have some itching," I said as I approached the exam table.

"Yes, it started two days ago. I didn't call because I knew I had this appointment."

Geena pulled her blue and white striped tunic up to her bra line. Bright red streaks caused by scratching covered the sides of her abdomen, so I slipped on gloves and inspected her skin closely under the exam lamp. There were no signs of a rash, blisters, or hives.

"I can see that your abdomen is very itchy. Anyplace else?" Her face and neck were untouched.

"The palms and the soles of my feet are itching nonstop. I can barely sleep."

Hm, those two areas were hallmarks of a certain condition. Strange how physical diagnosis was so like solving a mystery.

"Has the baby been active?"

"Yes, very active."

I continued my physical exam of Geena, noting that her vital signs and the baby's heart rate were within normal parameters. Pulling up the stool next to the exam table, I began to tell her my concerns.

"Geena there is a condition called cholestasis of pregnancy. In some pregnant women, the liver doesn't function as effectively as it should. This causes bile to build up, and if the levels get high enough, women develop itching."

I paused for her to digest this information. I always found it best to present the possible diagnosis briefly and outline the treatment path. Patients often didn't hear the facts on first discussion. I tried to put myself in their position on hearing unsettling news and allow them time to fully process the situation. She waited for me to continue.

"The next step is getting a blood test to check your liver function and bile levels. If those confirm the diagnosis, you will need to start medication."

"What about my baby? Did I cause this?"

I felt my shoulders droop. I had heard variations of this question so many times from pregnant women. When faced with an abnormal result that might affect their fetuses, they immediately blamed themselves. Why were women so quick to assume they had done something wrong? I'd pondered that so often, but this was not the time. For now, I needed to strongly reassure Geena.

"You did nothing to cause this. We don't even know why it occurs. Cholestasis may cause complications in the fetus, so if the tests are positive, we will monitor you and your baby extremely closely. We'll get the test immediately to learn what we're dealing with, and the results will come back quickly. Right now, though, let's talk about comfort measures to deal with the itching."

I answered a few more questions, and then Geena headed to the lab and ultrasound.

As I finished my notes, Jayda came and sat down so we could debrief.

"I'll watch the labs for Geena's results," Jayda said. "The odds are good she'll be positive. If so, I know you'll want to discuss her care with an MFM and book extra monitoring."

As usual, Jayda was right on target. The Maternal-Fetal Medicine staff at Creighton was simply the best. The midwives always notified them of patients who needed extra surveillance. They, in turn, always kept us in the loop.

"Thank you, Jayda. You are always a step ahead of me. I appreciate you so much."

"Back at ya. Let's look over the schedule for next week. I won't see you until then since you are deserting me for Rosemont College."

I smiled, shrugging at her while we reviewed the caseload.

When the clinic finished for the day, I got an iced hazelnut latte at the first-floor coffee shop. As I waited in line, my thoughts returned to the death of the morning jogger. The ED staff must have had a tough day. One of their people lost a family member at their own facility. What could I do to show support?

Refreshment in hand, I quickly stopped at the Creighton Memorial Gift Shop, where I bought a large box of the locally sourced Harbor Delights milk chocolate bark. That company had been through great turmoil recently, but now, newly employee-owned, it had regained its footing. They'd even been featured on Oprah's Favorite Things List.

As I entered the ED waiting room, I saw MJ conferring with the receptionist. When she finished, she turned to me.

"Decided to give up midwifery and come over to the dark side?"

I smiled and handed her the box of candy. "I witnessed the field CPR on Jeremy Archer's brother. I wanted the staff to know I was thinking of them. I mean, I am an auxiliary member now."

"Come right this way," she said, pointing toward a side door.

MJ led me to the staff lounge and pointed to a round table. The room was empty, except for us.

"The staff inhales snacks. This will be gone in an instant. Thanks so much."

Briefly looking up at the ceiling, she then closed her eyes momentarily as if to clear her thoughts. "What a day we've had. Jeremy Archer has been at Creighton Memorial for about four years. He came to us as a traveling nurse and, after a five-month assignment, decided to settle here. He's smart, has a great sense of humor, and is a regular magician with sick kids. Jeremy's a staff favorite. Unfortunately, he was also the charge RN today and was front and center for everything that happened with his brother. We all stepped in to help and quickly realized it was too late, but we tried to resuscitate Theo Archer for a long time anyway. Of course, Jeremy was just heartbroken. They are—well, they were very close. Jeremy loved the challenge of working in different ED units and traveling the country but stayed at Creighton Memorial to be near Theo."

"I can't imagine being a professional and seeing a loved one in that condition," I said. "If I were ever at the receiving end of a tragedy involving one of my family members, I would be unable to function for a very long time."

We sat in silence for a few minutes. MJ opened the candy and took a large chunk.

She grinned as she took a bite. "Chocolate is always the answer."

"I knew we would be friends," I said, taking a piece.

MJ leaned back and had a faraway look in her eyes. It seemed as if she was wrestling with what to say. In a slightly strained voice, she abruptly sat forward and said, "Jeremy is taking this very, very hard. He doesn't believe that Theo had a cardiac event. Even though we have all talked to him, he thinks foul play was involved."

"What? How?"

At that moment, MJ's beeper went off, and she leapt to her feet. "Oops. We are in overflow. Gotta run. Thanks so much for the sweets, Maeve. I'll tell the crew you stopped by."

Foul play? How? The jogger was running down the stairs of First Light. He came outside and collapsed. Maybe Jeremy was still in shock and looking for someone to blame.

Wait. Was I going to begin to start investigating? Well, I was a witness to the shocking death, and Jeremy *was* part of my Creighton family. Hm, might as well change my name to Alice. I apparently loved rabbit holes.

CHAPTER FIVE

————

American nurse-midwifery began in 1925 at the Frontier Nursing Service in Hyden, Kentucky.

Thursday, as I approached the Hadley conference room for our weekly midwifery meeting, I saw a middle-aged guy with graying, short-cropped hair waiting at the entrance. On second glance, I realized it was Jeremy Archer.

"Good afternoon, Maeve. I hoped to find you here."

From my memory of the jogger felled at First Light, I did see a family resemblance.

"Jeremy, hello—I am so sorry for your loss. I can't imagine what you're going through."

He looked at the floor, composed himself, and then met my gaze. "Thank you so much, and please forgive me for ambushing you like this. MJ told me that you stopped by to offer condolences and brought goodies for the staff." He gave me a weak smile. "Do you have a few moments so we could chat?"

I glanced at my watch and saw I had twenty minutes before Maddie started the meeting. "Of course. Let's sit in a corner of the patient waiting area. It will be empty for a while."

Taking a seat on one of the plastic molded chairs, I turned to face Jeremy and looked at him expectantly.

"Maeve, I heard that you were on the scene when Theo was being resuscitated."

I explained to Jeremy that I had been rowing and came upon his brother after others tried to help him.

"I wanted your thoughts on my brother's condition. I know that as health professionals, we often see what others miss. Also, I heard about your prior success in identifying murderers." He looked down at his hands for a few brief seconds and then continued. "Let me explain. Theo was in excellent shape. In fact, he was training for an Ironman competition. I know I will sound crazy, but I think foul play was involved."

I held his gaze. *Was he just distraught, or did he know anything more?*

"Why do you think that, Jeremy?"

"Theo was extremely wealthy. His company was sold, along with a very lucrative software application, to a tech giant. It was one of the highest sales recorded in the industry. Theo really was a genius. Unfortunately, he was also going through a divorce."

Was he saying that Theo's wife was somehow involved?

"He had an ironclad prenup, but of course, that is nullified by his death."

Yup.

"After the monster sale, he had time on his hands and decided to write a thriller. There was a glowing description of it in the *New York Times Book Review*. His agent sold the film rights to the Avalon Group."

My eyebrows went up a notch. The Avalon Group holdings included one of the up-and-coming streaming networks. "How fortunate," I finally said, "to get a bestseller and a movie deal with a debut book. That's incredible."

Except, now he was dead, Maeve. Not fortunate enough. Ugh, talk about foot-in-mouth issues.

Jeremy was silent for a long moment before continuing. "Theo was a great guy. He was also my big brother, and I loved him. Hey, he's why I'm here in Langford." Jeremy's face clouded over. "He also had a type A personality and was brilliant. There were people jealous of his success. Too many people." He sighed. "Also, with the divorce looming, Savannah, his soon-to-be ex, was about to be cut off from her extravagant lifestyle. She does well with her branding, but that is nothing compared to Theo's wealth. She was about to lose the Cabo villa and the Aspen ski house. Theo also asked for partial custody. They have two girls, ages two and four, that Theo cherished." He paused for a moment. "Look, Savannah's an awesome mother. I just know"—his voice broke—"or I guess I knew from Theo that there was a lot of conflict in the marriage." He paused, caught his breath, and looked at me solemnly. "Now, I'm rambling."

He got up and walked to the large window overlooking the bay. After a few minutes, Jeremy turned and said, "Maeve, Theo did not have an underlying cardiac condition. Did anything look off to you when you saw him?"

Now my mind was a jumble. I mean, I had seen a jogger in full cardiac arrest lying on the shore. Of course, he didn't look great. Can we just say it's not a natural state? I tried to think back and remember if anything at the scene looked off, but it was difficult. Every emergency, especially one taking place outdoors, was chaotic. I tried to focus on the details. I did remember his face was blue-tinged, as well as his hands, but I couldn't see how that could be chalked up to anything but cyanosis due to oxygen deprivation.

"Jeremy, you're the expert with cardiac arrest but your brother was cyanotic. I didn't see him collapse. It took me time to come ashore, and I don't know how long he had been down before I arrived. All I was thinking at the time was that he was in dire straits."

Jeremy hung his head. He had become more distressed as we talked. "I am so confused, and I want to be rational. Theo had a full cardiac workup a few months ago. He was in a boutique medical group, and they suggested an evaluation before he started Ironman training. He was incredibly disciplined. Theo always carried electrolyte drinks and followed a strict diet. If CPR was started immediately, why didn't he have a chance?"

He stopped speaking and looked down at his clasped hands. Finally, he continued. "The coroner ordered a toxicology screen, but that only covers standard medications. I insisted on having full-blown testing done for every drug possible. I was his healthcare proxy, and I will demand answers. I should have the results soon."

Jeremy was clearly in pain. He wanted no stone left unturned at this point, and I understood why.

From the main corridor, four midwives appeared, heading to the conference room. Jeremey must have seen them, because he said, "I know you have to go to your meeting. Thanks for your time."

"Jeremy, let's exchange contact info in case I think of anything."

"That would be great. Thanks, Maeve."

As I watched him walk away, a wave of sadness came over me. Losing a loved one was so hard, and sudden death was always so shocking. I didn't think I could help him, but I had felt the need to offer something. Jeremy had alluded to many people being jealous of Theo. Had he also made enemies along the way? Why was my mind already searching for clues? Theo had probably died of natural causes, I assured myself.

Well, maybe.

Did Meg and I, or as Mom had called us from childhood, the M&M's, need to hit the streets? Only time would tell.

CHAPTER SIX

———

A well-woman gynecological visit focuses on preventative care as well as a complete physical examination.

For some reason, even after a night full of mac and cheese, playtime, baths, and picture books, I had a restless sleep. Thoughts of Jeremy Archer's sorrow had kept me awake off and on.

In the morning, I dragged myself out of bed, showered early, and then struggled to decide on an outfit for my first official day as a faculty member at Rosemont College. It was brisk outside, so I dressed in my black woolen slacks and a pale pink mock turtleneck. But I still needed a little more pizazz.

I wasn't the scarf-wearing type. My many attempts in the past always made me look like I was wearing a Halloween costume gone wrong. Scrubs or slacks and a shirt under a white lab coat were my customary garb. This was an entirely new experience for me.

Taking a deep dive to the back of my closet, I found a waist-length, rose-patterned kimono with ribbon ties that I quickly slipped on over the turtleneck. Not bad, I thought, on making a confirming check in the mirror. It probably wasn't the usual academic attire, but I wasn't a full-time staff member, and everyone knew that midwives marched to a different drummer, right? Besides, it made me feel a bit sophisticated.

Ready at last, I said goodbye to Kate, the girls, and Fenway, and then headed out the door to Rosemont College. I'd get there comfortably early since my first class didn't start until 9:40. In the future, I'd need to adjust my life a bit since hospital shifts began so early, and, until now, they were the only professional work I'd known. This college start time felt like midday to me, but for today, I wanted to arrive early to get my bearings and review my notes.

Rosemont College had approximately 2,500 undergraduate and 500 graduate students. It consisted of a central campus which fronted a large, open green. Outbuildings and dormitories extended away from the central buildings for a half mile in all directions. Tall pines and a centuries-old rock wall sheltered the quiet campus from the bustle of the main street. Passing through the massive gates gave one the feeling of entering another world.

I couldn't help but compare this to my alma mater, the University of Massachusetts at Amherst. That was a bustling hub, a mixture of old and new set in the verdant pioneer valley of western Massachusetts. It enrolled 25,000 undergraduates and 8,000 graduate students. I loved my time there and still remembered those days fondly. My professors had been top-notch, my rowing team fostered great camaraderie, and there was always a theater production, art exhibition, or live music show to attend. For me, its appeal resulted from its size and variety. However, seeing Rosemont made me wonder what a small college experience was like.

My first answer came when I found the faculty lot quickly, without needing to drive for an extended period or go searching numerous far-flung lots for my assigned space. I pulled in beside a spring blue Citroën and was surprised to notice a Windsor College parking sticker on the car's side window. Must be a faculty transplant, I thought, and then put it out of my mind.

After shutting off sports radio, I attempted a two-minute meditation to steady myself and then gathered my belongings and headed out onto the campus.

I'd gotten halfway across the green when I was stopped by a familiar voice behind me.

"Maeve, is that you?"

I turned and saw Tom Locke, the nephew of my late friend Ingrid Olson. We had met under challenging circumstances, but had bonded over a shared loss.

"Tom, what are you doing here?"

"I could ask the same, Maeve. Are you going back to school?"

Before I could answer, we hugged, and then he turned to the shorter, dark-skinned man beside him. He was dressed in a camel cashmere overcoat and long dark brown paisley scarf, which I immediately decided fit well into this New England college scene.

"Maeve, this is my husband, Mike Grantham," Tom said. "He is the new chair of the English department, freshly recruited away from Windsor College. Mike, this is Maeve O'Reilly Kensington. She was a close friend of Ingrid's. She and her sister Meg ran Ingrid's estate sale."

"It's nice to meet you, Maeve," Mike said. "Do you teach at Rosemont?"

I explained that I had a dual appointment and that this was my first foray into undergraduate education. "Are you on the faculty too, Tom?" I inquired.

"I headhunt for Sphere, a global software firm, and I'm mostly remote. I'm here to explore and spend some time in the library."

"Well, this is marvelous news. Have you found a new home?"

"Mike and I bought an old farmhouse in Shipley and are in the process of updating it. Hey, we'll have you and Meg for dinner."

"That sounds like fun. We'd love to visit."

We exchanged contact information as we approached the nursing college and then said goodbye.

Since this was the first time a dual appointment between Creighton Memorial and Rosemont had been attempted, I felt a massive weight of expectation. It returned in full force after the welcome distraction of running into Tom. This morning I would meet with the six students who would be with me at Creighton Memorial for their fall clinical rotation. This afternoon, I would meet the entire class.

Nightingale Hall was a large white clapboard building with black shutters on the right side of the green. Terracotta pots full of blooming yellow mums lined the sides of the wide stairs, and a massive wreath made from stems of bright orange Chinese lantern flowers adorned the black steel door. Autumn was out in all its colors at Rosemont College.

As I stepped into the oak-paneled foyer, the door shut behind me and I was enveloped in silence. I looked at my schedule again and confirmed I was assigned to Room 204. I assumed the number corresponded to the second floor, so I began to ascend the foyer's wide staircase. About halfway up, I heard the front door open behind me.

Someone called out in a melodious sing-song voice. "Hello, hello, are you the new nursing faculty?"

Turning around, I saw a diminutive thirty-something woman dressed in dark gray and wearing knee-high black leather boots with three-inch heels. Her short brown hair had streaks of bubblegum pink. "Yes," I said with a smile. "I'm Maeve O'Reilly Kensington."

Taking purposeful strides toward an office door, the woman said, "Welcome, welcome. I'm Trudy Delchamps. I'm Dr. Allen's administrative assistant. She won't be in until one because she has a meeting in Boston with the Rosemont Board of Trustees. Come on in. Ask me anything. I have your badge. You'll need that to get around campus."

I backtracked down the stairs and followed Trudy into her office. The room was awash in color. Files were neatly stacked on her desk in every hue of the rainbow. A large, round neon yellow porcelain cup held pens and markers of every shade. Some even had feathers on the ends. A vast bay window behind her held multiple species of plants. Cyclamen, African violets, coleus, a few bonsai, and all types of cacti surrounded a massive jade plant in a blue and white glazed pot, which took pride of place. On her desk there was a chorus of jewel-tone vases with pink roses, red calla lilies, and yellow sunflowers.

To tell the truth, I was expecting something much more austere, judging by her outfit. I should know better by now than to judge a book by its cover.

"Let me see," Trudy said as she picked a notepad off her desk and read it. "Here's your agenda for the day." She passed me a sky blue sheet of paper with the date emblazoned on top. "Dr. Allen personally went over the timing." Taking in the fancy calligraphy font and the floral margins, I smiled at Trudy's special attention to detail.

Dr. Claudia Allen was a leader in the nursing community. She had done her doctoral thesis on addiction and then spent many years setting up rehab centers. Given her leadership and management skills, Rosemont had worked hard to recruit her to grow and recharge the nursing curriculum. Too often, colleges were only staffed with faculty who had not taken care of patients in years. Did knowledge of nursing theory substitute for clinical expertise? I believed a mix was the best for the students.

This dual appointment was the trial run of that idea, and that was the aspect that had me so anxious. Although being a part of a woman-run faculty was exciting, I knew all eyes would be on my results. I couldn't help but worry if I would measure up and if the current nursing faculty would be supportive. And, of course, I so wanted to showcase the midwifery profession in a positive light.

"Here is your packet," said Trudy, handing me a large magenta envelope she had just assembled. As I took it, she added a binder of the same shade.

"I try to match colors with people's aura," Trudy explained. "You're warm and serene, but I sense a will of steel."

Before I could react, Trudy was around her desk and running out the door. She motioned me to follow her down the hall, speaking loudly while her heels clicked on the expansive hardwood floors.

"This is the faculty lounge," she said as she swung a heavy door open. "I gave you the mug with the puppy motif. Isn't it cute? You know… a midwife… newly hatched puppies. I thought it fit. Oh, and I'll have your official office assignment soon."

The faculty lounge resembled an old English hunting lodge. Along both side walls, steel-blue drapes covered leaded windows, which filled the spaces not taken up by floor-to-ceiling built-in bookshelves. In the center of the far wall, tobacco-colored leather club chairs flanked a large marble fireplace. As I took it all in, I felt like Harry Potter arriving at Hogwarts.

I was about to say something but didn't have time as Trudy continued nonstop.

"Don't worry—Dr. Allen will change this old boy décor soon. She already has some plans, but she wants faculty input."

After showing me how to use the beverage machine, giving me a tour of the snack stash, and ensuring I could find my classroom, Trudy bid me goodbye. Then she was off, trailing a light scent of lavender in her wake.

Despite Trudy's directions, I wandered around the second floor of Nightingale Hall until I stumbled onto Room 204. It had a beautiful view of the grounds and a large round wooden table with twelve chairs. Clearly, this room was used for small groups. I pulled out a chair and, sipping hot cocoa from my puppy mug, I opened the magenta file.

A list of the six students, clinical dates, and a faculty directory were included. Trudy was both colorful and organized.

At 9:30, a lone student lightly knocked on the open door. "Hello, Mrs. Kensington? I'm Lilly Brewster. Nice to meet you."

"Welcome, Lilly. Come in. And please call me Maeve."

"Before we start, I wanted to tell you that I'm so excited to have a midwife teaching this course. We all are."

"I'm delighted to be here." And hopefully, I would feel more comfortable soon.

As she took a seat, four other students entered. As they made their greetings, each settled into a chair. I mentally made note of their names—Lilly, Edgar, Jenna, Sophie, and Helene. The taller redhead raised her hand.

"Yes, Helene," I said with a smile.

"Do we get to watch a cesarean section at Creighton?"

"Routine surgeries are booked for the mornings. I will talk to the patients and their families and to the surgeons. Hopefully, you can all see one."

"That sounds great." Helene beamed. "I'm very interested in operating room nursing."

"That's an exciting area. Maybe we can speak with some of the GYN OR nurses when we're there."

I checked my watch. It was 9:40, and one student was missing.

To start? To wait? What tone did I want to set?

Before I could decide, a tall, brown-skinned young woman with long black beaded braids burst into the room.

"I know, I know. Set the alarm earlier. But today, I am right on time. I'm Haley Wilson. Nice to meet you."

I had to smile. I admired her confidence. She had a presence, and the profession needed that.

Haley continued, "Now, if I didn't have to work, was more vivacious, and had a Spirit scholarship, I would be prompt." She added air quotes with her fingers on the word *scholarship*.

The reactions from the other five students varied. One blushed deeply, and the others laughed quietly. Edgar pointed to

his chest and said, "Wrong gender. I'm not your competition."
Helene stared at Haley with her hand on her right hip.

"What, Helene? You know it's the truth."

Whatever this was, I needed to get a handle on things.

I cleared my throat loudly, and after describing my background, I had each student talk about their goals and what they hoped to get out of the rotation. They seemed very pleased they would be at Creighton Memorial and had been paired with a midwife for their obstetrical clinical experience. The seminar portion of the class would be split between the traditional professors and me. This semester, I was responsible for four of the lectures.

The small group session ended, so I gathered my belongings and headed to the main auditorium. Today's talk would only entail a brief orientation and a general overview of the course.

As I sat in the last row, I saw that tweed blazers, in brown or gray, were practically a uniform among the faculty. So, when I stood to be introduced, my rose kimono marked me as an outsider and a colorful one at that.

I mused briefly about whether my attire would earn me an association with the colorful Trudy in the minds of the regular faculty. Oh well, I was a bit of a fish out of water here, anyway. All I could do now was hope that the rhythms of academic life would soon become second nature to me.

CHAPTER SEVEN

———

Menarche is the name given to the first menstrual period.

As the orientation finished, I waited to greet the other nursing faculty. Three women, ranging in age from mid-forties to early sixties, stopped at the back of the auditorium when they saw me.

"Welcome to Rosemont, Maeve. I'm Gwendolyn Birch, the OB faculty chair. Prudence Owens and Margarita Rodriguez make up the rest of the OB contingent. We're so happy to have you join us. Please ask us for anything you need."

"Thank you so much. I'm thrilled to be here and to introduce the students to midwifery."

"I had a midwife for my two births in New York. It was a wonderful experience," Margarita said, smiling.

Prudence Owens, the third member of the group, was silent. Her mouth was in a thin line, almost a grimace. As Gwendolyn and Margarita turned to greet students, Prudence leaned closer and, in a quiet voice, said, "Remember, the OB curriculum is not based solely on midwifery philosophy. Students must be well rounded to pass our exams and the national nursing boards."

With that, she marched off in her black pumps and steel-gray gabardine suit.

Okay, so not everyone at Rosemont was in love with midwives—nothing I had not encountered before. As usual, I would have to prove myself worthy. Just another day in the life of a midwife.

Looking at my watch, I was surprised to see it was only noon. I knew that reading papers, completing evaluations, and attending meetings would soon call for longer hours. For today, though, the free afternoon was a gift I was going to enjoy.

Since it was early, I texted Meg to see if she had time for a quick break.

Her reply was immediate: *Hey, professor—see you at On the Rocks in forty.*

Excellent! That gave me time to quickly visit the campus health center and then meet Meg.

At the far edge of campus, a foursquare red brick building held a small copper plaque that read *Rosemont College Health Services*. If it weren't for the sign, I would have thought it held small, drab administrative offices. Once past the front door, though, I found myself stepping into a bright, modern waiting room. Walking up to the front desk, I was warmly greeted by a striking blonde woman dressed in a Kelly green roll-neck sweater.

"Oh, there you are. Welcome. I was hoping that you would stop by. I'm Kristin, the nurse manager. You're our midwife, right? I saw your photo in the faculty email."

Smiling, I said, "Yes, I'm Maeve. It's nice to meet you."

Kristin got up from her chair, shook my hand warmly, and beckoned me to follow her down the hall.

"Let me give you the tour. Dr. Tim is at lunch, but I'll show you the GYN room. We're thrilled that you'll be joining the staff."

The exam room was immaculate and well-stocked. However, what really drew my eye were several beautiful photographs on the walls. They featured iconic locations and whimsical city and country scenes from around the world. Kristin saw me admiring them.

"Those are Dr. Tim's. He's a world traveler and practically a professional shutterbug."

When the clinic tour was finished, Kristin went over the dates I was available and explained the booking system. Luckily, Rosemont College used the same computer system as Creighton Memorial for its medical records.

"I assume that most of my patients will be students, right?"

"Yes, I've heard from several of our coeds that they are excited that there will be a woman practitioner for GYN issues.

I've also had calls from female faculty asking if you treat women of all ages."

"Certainly. Midwives provide care throughout a woman's life."

"That is great to hear. I think as word spreads, your schedule will be fully booked."

Kristin gave me a big smile as we sat in her sunlit office. With such a positive, engaging personality she made a perfect match for a college health service. I decided to ask her for more information about the composition of Rosemont.

"Kristin, I've heard about the Spirit scholarship. Is there a wide divide between students who have that scholarship and those who don't?"

"Did you hear some rumblings?"

"A bit. It made me wonder how many students receive financial aid at Rosemont."

Kristin took a swallow of coffee before answering. "About sixty percent of our students receive some type of financial aid. That can be made up of grants, loans, work-study, and various scholarships." She gave me a look I couldn't quite interpret. "Saying that, the Spirit scholarships are the top of the food chain. They cover all of an undergraduate's costs, and I mean soup to nuts. Apparently, it's endowed by some rich alumni for female students only. I hear that it is a rather secretive but rigorous selection process." She paused for a moment as if debating whether to add her next comment. "I suppose it doesn't help that all the Spirit women are both intelligent and extremely attractive."

"A scholarship that covers all needs. I can see why there might be some hard feelings."

"Well, Rosemont really strives to help all students with financial issues. The administration is very committed to this."

"That's good to know. Well, thanks so much—I look forward to working with you."

"Can't wait. See you soon, Maeve."

Must be some very wealthy alumni. I wonder if there are matching scholarship funds for male students.

As I pulled into On the Rocks, I thought of the old *Cheers* theme. Everyone here probably did know Meg and me. The popular restaurant was a cozy combination bar and grill that sat directly on the waterfront overlooking Langford Harbor. It was one of our favorite haunts.

As I entered, Sandy, the longtime waitress, greeted me at the door. She wore several hats at On the Rocks. One of these was keeping Arlo, the hit-or-miss chef, in line.

Sandy whistled loudly when she saw my kimono. "Pretty fancy schmancy, Maeve. This is a change. Going somewhere special?"

I filled Sandy in on my new position as she led me to my usual table.

"So, you're a professor now! Well, la-de-da! Here, take a load off—and please steer clear of today's special, the Chef's Kiss Chicken Salad. Arlo must have concocted the recipe during a nightmare."

As usual, Sandy would inflate and gently mock my new position and then balance that by saving me from digestive issues. Sandy could be caustic at times, but because of some shared history she had decided I was okay.

I sat perusing the menu, even though it rarely changed. As I read, Meg came through the door, waving to me as she did. Six feet tall, reed-thin, fashionably dressed as always, and impeccably coifed, she was a fashion statement. Meg had paired a sapphire blue pencil skirt with a fitted lamb's wool jacket and her customary two-inch black heels. Even though we were both six feet tall, she was the one blessed with a model's figure. The eternal mystery was that she kept it effortlessly while holding chocolate, a *lot* of chocolate, to be one of her five major food groups.

"Hi, Meg. You're looking dazzling, as usual."

She stopped before sitting in the booth and gave me the once over.

"A kimono? A silk kimono?" she asked in astonishment. "I would have thought an understated jacket with leather elbow patches would have been *de rigueur* at Rosemont."

"Well, you would be correct. As usual, I didn't get the dress code memo."

She grinned. "Who cares? The important thing is they won't forget you. Did you like what you saw?"

"There's a recently installed president and a new dean in the nursing college. Both are women who are forward-thinking and very welcoming. One faculty member, though, let it be known she was not thrilled to see a nurse midwife hired."

"Well, she needs to step into this century. You'll blow them away, Maeve."

Before I could respond, Sandy appeared at my elbow.

"What will it be, ladies? Or should I say lady and the professor?"

"I'll have a Reuben with fries, coleslaw, and a large Coke," Meg said.

"A tomato and cheese melt for me and a side salad with house dressing. I'll have a cup of decaf tea too, please."

"Coming right up."

When Sandy left, Meg leaned back and surveyed the room. On the Rocks was relatively empty because we'd come after the lunch crowd and before the pre-dinner rush.

I filled Meg in on my encounter with Tom and Mike, and she was excited about seeing them again. However, I could sense that she was a bit distracted. Was it something to do with Henry, her son? Work? Josh, her 'friend'? I decided to start off with a softball.

"How's the real estate business?" I lightly asked. Meg was the top real estate agent in the area and always had the latest market analysis at her fingertips.

"Fine, but everyone is a bit concerned about rising interest rates. As always, the market goes up and down. Property in Langford holds its value, though. The combination of beach, recreational activities, top schools, and a great medical facility is hard to beat." The words were upbeat, but Meg was chewing her lower lip.

"You look like you have something on your mind," I ventured.

After a moment of silence, she sighed. "I got a call today from Savannah Archer. She's the wife of Theo, the jogger who died. She and Theo had been trying to sell the house because they were divorcing. They've had no luck, and she wants a second opinion. I can already tell it's overpriced, but I'll stop by to take a look." She paused and then added with a grimace, "The home is in Mariner Heights."

I knew that Meg had issues in the past with the developer of Mariner Heights. The builder hadn't allowed local real estate agents to be involved, and all the buyers paid far above market value. Meg was honest to a fault and despised unsavory selling tactics. The whole saga was still a sore memory with her.

Mariner Heights, itself, was a relatively new gated development in Langford. It was a community of thirty homes built adjacent to a designer eighteen-hole golf course. As might be expected, each homesite offered pond, bay, or ocean views. Meg had told me that there were six elegant house models, each of which could be fully customized for even the most demanding buyer. The smallest home was 5,000 square feet, and many backyards sported pools, cabanas, and outdoor kitchens. As the developer intended, it was an enclave of very wealthy, demanding residents.

A legion of housekeepers, nannies, landscapers, and property managers arrived daily to keep the development running. Dinner parties, golf tournaments, book clubs, and children's outings dominated the residents' schedules. As if to announce their arrival, the Mariner Heights Community Association had entered a float worthy of the Rose Bowl Parade in the Langford July 4th contest last year. It easily captured first place.

Although some longtime residents of Langford bristled at the lavish displays of new money, the same Community Association also raised funds for the schools, the senior center, and the Langford Library.

I waited to speak because I knew she had more to say.

"I know they were divorcing, but they have kids," Meg finally went on. "And speaking to her was unsettling. Even though it was such a sudden and tragic death, one that must have shocked her and the family, she was very matter-of-fact. There was no hint of sadness or loss in her tone. By the end of our call, I was totally convinced no love was lost because of Theo's death."

Sandy arrived noisily with our meals. She obviously had overheard snippets of our chat. As she set the plates down, she immediately weighed in. "Mariner Depths is what I call them. They're all so entitled and haughty. Plus, they demand lime wedges with everything and are lousy tippers. But I know they are gonna love Arlo's Kiss of Death Chicken Salad today."

The tribe has spoken. It was a reminder to stay on Sandy's good side.

Meg nodded slightly in agreement and took a bite of her Reuben before continuing her train of thought. "I know divorce is hard. Look at my life."

Meg's ex-husband, Artie, a financial titan, had been very generous in the divorce and always provided for their teenage son, Henry. Meg was wealthy in her own right, but Artie insisted on providing the best for both Meg and Henry. I suspected it had to do with some paternal guilt. Although Artie loved Henry, he was often away on business trips, both national and international, and so the lion's share of raising Henry had fallen to Meg.

"Even though Artie and I aren't together, I'd feel terrible if something happened to him. I mean, we had a baby together."

So many thoughts came into my head then. Was Theo's death due to cardiac arrest? Or was there a killer on the loose? Must I open Pandora's box or should I stop now while I was ahead? Finally, I looked at Meg and sighed.

"What?" she asked.

"Well, as you know, the jogger's brother is an RN in Creighton Memorial's emergency department. I spoke with him today, and he doesn't believe Theo Archer had a cardiac event. Jeremy suspects foul play."

Meg dropped her fork and shook her curls, which today shone in a glossy raven color.

"No! No, no, no. Do *not* even begin to go down this road, Maeve. We've retired as private investigators, remember? We turned in our badges long ago. I mean, our last adventure almost finished off the both of us."

I was quiet. She was right. Our last caper had placed many people in harm's way, not the least ourselves. I needed to leave Theo Archer's death to the police.

Sipping tea, I looked down at my plate and nodded in silent agreement.

However, when I looked up again, she was drilling her baby blues into me, and I detected a bit of a twinkle.

"But then again, what if he was murdered? And what if we can help? Who better than the M&M's?"

I didn't respond. But I felt the rabbit hole suddenly becoming crowded.

CHAPTER EIGHT

———

Menses is the term used to describe the menstrual flow.

After a long day of postpartum rounds and a GYN session, I called Geena Sheehan to see how she was doing. Her blood test had confirmed cholestasis, and she had already been called by a fellow midwife. However, I knew her well and suspected she had googled the disease. In the past this had led some patients to focus on the worst aspects of their condition. I wanted to follow up with her about any concerns.

She answered on the first ring. Geena told me her baby was very active, and her itching was fairly controlled by the comfort measures we had previously discussed. We reviewed her medications and went over follow-up appointments and what symptoms to report to the midwifery practice.

Geena and I conversed for a fair amount of time. After hanging up, I realized I'd have to scramble to get to family dinner on time. On the way to my car, I grabbed a small autumnal flower arrangement featuring red and orange maple leaves and yellow tea roses from the Creighton Memorial gift shop. I knew Will was bringing chocolate cream pies for dessert, but I wanted to contribute a little something, too. Aidan and Sebi decorated thoroughly for every season, and I wanted to enhance their dinner table.

They had designed their dream house for six months before Sebi and his team started construction. It looked like a classic antique Victorian from the outside, but the inside was tailor-made for a modern family with state-of-the-art features in every room.

From the number of cars parked in front of the house, I saw that I was the last to arrive and so I hurried up to the door. As

I entered the foyer, which showcased an intriguing mural of a pastoral countryside done by a local artist, the first person I saw was Mom. She was dressed to impress in dark brown slacks and a peach and white raglan-sleeved sweater. And, of course, there were crisscrossing rows of glittering sequins across the front.

Mary Margaret Callahan O'Reilly, my mother, was a force of nature, often on the order of hurricanes, tsunamis, or devastating floods. The oldest of fourteen, she loved family, friends, animals, the oppressed, all things Irish, St. Jude, the Red Sox, and a good party, or as she called it, a time. She had been widowed young and now used a wheelchair full-time because of debilitating arthritis. In her signature style, sequins were a necessity for daily wear.

"Hello, Maeve! I'm so happy you got out on schedule. Rowan and Sloane are having a great time in the living room with their cousins."

"Hi, Mom, you look festive," I said as I leaned down to kiss her.

"I found three new tops at Bargain Alley. I also got the grandchildren bubbles, jump ropes, and coloring books. I do love that place. It's one-stop shopping."

Seeing what Mom had discovered at the warehouse-like store where odd lots were sold was always an adventure.

"They will be thrilled," I said, hoping the bubbles stayed unopened until after we left the house.

I then headed into the kitchen to say hello to our hosts.

"Hi, Maeve," Sebi said, hugging me. "Wonderful timing."

He was tall, dark, and handsome, just like the cliché. He was also an incredible brother-in-law and an accomplished cook. He noticed the bouquet I was holding and took it from me.

"Thank you for these," Sebi said, placing the flowers in a light tan ceramic vase. "They'll go beautifully on the table."

Aidan sidled up to us and said, "I think we're ready to eat. Dinner for seventeen, can you believe it?" He was smiling broadly. These two loved hosting large dinner parties, especially ones for family.

I settled next to Will at the table after saying many hellos and exchanging hugs and kisses. Then I looked around the table and couldn't help but smile. Family dinner! We tried to meet weekly and took turns hosting. The dinner itself could be anything the cook desired, even takeout. It was just important that we were together.

Aidan and Sebi went full-out Italian tonight, which was a fan favorite.

A huge antipasto selection and large platters of spaghetti and meatballs were on the table. I also saw a plate of stuffed shells being passed around. It was a pasta feast, and Rowan and Sloane loved it. All the kids did. And all the adults, too.

After surveying the table, Olivia, Patrick's wife, exclaimed, *"Magnifique!"*

I immediately found Meg's eyes. Why was Olivia speaking French? In return, Meg gave me *The Look*. All sisters know it. We didn't need words. Sister ESP was foolproof. We would hash this over later.

The truth was, Olivia changed her wardrobe and persona on a dime. Watching her go through life was like watching a runway show of different lifestyle choices. I'd witnessed her organic cotton days, her raw food eating era, her ponytailed hipster phase, and, last but not least, her 1950s shirtwaist time. I had to admit that Olivia was nothing if not dedicated once she committed to a theme. Her dress, home décor, and meals quickly followed suit, and Patrick and their four girls were also pressed into serving the trend.

Well, at least the girls were.

I took a close look at Olivia. Since I had arrived just in time for dinner, I hadn't looked at her outfit until now. The first thing I noticed was that her hair was cut in a sleek, chin-length style, which suited her. Next, dark red lipstick, a jaunty paisley scarf, and a white silk fitted blouse made her look like a young sophisticate. Then it hit me. I looked at Penelope, Sarah, Becca, and Cassie. They were all wearing tiny red berets. How had I missed this? Olivia was channeling *Emily in Paris*.

I could hardly wait to see this play out.

The dinner was scrumptious, but the conversation was even better. The dominant themes were playgrounds, Thomas the Tank Engine, wrestling, and Lawrence the Lion. Aidan was the bestselling author of a series of children's books featuring Lawrence, and the nieces and nephews always wanted to know what the lion would do next. The adventures of Thomas and his friends placed a close second.

During a lull, Mom looked around the table and said, "I've been thinking about Ireland a lot lately. Maeve, talking to your darling Kate really makes me want to visit. I want all of us to go."

The entire O'Reilly clan in Ireland? The country might never recover. Plus, how could it ever be arranged with our various schedules, not to mention the cost?

"Maybe that's something we could plan for, Mom," Patrick said. "Perhaps you and Meg and Maeve could go."

"But Patrick, I want the entire family to experience the beauty and to meet my family and Dad's."

We were all silent for a moment. Mom rarely asked for anything. I looked at Meg. I knew she was silently calculating costs. She would always help bankroll anything for the family, but this was a big ask.

"Mom, let's think about this," Aidan said. "It requires a lot of thought, but it's a great idea."

"I agree," Henry joined in. "I've read a lot of Irish history and would love to explore castles and see the Cliffs of Moher."

Suddenly, everyone began weighing in on what they wanted to see in Eire. To pull it off, though, the O'Reillys would need to be magicians. And Mom wasn't getting any younger.

As the dinner ended, it was decided that Meg and Henry would drop Mom off at Hanville Grove, the senior residence where she chose to live.

Will took Rowan and headed out to the van as I gave last-minute hugs. When I got to Meg, I had to wait while she reapplied lipstick and put a few drops in her eyes.

"Meg, I wish you would stop using those eye drops," Mom said with an exasperated sigh. "They can kill you, you know."

"Mom, they refresh my eyes and take the red out. Seriously, they're just eye drops."

"I know what I read," Mom said.

Hearing that exchange, I knew it was time to make my exit. Mom was a dedicated consumer of every tabloid available, and she had a lot of time to read. But she also seemed to believe that anything in print had attained the gold standard for truth and objectivity. As a result, Meg and I had been on the receiving end of some strange bits of advice over the years.

I couldn't wait to spring a mention of 'killer eye drops' on Meg at some appropriate future moment. Chuckling over the thought, I picked up Sloane and headed out.

The night air was chilly, with just a whisper of winter. I took a deep breath and drank it in. New England. Was there any better place to live? Not for me…even if my sleepy town could occasionally be featured on a true crime podcast.

CHAPTER NINE

———

The duration between menstrual cycles is counted from the first day of one menstrual cycle to the first day of the next cycle.

Looking out at a few hardy roses still blooming in our garden, I poured coffee into my thermos while waiting for Kate to arrive at Primrose Cottage. It still felt strange being in the house this "late" in the morning on a workday. My internal clock hadn't recognized the shift to academic life yet. Today, my girls were already fed, changed, and ready for their day. It was heavenly to have this early morning time with them.

When I arrived at Rosemont, I knew my slides and detailed notes were ready for my first lecture, but was I? I hoped so.

My stomach did a few flips as the students were filing in and settling down. Why had I not realized that over fifty people would be present? Fumbling with the cable, I momentarily struggled to get my laptop connected to the school's equipment. Was that sweat on my brow? *Come on, Maeve, pull it together.*

As I began to focus and relax a bit, I noticed that Gwendolyn Birch, the obstetrics faculty chair, had taken a seat in the last row. *Great! Let's raise that anxiety meter some more!* Breathing exercises were not going to help me now.

I opened my notebook and saw a pencil sketch of a woman lecturing to a packed auditorium of cheering students. Red hearts floated above them. Will! Smiling, I gathered my thoughts and began.

"Good morning. As you know, I'm Maeve O'Reilly Kensington, a nurse midwife at Creighton Memorial Hospital. This year, Rosemont College is experimenting with a dual appointment position. I will give some of your lectures and have a group of six students per term for clinical rotations at the hospital."

A few nods, a few heads bent over phones, and more than a few closed eyes. It looked like I was starting with less than a bang. But then, in the right near corner of the auditorium, I spied Lilly, one of my clinical rotation students, giving me a wide grin. *Okay, score one for the rebel alliance.*

"Today, I'll discuss fetal development." I knew this could be a dry topic, so I had interspersed it with maternal symptoms and real-life vignettes for the appropriate gestational weeks. The audiovisual department at Creighton Memorial had been incredibly helpful in making superb slides, and I felt the tension leave me as I warmed to my subject.

After discussing first trimester anatomy, I listed the signs and symptoms that pregnant women often felt. More than anything else, the real-life examples seemed to captivate the class. In the middle of the auditorium, I saw Edgar and Helene listening intently and taking notes. All eyes seemed to be on me as I talked about comfort measures and warning signs, using case studies. Before I knew it, I only had five minutes of class time left. After assigning reading for the next session, I reviewed my office hours and email address for the class and told them I was happy to meet for any reason.

My first lecture was over. I packed up, and the classroom emptied.

Okay, I was still standing. I found my office key in my faculty mailbox and went in search of my assigned space. Opening the door, I discovered a small room that somehow managed to contain an ancient oak desk and chair, a set of bare bookshelves, and a well-worn tan leather side chair. Clearly, new faculty were at the bottom of the pecking order when it came to office allocation. Luckily, the window looked out into a small courtyard.

As I opened my tote to retrieve my laptop, Trudy Delchamps appeared at my door. She was attired in head-to-toe black and carried an overflowing box.

"Hello, hello, Maeve. I know it's a dreary little space. The newbie always gets the leftovers. But you, my dear, have me," she said in her ratatat way of communicating.

Trudy pulled out two flowering purple hyacinth plants in orange and red enamel pots and placed them on the wide windowsill. Next came file folders in every color of the rainbow. Trudy piled them on one of the bookcase shelves.

"I've requested a small filing cabinet for you. It will be here later today."

A yellow pen holder, a green glass bankers' lamp, and a sunset-orange ceramic mug filled with chocolates were all arranged on my desktop.

"I'll bring more, Maeve. This is just to get you started. There are blueberry scones in the staff lounge. Whatever you need, just ask me," Trudy said. Before I could speak, she picked up her empty box and hustled down the corridor.

Well, there was no question that she had elevated the décor. It reminded me a bit of Willy Wonka's Chocolate Factory, though. It also occurred to me that finding space for a filing cabinet might be problematic.

It seemed like a good time for some refreshment, so I made my way to the staff lounge. Since I was looking forward to a few quiet moments, I wasn't disappointed to find it empty. It took a minute, but I found my puppy mug among the many others. I filled it with Earl Grey tea, wrapped up a scone, and returned to my office.

Shutting my door, I stretched and relaxed. Maybe I could get used to this academic life. As I sipped from my new cup while reading Rosemont's morning announcements, I saw an email pop up from Gwendolyn Birch, my department head. *Hi, Maeve. Your lecture was excellent. The students were fully engaged. Strong work!*

As I basked in the glow of the praise, my phone vibrated. The caller was Jeremy Archer.

"Hello," I answered.

"Hi, Maeve. Are you on Labor and Delivery?"

"No, Jeremy. I teach at Rosemont College for part of the week now. I'm on campus today."

There was a brief silence.

"The extensive toxicology report just came back," he said in a choked voice.

What was Jeremy Archer going to tell me?

"It was tetrahydrozoline. Theo died from tetrahydrozoline poisoning."

His words didn't register. "I'm not familiar with that, Jeremy."

"It's the main ingredient in many eye solutions. It's harmless when dropped in the eye but fatal if consumed in large quantities."

What? I was silent. I didn't know how to respond. I had no knowledge of this medication.

"My brother was murdered, Maeve."

CHAPTER TEN

———

The ovaries, which produce and store a female's eggs, are located on each side of the uterus.

After reviewing the information again, Jeremy and I made plans to talk later. Then he hung up to attend a meeting with the Langford police.

My thoughts were jumbled, and I needed someone to help me sort things out. Will was off catering a luncheon at Langford's Nautical Society, so I couldn't call him. Meg's phone went directly to voicemail, and I figured she must be with a client. I finally settled for texting her to call when she could.

For now, I decided the best thing I could do was to google tetrahydrozoline. I saw that it was just as Jeremy had described. The ingredient was indeed in many over-the-counter eye drops, but it was only lethal if ingested. Of course, it was not intended to be placed anywhere but the eyes. To inflict harm, it had to be consumed orally in much larger amounts than one of those little bottles held. Could Theo Archer have confused his meds? Obviously, that didn't make sense. He wouldn't drink eye solution. As I read on, the realization hit me. Theo Archer may have indeed met with foul play.

My phone pinged. *Meet you on Rosemont Green at 1? I'll bring lunch.*

Meg must be texting from her real estate meeting. I responded with a thumbs-up emoji and then tried to concentrate on writing my next OB lecture. It was no use, though. My thoughts were firmly stuck on eye drops.

Suddenly, it hit me. Mom! What had Mom meant when she warned Meg to be careful with her eye drops? Why did she say that? What did she know?

I grabbed my phone and tapped her name on my list of favorites.

Mom answered on the first ring. "I'm just off to my painting class, Maeve. How are my girls?"

Mom had a very full social calendar at Hanville Grove.

"They're great. Mom, I need to ask you something. What did you mean about Meg and her eye drops?"

"Those darn drops can be perilous. I read in the *New York Post* that a woman in Montana killed her husband by putting them in his coffee. I always tell Meg that I wish she wouldn't use them. Oh, here's the elevator, Maeve. We'll talk later."

There was no use explaining to Mom that eye drops were fine if used appropriately. Mom always knew best and believed any news report originating in the Big Apple was gospel.

She hung up, leaving me with my own thoughts once again. Since it was apparent that the lecture wouldn't get written now, I decided to find out more about the murder Mom had read about.

Again, I pulled up my search engine and tried to find mention of the case. First, I tried *tetrahydrozoline*, but that only got me a string of notifications for various brands of eye drops. I groaned, knowing this meant I'd be inundated with advertisements for all things optical on the internet for a while. Then I added the words *murder* and *eye drops* and immediately found what I sought.

The article was from three years ago. A thirty-eight-year-old mother of two had laced her unfaithful husband's coffee with large amounts of tetrahydrozoline, and he had collapsed and subsequently died. The murder was only discovered because the wife, who was racked with guilt, confessed to her best friend.

An involuntary shiver ran up my spine as I wondered how often this cause of death was overlooked. And how had it happened to Theo? Who could have planned this? Could it have been Savannah? She had the motive of an acrimonious divorce and a tough prenup. She and Theo still shared a home, so she had access to his beverages. Was it possible that she was a murderer?

I decided the best thing I could do was to venture out to the green and wait for Meg. Maybe getting outside would bring me some clarity.

The day had warmed to sixty-two degrees, and the quad was filled with students. This was no surprise since, in New England, it was a given that one had to take advantage of every sunny fall day. Everyone knew that wintery weather would soon be on the horizon.

Frisbees were flying, and I heard strains of "Shake It Off" by Taylor Swift as I commandeered a bench near the arts center, away from the hubbub. Texting Meg my location, I sat down.

I felt very decadent as I waited, doing nothing. Often at Creighton Memorial, the staff barely had time to inhale a cup of yogurt at lunchtime, let alone loll in the midday sun. I realized the tradeoff, though. The college faculty put in many off-campus hours preparing classes, advising students, researching, writing for publication, and grading papers. It was all a balance. Could I adjust to this sort of schedule? Time would tell, I supposed. For now, I was delighted to have a foot in each world—and to sit in the sun.

"Is this bench reserved for faculty only?" Meg grinned as she sat beside me.

An Eileen Fisher plum boiled-wool jacket and matching shell accompanied her pleated black slacks and low-heeled ankle boots. I knew Meg took great care with her wardrobe, but I couldn't help envying how effortless she made it look.

"Hey, I was lucky to get seats on a beautiful day like this," I pointed out.

She opened her massive Louis Vuitton tote and pulled out toasted lobster BLTs, Cape Cod chips, and bottles of lemonade. I knew dessert, undoubtedly chocolate, wouldn't be far behind.

Meg took a sip of her drink and gave me a long stare from behind her thick, black lashes. She finally said, "Spill. I can tell you have news."

My sister. I never could hide anything from her.

"I just heard from Jeremy Archer. There was a lethal dose of tetrahydrozoline in Theo Archer's system. Someone killed him."

"Murder. It's always murder with you." She had begun a head roll for the ages but then snapped her gaze back into focus. "Wait. What is tetrahydrozoline? And how does it figure into Theo's death?"

I couldn't help myself then. "You should listen to Mom more, Meg. Those eye drops really can be lethal."

Meg stared at me, knowing I'd explain myself sooner or later. She was right.

"Many eye drops contain tetrahydrozoline," I explained. "It's harmless in the eye, but it's lethal if you drink enough of it."

"So, you think Theo Archer suffered murder by eye drops?" Meg asked. She suspected I had taken to seeing foul play in every dark happening in Langford. Maybe I shouldn't have led with the remark about Mom.

"Well, not by eye drops exactly. But from the main ingredient in certain ones."

I started at the beginning, going from Jeremy Archer's call and ending with the story I found online.

Meg was quiet when I finished. Then she said, "Well, I guess Mom was right again. Killer eye drops for the win."

"Yup. We should know by now to never underestimate her."

"Disabled? Elderly? Senior living? Nothing slows her down. I'd bet on Mom every time. She's unstoppable."

I nodded in agreement.

"We'll need to know more about Theo Archer's life," I said tentatively.

Meg pulled out two sizeable double chocolate whoopie pies from the recesses of her bag and passed me one—dessert at last.

"Maeve, are we going to put ourselves out there for Jeremy Archer? Really, you just met him. Let's be rational for once. Maybe we should just see what happens next."

I said nothing as I bit into the pie. Maybe chocolate couldn't solve all problems, but it was momentarily chasing all my thoughts of murder far away.

CHAPTER ELEVEN

———

Ovulation refers to an ovary releasing an egg. In a twenty-eight-day menstrual cycle, ovulation usually occurs around day fourteen.

The next day I woke early, showered, and made a cup of tea while the girls still slept. A weekday off with my girls. Heavenly! And it didn't hurt that I had found a note from Will taped to the mirror in the bathroom. It was a line drawing of me, or rather a stylish version of me pushing Rowan and Sloane in a royal-looking carriage with Fenway trailing behind. A flurry of red hearts floated behind us. *My women...love you all* was written at the bottom of the card. Smiling and thinking of my honey, I got yogurt and blueberry waffles ready.

After breakfast, Rowan, Sloane, Fenway, and I were listening to Raffi in the sunroom when the doorbell rang. Taking Rowan's hand while carrying Sloane, I slowly approached the front door. Of course, Fenway had gotten there first and was crying and running in circles. Since she wasn't barking, I was certain it was someone she recognized. Looking through the side window panel, I saw Kate. My first thought was that she had mixed up the schedule.

I let go of Rowan and quickly opened the door. "Kate, good morning. Come in. You do remember today's my day off, right?"

"I know, I know, Maeve. Sorry to barge in, but I just need to have a wee chat." She bent down and said, "Hello, my beauties," as she kissed the girls and picked up Rowan. "Yes, I see you, too, Fenway love." She bent again to pat her.

Kate was always neatly dressed and ready to roll when she came to work at dawn. Today, though, she looked disheveled and exhausted. Her hair was unwashed and pulled back with a headband, and her jacket buttons were fastened incorrectly. Maybe she'd had a late night, I thought, but even then I knew something was off.

Putting the kettle on, I watched Kate put the girls in the gated playroom so we could easily keep an eye on them. She took a seat at the kitchen table. After pouring mugs of tea and putting out an apple cider cake, I sat down across from her.

"What's wrong?" Selfishly, my first thought was to hope it was nothing that would stop her from being our nanny. Our last nanny had moved across the country, and although we were happy for her, we were devastated for ourselves. But now the girls were thriving with Kate, and I hoped she would not tell me that Ireland was calling her home.

"Oh, Maeve. I haven't slept a wink all night." She sat on the edge of the chair, looking at me with bleary eyes. Then she took a long sip and revealed the cause of her worry. "Fiona is in a world of trouble."

"What happened?"

"She nannies, or rather was a nanny, for the Archers over in swanky Mariner Heights. You know who they are. The husband was the dead man you found."

Fiona was the Archers' nanny? How had I never heard this before?

And, technically, I didn't find Theo.

"Well, everyone thought he had a heart attack, but now the town is buzzing that he was poisoned."

The Langford unofficial hotline must be in overdrive. No information was sacred in a small town.

Kate tapped her foot nonstop while she continued, "Mrs. Archer called the *Garda* yesterday and told them that Fiona was having a romantic relationship with her husband and had probably murdered him!"

My eyes widened. I knew by the Irish term, *Garda*, that Kate was referring to the Langford police.

"What? Where is Fiona now?"

"She's with Bridie. The police want her to come to the station at noon. Can you help her, Maeve?"

Kate and I talked at length, and then I dialed Meg. Fiona needed help, and I wanted to ensure all bases were covered.

After a conference call, Meg and I assured Kate that Fiona would have skilled representation against the well-heeled Savannah Archer. To this end, Meg told Kate she would call Indigo Mitchell, a friend and highly sought-after criminal defense attorney, to meet with Fiona and accompany her to the police station. When Kate raised the cost issue, Meg immediately cut her off, and I surmised that, as usual, the Bank of Meg would be footing the bill.

We ended the call, and Kate left to fill Fiona in and support her. For my part, I had promised I would call Patrick and attempt to get a few answers. When I tried to reach my older brother, though, his phone went to voicemail.

Since it was a glorious day, I decided to stick to my original plan, and Rowan, Sloane, Fenway, and I took a trip to the playground at Starfish Park. Once there, we made a beeline for the two rows of baby swings that were just the right size for my girls. They both squealed with delight as I pushed them back and forth. As I looked around at the twisty slides, climbers, and merry-go-rounds, I realized a playground trip would truly be an adventure when both of my daughters were mobile and had competing interests.

A group of nannies, dressed in long gray formal coats and all with short hair or tight buns, huddled with their charges on the dark green benches at the edge of the children's section. Since I had researched the school online, I recognized the uniforms and realized that this must be the cadre of Bloomsby nannies from Mariner Heights. Seeing them made me wonder how Fiona was faring. Had Theo Archer cheated on his wife, and if so, was it with Fiona? Was that the reason for the divorce? Who murdered Theo? So many unanswered questions swirled in my mind.

After many more pushes on the swings, walking every inch of the playground multiple times, and chasing Fenway back and forth endlessly in the gated grassy area, the four of us were ready to leave.

On the way home, the girls fell quickly asleep in their stroller. I bundled Fenway into the stroller's bottom storage, wrapped in her cozy red blanket, and she soon followed suit.

Since everyone was asleep, I decided to stop at A Child's Garden, a high-end clothing and toy store in downtown Langford. The clothes were exquisite and very costly, but I had found some treasures for my daughters on their sale rack.

The shop owner, Felicia, held the door open as I pushed the stroller inside.

"Hello, Maeve. I see your girls are sleeping soundly. They are beauties. Are you looking for anything special?"

"Good to see you, Felicia. No, I'm just browsing. You do have the sweetest children's clothes."

The shop was small enough that I parked the stroller next to the dressing room and surveyed the baby girls' area. Embroidered silk, cotton, and linen dresses in every color of the rainbow graced the racks. Palming a price tag, I saw that a pastel yellow smocked number that would look stunning on Rowan was $245. Yikes! Beautiful, yes, but who could afford these prices? Well, someone must because I knew from Felicia that the shop was thriving.

I perused the sale rack, looking for a Thanksgiving dress for Rowan. Sloane could wear the fetching champagne colored one Meg had bought her big sister last year. That was another benefit of having girls eight months apart.

Moving the mini hangers, I spied a pale gold and cream smocked dress with a white Peter Pan collar and puffed sleeves. It was gorgeous. Flipping the tag, I saw the frock was on final sale because it was from the spring line. It had been marked down from $280 to $30. What a bargain! This was coming home with me.

I rolled my stroller toward the checkout register hoping I would be out of the shop before my threesome woke up. As I did, I saw a deeply tanned, very fit woman in a black and white Chanel suit and pearls talking to Felicia.

"Alasdair will need a complete ski outfit as well as formal and casual holiday attire. We are going to our lodge in Jackson Hole for Thanksgiving, and I would like everything ready a few weeks before we leave. My assistant can send you a list of our activities. Please put together a few options for each event and send me photos. Then, I can make my final picks. Oh, I'll also need some gifts for the nieces and nephews—something cute for when they tire of outdoor play. But remember, the toys must be educational. I'll have a list emailed to you with the children's ages and gender. I'd like this as soon as possible."

"Of course, Mrs. Talbot. I'll get right on it," Felicia said with a smile.

As the woman turned, she looked at me and the girls. "Oh, so sweet. Are they twins?"

I got this question a lot, and it always made me chuckle. The girls would have had to grow at vastly different rates to be twins.

"No, they're eight months apart."

"Oh, you used a surrogate. How smart. I should have done that. Well, cheerio, Felicia. I'm off to a luncheon."

The bell on the door gently tinkled as it closed.

Felicia said nothing. Clients like this were her bread and butter. She rang up my purchase, wrapped it in tissue, and placed it in her signature silver shopping bag with a garden motif. I kept thinking of Mrs. Talbot and her worldview. Surrogacy was usually a miraculous and joyous occasion after a long fertility journey. But apparently Mrs. Talbot only saw it as a convenience.

As I signed the credit card reader, I saw Felicia writing a label with Mrs. Talbot's address. She resided in Mariner Heights.

A different breed, all right.

When I returned home, the girls were still sound asleep, so I put the stroller in the nursery, turned on the baby monitor, and started to get some laundry done. My phone pinged, and I saw a curt message from Meg. *Don't want to ring bell. Open door.*

When I followed orders, Meg marched in like a woman on a mission, putting two large bags on the kitchen table and flinging her maroon Kate Spade crossbody bag on a chair.

"Well, this day is becoming a challenge," she declared. "Fiona has an appointment at the police station and, luckily, Indigo will be with her. On the heels of that, I'm meeting Savannah Archer at three to discuss strategy for selling her house and will have to be very careful about what I say."

She stalked over to the table and began pulling out muffins, scones, two large cranberry seltzers, and two jumbo-sized fruit and nut chocolate bars--all the essentials necessary for a midday debriefing.

Handing me a large chunk of candy, she said, "Chocolate is healthy, and these even have fruit."

Well, she wasn't wrong. "Did you talk to Fiona?"

"No, Indigo said to let her handle it."

"Meg, Fiona's a kid. An Irish kid who has no family here and is now being cast as a murderer."

"There's got to be more to the story. Did Savannah just discover that Theo was cheating? Does she truly believe Fiona would murder Theo? Kate said that Savannah called Fiona a thief in the past, and then her bracelet magically appeared. What is really going on?"

"Do you think Savannah made it all up?" I asked.

Meg narrowed her eyes slightly. "I don't know. But this whole thing is struggling to pass the smell test, Maeve. So, I want answers, and I want the truth. If Fiona is blameless, she cannot be left high and dry."

Meg had long ago been denied employment at the hands of a rich and devious male boss because she refused his advances. Now, her hackles were raised by any possible injustice towards young women, and she had the resources and contacts to back up her inclinations.

"For now, Fiona is out of a job and also accused of sleeping with her boss and possibly committing murder," I pointed out. I told her that Kate said that Bloomsby nannies had replaced almost all the Irish nannies at Mariner Heights.

"Of course. Those women all have the 'fear of missing out' if they're not in lockstep with their peers." Then she deliberated, "I wonder if Savannah Archer has any real proof for her accusations."

"Do you think you'll have any problems representing her in the house deal?"

"Oh, I'll give her my honest opinion about pricing and staging. And I've never met Fiona in person…at least, not yet. Maybe I'll get a better read on Mrs. Archer and the late Mr. Archer from our meeting. Remember, I don't represent Savannah yet."

Meg would undoubtedly use her X-ray vision to size Savannah up. It would be an unfair contest.

"I need to run," Meg suddenly said. "I'll fill you in once I hear from Indigo and after I do the house assessment."

She was off in a cloud of Coco Mademoiselle, heels clicking.

Meg didn't call back for the rest of the afternoon. Dinnertime arrived, and I was still wondering what had gone on with Fiona and the police, not to mention what Meg had learned about Savannah Archer.

Meanwhile, Will brought dinner home from the café's daily fare. After a bit of rewarming, the four of us sat down to a meal of my favorite sort of "leftovers."

"Off to Rosemont tomorrow?" Will asked. He was trying to catch Sloane's mouth with a spoonful of mashed avocado, but it was a moving target, and the results were pretty much hit-and-miss.

"Yes, it will be a full day, starting with a faculty breakfast."

"Maeve O'Reilly Kensington, midwife and college faculty—my multi-talented wife." Will beamed at me.

"Wait a minute—a dual appointment is not a full faculty member. I'm looking forward to going behind the scenes in academic life, but I have more than a few butterflies. Truthfully, in the end, I just hope I don't bore the students to death."

"Maeve, you have so much clinical experience to share. They couldn't possibly be bored. You're also a great public speaker, so I know you'll do well."

He hugged me reassuringly. Will was always in my corner.

When the girls had finished dinner, I cleaned the kitchen while Will got their bath ready. Then we both did baths and bedtime. Once they were asleep, Will went to the sunroom, where he kept an antique desk he had restored, to catch up on some catering paperwork.

Meanwhile, I turned on the latest episode of *Annika*, which I had recorded. Only Nicola Walker could take my mind off the events of this day. Well, that along with a bowl of mint chocolate chip ice cream with sprinkles might do the trick.

Just as I brought up the first spoonful, my phone rang. It was Meg.

"Hey, Meg, I've been waiting to hear from you," I said, sitting bolt upright.

"I figured. I got home late and knew you would be busy with Rowan and Sloane."

"True. We just got them to bed. So how was the grieving Mrs. Archer?"

"Well, she wasn't exactly the weeping widow. She's probably in her late thirties, and strangely enough, she's even more attractive in person than her videos suggest. She has two little girls for whom a British nanny was caring. I tried subtly asking if the nanny was new, but I didn't want to push it."

"Are you going to represent her?"

"I gave her all the comps and told her that the house was priced too high for the current market. She may listen, but she has her eye on a pricey large contemporary on Eagle Cove Road, the last street in the Mariner Heights complex. I told her to think it over and get back to me. We'll see what she does."

"Have you heard from Indigo? I didn't call Kate because I feared she would be with Fiona."

"Yes. Savannah insists Theo and Fiona were having a romantic tryst. She also claims Theo came to his senses and ended it, and Fiona retaliated by poisoning him. Kate told me Fiona is shaken up, and Indigo left her with Bridget and the nanny group. She believes they'll be able to take care of her."

My mind was troubled. Would Savannah blame Fiona for no reason? And if she did, why? Had Fiona and Theo been romantically involved? Doubtful, but who knows? But most importantly, would Fiona's name be cleared?

"But Meg, how can Savannah blame Fiona without proof? Maybe she killed him herself. I mean, it happens when infidelity is uncovered."

"Already lining up suspects, Maeve?"

"Fiona needs us. I'll be at Rosemont all day tomorrow, but I'll text you when I'm done."

"Fiona does need us. The M&M's *are* back. Now, get some sleep. Did you get a new houndstooth suit or perhaps a pair of pumps with front buckles?"

"Good night, Meg."

CHAPTER TWELVE

———

Women are born with approximately one to two million eggs. At the time of menopause, a woman has about 1,000 to 2,000 eggs left.

After a long day of faculty meetings and lecture writing, I got to my car. I had just clicked in the seatbelt when a text came in from Meg: *Langford police having press conference at station. Meet me there.*

Yes, ma'am, I mumbled before pulling out of the lot.

At the Langford police station, I saw several news vans parked along Main Street. Of course, the media would be here to cover this murder. It had all the sensational elements—small seaside town, a tech titan who was also a bestselling author, a foreign nanny, and rumors of illicit entanglements. Death by poison just sweetened the pot.

I parked on a side street, and approaching the station, I saw four Langford police officers gathered by a microphone out front. A small crowd was forming on the lawn. As I scanned the knot of people, I spotted Meg standing in the back and made my way over to her.

"What's happening, Meg?" I asked, giving her a quick hug.

At that moment, Chief Mike Petrucelli tapped on the mic and began to speak. "Good afternoon, ladies and gentlemen. We will issue a brief statement on the death of Mr. Theodore Archer. It appears that Mr. Archer died from an overdose of tetrahydrozoline. At autopsy, his blood tested positive for that chemical. The investigation is still in the very early stages. As we develop a timeline for the murder and question several people, we will keep the public informed. We do not believe that the public is in any danger at this time. Deputy Chief Patrick O'Reilly will take your questions now."

"Of course, he will," Meg scoffed sotto voce.

Our brother Patrick was a master at speaking to the press. He was well respected and often the public face of the Langford Police Department. Meg and I firmly believed that he should be the next chief.

Five reporters started speaking at the same time.

"One at a time, please. I'll take all your questions, but one at a time."

"Do you think this was a crime of passion?" Libby Stewart from Channel 3 asked.

"We have no evidence of that," Patrick responded with a steely look.

"Way to take charge, Pat," Meg whispered.

"I heard that the Archers' nanny was brought in for questioning," Ted Gleason from Channel 9 commented.

"As Captain Petrucelli said, we will be bringing several people in for questioning. The investigation is in the early stages."

"He's a wizard at deflection," Meg said proudly.

"Is it true that the poison was in his water bottle?" Mira Johnson from the Langford Times asked.

"All evidence is being examined now, and we will update statements as the results become available."

"In other words, pound sand until I release any info," Meg said softly.

Listening to Patrick, I surveyed the crowd and saw Jeremy Archer standing a few feet from us on the right. Thank goodness he had pushed for a complete toxicology investigation.

The press conference continued until questions were being repeated. Finally, Patrick said, "Thank you, ladies and gentlemen. As I said, we will keep you updated on any new developments."

The crowd began to disperse, and I caught Jeremy's eye.

"How are you doing, Jeremy? This must be so hard." He had deep circles under his eyes.

"Hi, Maeve. I'm okay. I'm just still in shock that I was right about Theo's cause of death."

"How's the family doing?"

"I don't know. Theo and Savannah's divorce proceedings were rather hostile, so as of now, I am persona non grata. Savannah has effectively cut me off. I hope she eventually lets me visit with the kids."

"I'm sorry. That's very difficult."

Meg joined us, and I introduced them.

"I hear that Savannah is trying to incriminate the nanny," Jeremy said solemnly.

"Yes, she is. The nanny's name is Fiona, and she was questioned about it today. I don't know her, but my nanny is her friend and believes she is innocent," I said.

"I don't doubt it," Jeremy replied. "I know Savannah's under a lot of stress, but she is also the type to cast blame. Savannah had been desperate to break her prenup. I hate to say this, but I need to be realistic. I do wonder if Savannah killed Theo."

Meg looked at me, but I was as speechless as she was.

"Jeremy!" called out an older man from the crowd. Jeremy looked up and waved.

"I need to go, but it was so nice to see you again, Maeve. And it's been nice meeting you, Meg. I'll be in touch."

As we watched him walk away, Meg shook her head. "For the sake of those kids, I hope Savannah had nothing to do with this murder."

In my head, I put Savannah Archer down as suspect number one. Weren't motive and opportunity always the key components to look for in foul play?

Wait a minute. Was I starting a suspect list? I guess I was.

Savannah?

Fiona?

Poison!

Hm, I was a long way from having any ducks in a row.

As the crowd dispersed, I saw Patrick motion that he wanted to speak with us. Was it about the case? That would be unusual since Patrick generally wanted us as far away as possible from any police action. We'd had more than a few confrontations in the past about that very issue.

We walked over to Patrick's truck, parked in the far corner of the police lot.

"Hey, girls, how are you doing?"

He would always be our protective big brother.

"We're okay, Patrick. Excellent press conference as usual," Meg said.

"How are you holding up?" I asked.

"Well, it's surprising that another murder has occurred in small-town Langford, and my youngest sister was once again front and center at the event."

"Technically, I was at the scene but was not the first to arrive."

He put his hands up in mock surrender and gave me a slight grin.

"Pat, I know you questioned Fiona today," Meg said.

"And *I* know you hired Indigo Marshall to represent her," Pat countered.

"Yes, I did. She's entitled to the best," Meg said, rising to her full height, which, with the help of her three-inch heels, put her eye to eye with our eldest, very tall brother.

Patrick wisely changed the subject. "There is so much we don't know for certain. We're examining the water bottles to ensure they were the source of the poison, although they probably were."

"Tetrahydrozoline is usually found in eye drops, so it's available to just about anyone," I said.

"That's true, but as you know, it has to be consumed in substantial quantities to kill someone, so it had to be a deliberate act."

"Well, I don't think Fiona had anything to do with it, but I know you won't tell us anything," Meg said.

"There's nothing I can say at this time, Meg. But..." He paused to weigh his words. "Well, I *am* asking for your help now."

"What? The Langford police are asking the M&M's for assistance?" I asked, truly shocked.

"On an unofficial basis, of course. You two have been involved in three tough cases and have done amazingly well. This case involves some very wealthy players, and you both know this elite high-society world far better than I do. The police, unfortunately, will have a hard time getting the facts with limited access."

I was stunned, and I knew Meg must be too since she had yet to say a word. Incredibly, Patrick was enlisting our detective services.

"Maeve, you have a nanny, and Meg, you employ a house manager. As you know, the 'help'"—he emphasized this last word and added air quotes—"sees everything. If you were to hear anything pertinent to this case, please let me know."

"So, are we deputies or something? I always wanted to be a deputy, but I won't wear that drab khaki clothing," Meg said, unconsciously brushing off her cashmere jacket.

Patrick winced a bit. He was probably already wishing he could rescind his offer. "No, this is unofficial, but it would seriously help me. Please be extremely cautious. I don't want either of you to be harmed. Just, if you could, keep your ears to the ground. I truly appreciate the assistance. I need to run, but remember, keep this under your hats."

He kissed us goodbye and walked back to the station.

"Well, well, will wonders never cease?" Meg marveled. "I feel very authentic."

"You know, Pat is correct that we can infiltrate that world a lot easier than he and his officers can, and especially you, Meg. You're the real estate agent to the stars."

"But you are connected to many of the nannies," Meg countered. "As Patrick said, they know everything behind the scenes. So, we need to get on the case. First, though, let's get iced Dunkin' coffees. I have a stash of Twizzlers in my car. It's good brain food. It will help us make plans."

My sister defied logic, but I happily went along. If red licorice was beckoning, I was helpless. It was my Achilles' heel.

CHAPTER THIRTEEN

―――――

There are two fallopian tubes, one on each side of the uterus. Eggs from the ovaries pass through them on the way to the uterus.

Yesterday, Meg and I had tried valiantly to start a list of suspects. As of this morning, it consisted of just one person, Savannah Archer. We had put Fiona on the list at first, but then immediately crossed her name off because she gained nothing from killing Theo. Plus we just couldn't bear to add her to the list. It already was clear we needed to pick up our pace if we wanted to help Patrick.

I had just finished a peaceful birth and was sitting in the midwifery call room when an Evite popped up in my messages.

Dinner at Riverbend
Please join us for an Autumn Evening of Fellowship
Riverbend
62 Beaver Dam Road
Saturday, October 5 at six in the evening
Mike & Tom
We look forward to meeting Will!

How fun! I would need to book Kate and ensure that Will's schedule was clear.

A few seconds later, my phone pinged with a text from Meg: *Excited for dinner. Josh coming too. I know the house they bought. It was for sale by owner and a mess. Will be interesting to see what they have done.*

I quickly texted back: *Sounds fun.*

My phone chirped with a message that I had a new patient. It was Audrey Davis. Winnie, my midwife partner on duty last night, had sent me a text that I might see Audrey today, and I had planned to call this morning to check on her. Audrey was a single woman who was pregnant with her first child. I remembered seeing her a few times for prenatal care as I brought her chart up on the workstation. A quick look through it told me she'd had an uneventful prenatal course and was now thirty-nine weeks. Without giving it much more thought, I headed down to the room where she was admitted. I saw the emergency light over her door flash on as I approached.

What?

One of the OB staff, Dr. Wendy Miller, came running from the main desk and entered the room just before me.

Robin, the admitting RN today, had already put an oxygen mask on Audrey's face and turned her on her left side. "There was a deceleration with her contraction," Robin said, gesturing to the monitor.

Audrey's face was bright red, and her eyes were wide and full of fear. A young woman who closely resembled her stood at the side of the labor bed, holding her left hand. She had tears in her eyes.

Dr. Miller donned exam gloves quickly and checked Audrey's progress as I asked questions.

"Hi, Audrey, when did labor start?"

"About 4:00 a.m. I called and spoke to Winnie. The contractions were very mild and she told me when to call. Then I fell asleep and woke up with contractions every six minutes. They were much stronger. I figured I was early but wanted to see how dilated I was, so we came along."

"Well, you were right about being early. Your cervix is long and closed," Dr. Miller said.

The fetal heart had returned to the 130s and was steady without contractions.

"What does that mean?" Audrey asked.

Dr. Miller waited for me to speak.

"That means your cervix has not begun to dilate or shorten yet," I explained. "Now we need to see how your baby tolerates contractions."

"One is starting now."

Audrey closed her eyes and breathed slowly. The woman beside her rubbed her arm and whispered, "I'm Aspen, her twin."

Robin, Dr. Miller, and I all watched the monitor. Once again, the fetal heart decelerated sharply, and this time, it stayed down longer. We changed Audrey's position a few times, but it did not help. Finally, the fetal heart returned to baseline as the contraction wore off.

"Was her heartbeat better?" Audrey asked tensely.

"No, it wasn't," I answered. "Her heartbeat slowed down with that contraction."

Dr. Miller and I exchanged glances.

"Ms. Davis, we can watch for a few more contractions, but your cervix is closed, and your baby is showing signs of distress. Changing position can sometimes help, but it doesn't seem to work for your baby."

"You're starting another contraction," Aspen said as she grasped Audrey's hand tighter.

"Again," she said, dropping her head back.

The contraction built up, and true to form, the fetal heart rate dropped severely.

"Audrey, it appears that you will need a cesarean section," Dr. Miller concluded.

Audrey nodded. She looked dazed.

"A cesarean? Okay." Aspen rubbed Audrey's shoulder. "We saw a movie about that in childbirth class. Remember, Audrey?"

"We're right here with you, Audrey. Let's get your baby born," I said.

"May I be in the OR?" Aspen asked.

"Of course," I replied, as one of the other labor nurses ushered Aspen out to get changed for surgery.

As the contraction finished, Robin and I sprang into action. Robin started an IV as I updated her chart and explained to Audrey what to expect. Dr. Denice Lynch, the obstetric anesthesiologist, briskly walked in and discussed anesthesia options.

"Ms. Davis, your baby's heartbeat is fine without contractions. I can quickly put in a spinal if you'd like so you can be awake for her birth, or you can be put to sleep. I'm sorry that we're moving so fast."

"I'd like a spinal, please," Audrey responded.

Several minutes later, the surgery was underway. I brought Aspen into the operating room and had her sit on a stool at the head of the table. The twins smiled at each other, and Aspen touched Audrey's cheek lightly.

"You got this. We've got this."

Stepping over to watch Dr. Miller's progress, I was curious to see what had caused the fetal distress. From the tracing on the monitor, it appeared to be an umbilical cord issue, but time would tell the tale. The pediatricians had monitoring equipment standing by at the baby station and warming table. The surgeons, the anesthesiologist, the operating room RN, and the technicians all worked together like a finely tuned ballet.

"Here she is," Dr. Miller said as she was about to bring Audrey's baby out. I saw her briefly stop and begin to unravel the umbilical cord from the baby's neck. It appeared to be coiled tightly. Dr. Maiya Wu, the MFM, helped her to untangle the newborn.

With the cord free and safely cut and clamped, the baby was handed off to the pediatricians, while the obstetricians turned back to deliver the placenta and finish the surgery.

"Is she all right?" Audrey asked.

At that moment, we all heard a loud "Waah." A lusty cry arose from the infant on the warming table.

"She looks great," the NICU pediatrician said. "We'll bring her to you in just a minute."

Dr. Miller looked up. "Audrey, your daughter had a tight, very short umbilical cord, and it was wound around her neck twice. That's why her heart rate went down during the contraction and why you needed immediate surgery. But she's fine now, and I'll go over everything when I finish."

I went over and gave Audrey a thumbs-up. She and Aspen were beaming. Silently, I breathed a big sigh of relief. Thankfully, this mother and baby would be fine.

When the surgery was over, Dr. Miller and I reviewed the course of labor with Audrey and Aspen. Baby Vivian was resting peacefully in her mother's arms.

As I went to get a cup of lemon ginger tea, my beeper chirped again. There were calls regarding labor issues from two of the midwifery patients. My tea would need to wait. Two active labor patients of mine were on their way to Creighton, and another had probably ruptured her membranes at thirty-five weeks.

I grabbed a power bar with my tea and added my new patients to the labor and delivery board. There would be no time to stop today and no time to contemplate poison, murder, or mayhem.

CHAPTER FOURTEEN

———

Some women experience lower abdominal discomfort with ovulation. It is called mittelschmerz, which is German for middle pain.

That Saturday, Will and I headed to Tom and Mike's for dinner. I wore my new cocoa-colored suede boot-cut jeans, a deep maroon tweed tunic, and brown ankle boots. The crisp autumn air sparkled around us as we left Primrose Cottage. I was ready for this change of seasons. I mean, I loved summer, but autumn in New England was cider, apples, and all things maple. And those were just a few of my favorite things about the fall.

This night with Tom and Mike promised to be a welcome engagement. Will had brought a bottle of Mountain Reserve, a small batch whiskey made by one of his suppliers in Brookton, Vermont, as a gift.

Following our GPS, we traveled past Rosemont College through bucolic farmland until we came to the town of Shipley. As we crossed the town line, it seemed as if we had journeyed into a Norman Rockwell painting. The main street was lined with shops, many of them painted yellow, white, or Swedish blue. In store windows, pumpkins, candles, autumn wreaths, and all the other signs of fall were on full display. Continuing, we passed out of the town proper and crossed a mint-green iron bridge that overlooked a churning river and falls. About a mile down a winding road, we were directed to turn left. A paved road led up a slight hill, and to the right, a polished wooden sign said *Riverbend.*

We pulled up to a rambling, newly painted red farmhouse with black shutters. A massive hedgerow bordered the driveway. The front porch was a tableau ready for a Hallmark movie. Various autumn-colored mums, asters, pumpkins, and assorted gourds surrounded black high-backed Kennedy rocking chairs. A large, exquisite magnolia wreath hung on the black lacquered front door.

It was a picture-perfect scene.

We rang the doorbell and waited as footsteps approached, and the door opened.

"Welcome to Riverbend, Maeve and Will," Tom said as he greeted us.

"Thanks, Tom. What a beautiful town. We've never been to Shipley before," Will said.

We passed through a pewter-colored foyer, where we were greeted by a handsome Irish setter.

"Who is this beautiful girl?" I asked, reaching down to scratch her head.

"This is Callie. She's our love."

I petted Callie's royal mane, and she sighed with contentment.

The hallway opened to a charming ecru colored living room with a vast sunroom beyond. Floor-to-ceiling windows enhanced the view of the broad, sloping meadow and the majestic river beyond. The tableau was so spectacular that I almost fell over the navy velvet Chesterfield couch.

"What an amazing panorama," I exclaimed.

"Hello, Maeve," Mike said, hugging me. "We should have a warning sign about the vista. So many people almost trip. We call this the fainting couch."

"The view is like a painting," Meg said, joining us. She wore a black and white houndstooth midi dress with a wide leather belt and knee-high boots. "I saw this house when it was for sale by the owner. You two have transformed it and made the most of the landscape."

"It's a work in progress. We thinned some trees to enhance the outlook, updated the sunroom, and have plans for a major kitchen redo. Down the line, we'll add a barn," Mike said.

Josh, Meg's boyfriend, was sitting in a lapis colored Queen Anne chair. Callie was sitting at his feet, staring at him adoringly.

"Looks like you have a not-so-secret admirer," Will said.

"It is all part of the job. She smells my patients," Josh said, smiling. He was a veterinarian in Norberg.

There were two other couples, as well, and Tom introduced us. "Maeve and Will, this is Carter Morrison, a teaching assistant in the Rosemont English department, and his wife, Estella. She owns The Book Nook, a delightful bookstore in Shipley, and writes a very successful historical fiction series."

Carter was a tall, very slim man in his early thirties. Estella was about five foot six with large brown eyes and a thick, long black braid woven with colored ribbon. As Tom told us more about their backgrounds, I noticed that the man's complexion had turned a deep red. *What was that about?*

"And this is Garland. He's currently with Sketch'd, a tech startup. His partner Curt owns Stems, an awesome flower shop in town. He's going to help us design the back flower garden."

After settling into the sunroom, Tom and Mike presented us with fried Halloumi cheese drizzled with lime and served with crostini. It was firmer than feta and nice and salty. It paired perfectly with the sparkling rosé, served in delicate antique wine glasses with gold rims.

"Delicious," Will said. "Do I detect a bit of coriander?"

"Well, of course, you would discover our secret ingredient. Can't fool a chef, can we?" Mike laughed.

The dinner discussion flowed from local politics, contractors, and dog breeds to winter holiday plans. It turned out that Tom and Mike were highly knowledgeable world travelers.

As we nibbled, the scents drifting in from the kitchen were intoxicating. About thirty minutes later, Mike ushered us into their dining room. It was tastefully wallpapered in a subtle gray floral motif. A large walnut oval table was set with distinctive celadon and gold china. White peonies in deep green glass basket vases enhanced the design. The armchairs were upholstered in ivory silk with embroidered gold bumblebees.

The impressive dinner consisted of chicken piccata, polenta with goat cheese, and roasted broccoli with garlic and lemon. Tom and Mike were obviously accomplished cooks.

"Will, I must say that we found it unnerving to cook for a professional chef," Mike said.

"Your food is delectable," Will said. "And to tell the truth, chefs long for friends to invite them for a home-cooked meal. I'm loving this." To emphasize the point, Will took a second helping of chicken and some broccoli.

Will and I were seated next to Carter and Estella, and I couldn't help but notice that his wine glass seemed to be emptying rapidly.

"Es suficiente!" Estella whispered harshly as a look of distress crossed her face.

All conversation immediately stopped.

"How about some coffee?" Tom asked, clearly trying to save Estella from any embarrassment. "We discovered an exquisite French roast in Honfleur and were lucky enough to have some shipped over."

There was a chorus of assents from around the table.

"I think you'll enjoy it. Let's have dessert in the living room," Mike said.

"Estella, please sit near me. I want to hear all about your books and your road to publication," I said. Carter shoved his dining chair aside and left the table, presumably to use the restroom.

As we settled into the living room, Carter entered the room and began pacing back and forth in front of the wall of floor-to-ceiling bookshelves. Estella looked wary, and Meg quickly glanced at me with questioning eyes. I shrugged slightly in response. I had no idea what was going on with Carter, but he had seemed agitated from the moment we met.

As Tom appeared with coffee and Mike followed with a scrumptious-looking chocolate hazelnut tart atop a yellow porcelain cake stand, Carter suddenly spun around so quickly that he almost crashed into Mike. His eyes were unfocused and wild.

"I'm glad Theo's dead. He stole my work. Bestseller, film rights…he took it all!" He took a shaky breath, then blurted out, "He was a thief."

At this proclamation, Estella abruptly stood up. "Thank you for your hospitality, Tom and Mike, but Carter and I need to leave."

She swung her purse over her shoulder and hurriedly proceeded to the front door. Once there, she barked, "Carter!"

Carter looked momentarily dazed but then followed her out into the night.

The remaining group silently sipped their coffee.

"It's a fantastic-looking tart," Garland said, trying to ignore Carter and Estella's abrupt exit.

"Come on now—what, or rather, who is the elephant in the room?" Meg asked, looking bewildered.

Tom and Mike both studied their vibrant Bakhtiari carpet for a long moment. They were obviously conflicted about breaking confidences. Finally, Mike sighed deeply and said, "Carter had too much to drink tonight. I think he had imbibed a bit before he arrived. In the past, he has claimed that Theo Archer stole his manuscript. It seems that a few years ago, Theo was taking a writing course at Rosemont College that Carter was auditing." He paused and seemed reticent to continue.

Tom refilled Mike's cup and lovingly rubbed his shoulder.

"Carter says that he was very impressed with Theo's background, and since he had set his thriller in the tech world, he asked Theo to read it and give feedback."

The entire room was riveted to Mike's story.

"Well, according to Carter, Theo stole his story, changed the main characters' names and the plot a bit, and sent it to his friends in the publishing world."

"And now Theo's book is set to be a runaway bestseller and will be made into a motion picture?" Meg asked incredulously.

Curt threw his hands in the air. "No wonder he's overindulging."

"Did Carter have no recourse? Couldn't he prove the manuscript was his?" Josh asked.

"He got an attorney, and the case went to court but was thrown out for lack of evidence. Carter believes that Theo had friends in high places who quashed pertinent findings," Mike added.

Silence enveloped the room as we thought of the implications of that statement.

"I wonder if Carter buys a lot of eye drops?" Meg asked, clearly unable to hold back.

"He's not the only one who had a beef with Theo," Tom said.

The group turned as one and looked at him.

"This is like a real-life *Clue* game," Garland said. "Colonel Mustard with a dagger in the conservatory can't compare. Come on, don't stop now. Tell us the whole story."

"Well, I've also gotten to know Carter. He's a nice guy. As unhinged as he looked tonight, I doubt he would have harmed Theo," Tom said. He stopped for a moment as if unsure whether to continue.

Mike took his hand and squeezed it, encouraging him to go on.

Tom continued, "As you know, I'm in tech. There are always numerous rumors flying around. Sometimes, I swear it's like high school. But the word on the street is that Philippe Duval, a software investor from New York City who bought Theo's company and app, is very disgruntled. I mean, like, blackest rage disgruntled. He says the app's projected sales were pumped up, and he will lose millions unless he can capture a huge market share."

"The plot thickens," Curt said.

"And then there's Aoki Yoshida," Mike interjected.

Tom's hands combed through his hair, and he suddenly looked weary.

"I'm gonna need a scoreboard," Garland sighed.

Tom sat down on the navy pintucked ottoman. "Aoki is an interesting young woman. She dropped out of Stanford because she was recruited by a few different startups. Aoki's brilliant but prefers to work alone. Somehow, Theo persuaded her to help him develop the app. He must have made her some big promises. Aoki claims she wrote the code and helped Theo expand his marketing plans. She says the unwritten understanding was that she would be brought in as a partner."

Tom stopped speaking and looked at the group.

"Is this a Winklevii versus Zuckerberg situation?" Garland asked, referencing the famous Facebook court case.

Tom shrugged. "Who knows?"

After more discussion, the dinner party began to break up as the night lengthened.

Meg caught me in the hall as I picked up my purse. "Delightful evening—so wonderful to meet new people and expand our horizons."

"Murder most foul," I responded, lightly pinching her arm.

Saying goodnight and promising to get together again soon, Will and I began the trek home.

"Gosh, Will, now we have so many suspects."

"Sounds like Theo had more enemies than most."

"The suspect list of the M&M's has expanded considerably. Philippe, Carter, and Aoki all felt wronged by Theo, and Savannah wanted out of her prenup."

"Just remember, Maeve, please be careful. There's a killer on the loose."

As he spoke, my phone vibrated with a text from Meg: *Our work has just begun.*

I read it out loud to Will.

"The M&M's are always on the same page," Will said, smiling and squeezing my hand, "but please don't let it be a thriller."

CHAPTER FIFTEEN

———

Amenorrhea is the absence of menstruation.

On Sunday afternoon, Will, the girls, and I headed to Parker Hill Apple Orchard to meet up with Will's family. Well, some of his family. Teddy, Will's youngest sibling was at college in New Haven and thus excused from the outing.

Lydia and William, or rather "Senior" as he now wanted to be called by the grandchildren, were dressed in twinning vermilion-colored cashmere sweaters and black corduroy slacks. Their outfits always matched. I sometimes wondered if they shared the same personal shopper.

Eloise, Will's sister, her husband Taylor, and their young son Nathaniel wore matching L.L.Bean red plaid flannel shirts. It suddenly dawned on me that Will had on a red turtleneck, and Rowan and Sloane were in scarlet overalls. Without a conscious thought, my family matched as well. The entire Kensington clan matched. Well, except for me, that is. I had felt very secure wearing my deep brown velvet hoodie, but now I realized that I was once again the outlaw. Somehow, the appropriate attire always eluded me at Kensington family events.

Taking this in stride, I consciously shook off the feeling of being an outsider and commenced apple-picking. The sun was high in the sky, the trees in the orchard were heavy with fruit, and the farm's apple presses must have been going at full tilt because the smell of cider filled the air.

Lydia and Senior notably didn't interact much with their grandchildren. They seemed to love them all, but at a distance. Hands-on childcare had never been on their agenda, and that wasn't about to change any time soon. Today, for example, they posed for carefully choreographed photos to eventually be placed on one of their many mantlepieces. Then they picked a few apples but spent most of their time greeting friends they knew from town, mainly from The Country Club.

My reaction to The Country Club was utterly different from that of Lydia and Senior. For them, it was a home away from home, filled with friends and pleasant memories. For me, it had been the scene of my first foray into sleuthing. The chief obstetrician at Creighton Memorial had been murdered there, and one of Will's employees had been falsely accused and arrested. Even after the dust cleared and the murderer was caught, I still felt a sense of dread when entering the building. Despite this, my in-laws, with much fanfare, had gifted their offspring with pricey memberships last Christmas. After much soul searching, Will and I had gone through the obligatory meet and greets required to formally join. We decided that accepting the gift gracefully was the better part of valor since it would keep peace in the Kensington family and help expand Will's business.

As the picking progressed, all thoughts of the Kensingtons and The Country Club fell by the wayside. Rowan, Sloane, and Nathaniel loved crawling on the grass and holding up fruit they came across. The sight of Will acting as an apple-craving dog brought squeals of delight. Best of all, I knew Will would bake a mean apple pie with our pickings.

At precisely 4:00 p.m., Senior tapped his Vacheron Constantin watch—or, rather, timepiece—to let us know it was time to decamp to Fairview, their oceanfront manor, for dinner. Traveling in a caravan, we pulled up next to the Positano cast-stone fountain in the front courtyard. In keeping with the season, a riot of yellow, orange, and red flowering plants filled the far side of the front staircase. It was a display that could make garden shops weep with envy.

As we filed into the black and white marble foyer, Roberts, the Kensington's live-in butler, welcomed us home. He had prepared the great room for our arrival. For the adults there were libations, mouthwatering cheese puffs and a large veggie tray. Roberts had also laid out Lydia's beautifully quilted ivory silk playmat for the children. It was not a color or fabric I might have chosen for small children, but Kensington babies were expected not to make a mess.

I changed the girls in the powder room Lydia had designated and outfitted for baby diaper duty, then turned them loose to roam on the mat. Thankfully, Roberts had added a temporary baby-friendly fence to protect the kids, as well as the Kensington's many valuable *objets d'art*.

As I sat on the floor with my girls, I heard a lot of chat about the financial markets. Taylor was now a partner in Oyster Cove Financial, and he and Senior reviewed the past week's market earnings. As they droned on and on, Will gave me a quick wink as he helped Rowan pull herself up to the couch.

"Terrible news about Theo Archer," Taylor said, finally changing the subject. "He was such a nice guy."

"Who would want him dead?" Senior asked. "He was a titan in the tech industry."

Obviously, Senior equated power and money with a noble heart.

"I heard that you were at the scene, Maeve," Taylor pointed out. "Did you attempt CPR?"

Before I could answer, Lydia piped up with a look of disgust, "At the scene? You can't stay away from mayhem and casualties, can you? Maybe you should have pursued a career as an EMT."

Always in my corner, Lydia.

I smiled broadly and said in my calmest voice, "I often row before work and use First Light Lighthouse as my measuring stick. As I was heading back to the Regatta Club, I saw that someone had collapsed and people were trying to resuscitate him, so I stopped. By the time I reached them, they had the situation well in hand. The ambulance arrived almost immediately."

"Not too well in hand, I suspect. Theo Archer died," Lydia replied.

I counted to ten. *Let it pass. Don't react.*

Will caught my eye from across the room. He knew I wouldn't want him to intervene. We had been through much worse with his family many times, and we would laugh about this later. Well, chuckle, maybe.

"Theo Archer made a fortune when he sold his software company," Taylor said.

"Yes, Pinnacle Endeavors had a huge market share. The buyout was phenomenal," Senior agreed.

"Didn't he live in the Mariner Heights subdivision?" Lydia asked.

Subdivision? It was more like a wealthy enclave.

"Yes, although his home has been on the market," I said.

"That's where the new money goes. My friends and I refer to that neighborhood as the chocolate chip streets. They all use the same designer and are cookie-cutter replicas." Lydia grimaced as if she had tasted something foul.

I guessed having money wasn't enough. One had to be born with a few architectural-worthy manses, preferably in both city and country venues.

"But at least they know quality in nannies," Lydia continued, turning to her daughter. "Didn't your nanny say that many of her Bloomsby classmates are employed there, Eloise?"

"Yes, Mother, they are a very tight group."

"There is simply no substitution for excellence." Lydia smiled widely at me, a bit of challenge in her eyes.

Oh, Lydia, do you always have to step over the line? Well, I was ready to expound on Kate's virtues. I'd met Eloise's nanny, Agatha, and while she was professional, she was also very rigid and only allowed Nathaniel to listen to classical music. As I opened my mouth to begin, I saw Roberts standing at attention at the great room door.

"Dinner is served," he announced.

Pork roast, applesauce, squash, and roasted potatoes were beautifully presented on the Kensington dinner table. Rowan and Sloane feasted on the applesauce and rolls. Thankfully, all talk of Theo Archer's demise and nanny selection was forgotten.

"Are you attending the Mom's Fall Meet and Greet at The Country Club?" Eloise asked.

"The Meet and Greet?" I said as innocently as I could manage.

Lydia seemed to sense something amiss. "It was in this month's newsletter. Didn't you read it?" she asked.

"Ah, I haven't gotten to The Country Club Newsletter yet," I demurred. Actually, I knew exactly where the newsletter was—at the bottom of the recycle bin.

"I saw it on the top of your 'to read' pile, Maeve," Will said, smiling.

He, too, knew exactly where it was sitting.

"It will be so much fun," Eloise said. "Please come."

I smiled and nodded. The last thing I wanted to do was to mingle with The Country Club set, but I needed to keep peace with the Kensingtons. Besides, Eloise, my sister-in-law, was very sweet and always inclusive.

Deliciously spiced carrot cake with cream cheese icing was brought out for dessert, and then Will and I packed up our tired girls and headed home. They were asleep before we got to the end of the Kensingtons' winding drive.

"Okay, on a scale of one to ten, with ten being the worst—hit me," Will said.

"Well, except for being roped into the Meet and Greet, it was child's play. I must be getting used to your parents. Truly, I wasn't rattled at all. I did miss Grand, though." Grand, Will's grandmother and the family matriarch, was kind and charming but did not suffer fools gladly. She was also marvelous to Will, me, and the girls.

"I missed her, too." Will agreed. "She's visiting her friends in Boothbay Harbor for the weekend."

"Good for her. I know how much she loves Maine."

We pulled into Primrose Cottage, and Will kept the car running. He reached over and took my hand. The fall foliage was displayed around us, and our home looked cozy. We could see Fenway standing on the back of the living room couch with her head cocked to one side. She was undoubtedly wondering why we didn't come in.

"I love you so much, Maeve. Sometimes, I can't believe how far we've come."

I leaned my head on his shoulder. I felt such deep contentment.

"Mama," Rowan called out, waking up because the car had stopped moving.

"Mmmm," Sloane said.

It might not be Mozart, but it was music to my ears.

"Okay, honey, showtime," Will sighed as he let go of my hand, and we began to unpack the car.

How our lives had changed. Parenting is hard, but I had no regrets. This is what I always wanted...well, this and maybe a live-in Roberts.

CHAPTER SIXTEEN

————

Painful menstruation is referred to as dysmenorrhea.

Labor and Delivery was humming the morning the six Rosemont nursing students arrived, and I assigned them to various patients. Most of the women were in early labor, but Kendra Danner, one of the midwifery patients, was finally pushing after a long, long labor.

I had already spoken to Kendra and her partner, as well as Maddie, her midwife, about having Haley observe the birth. Both were fine with the plan. Haley had peppered me with questions about nurses in expanded roles after our last class, and I wanted her to see an experienced midwife in action.

Haley and I reviewed Kendra's chart. She was a primipara, had a large baby, and was undoubtedly very tired at this point.

"Primipara means that Kendra's giving birth for the first time, right?" Haley asked.

"Exactly, Haley."

As we sat at the main labor desk, we talked about the second stage of labor and how Haley could best assist with Kendra's care. I also pointed out that both shoulder dystocia and postpartum hemorrhage were issues that a midwife considered with a big baby and a long labor.

"Shoulder dystocia occurs when the baby's head has been delivered, but the shoulders get stuck," I explained. "This complication strikes terror in the hearts of all delivery room personnel because sometimes babies are injured or worse when it occurs. Even with the best planning, it can happen suddenly and unexpectedly."

I knew that Maddie had already discussed Kendra's progress with the attending physician, and help would be available if necessary.

I reviewed with Haley that postpartum hemorrhage was another concern because of the length of Kendra's labor and her enlarged uterus. The usual course after the placenta is delivered is for a woman's uterus to clamp down and squeeze off the blood vessels where the placenta had been attached. This stops the bleeding and prevents a hemorrhage. Sometimes, after a long labor, though, and especially if the uterus has been stretched out by a large baby, the uterus does not contract properly. Then, heavy bleeding occurs. When this happens, medications and other procedures may be necessary to control the blood loss.

Haley nodded her understanding. I told her that I would be with her throughout the birth. Seeing a baby born was a wondrous experience, especially for first-time observers. Every birth was special for me, but I wanted to make sure Haley could take in the entire moment.

As we quietly stepped into the labor suite, I could see that the birth would occur soon. Robin, the labor nurse, had the lights turned down low and the delivery kit opened. Maddie was sitting on a stool, watching as a circle of dark hair appeared. Kendra was fully concentrating on pushing. Her partner Miguel rubbed her back slowly and whispered encouraging words to her. The room was very peaceful, but there was great anticipation.

"Ahh," Kendra moaned as the next contraction set in, and she gave a long push.

"That's it," Maddie encouraged. "Your baby will be here with the next push,"

Kendra took a deep breath, let it out, and put her head back on the pillow. Miguel gently kissed her forehead.

Haley had one hand on the end of the bed rail while her other was clenched in a fist. I knew from experience that she was probably pushing along with Kendra. I stood on the opposite side of the bed, ready to help if shoulder dystocia reared its ugly head.

Suddenly, Kendra sat forward with a fierce look, grabbed her knees, and gave a mighty push. This was it! Little by little, the baby's head was born.

"Okay, Kendra, you can stop pushing now. Blow out. Look down and see your baby," Maddie said.

The baby's head rotated to the right, and Maddie stood up to assist with the shoulders. This was the moment of truth. Would they deliver easily? Maddie and I locked eyes over our masks. We were ready, no matter what came next.

Maddie gently pulled down, but the anterior shoulder didn't emerge.

"Give me another push, please."

Kendra closed her eyes and complied.

Watching Maddie's hands, I saw downward movement, and the shoulder came into view.

Yes!

Then, the rest of the baby's body slid out quickly. Maddie placed the baby on Kendra's chest, and Robin gently wiped the newborn's face and then placed a warm blanket over the two of them.

"Hello, sweetie," Kendra cooed.

"Miguel, you can cut the cord," Maddie said as Robin handed him a pair of scissors.

Haley smiled widely while also biting her bottom lip.

"Okay, Kendra. Now your placenta is coming."

Maddie expertly controlled the umbilical cord, and the placenta easily slid out. I watched as Maddie placed the placenta in the basin and began to massage Kendra's uterus.

"Robin, please add oxytocin to the IV now."

Working with Maddie for so long made me realize by the tone of her voice that there was an issue. Kendra must be bleeding heavily. I lowered the head of the bed and said quietly, "Miguel, can you hold the baby, please."

Robin and I waited for Maddie to speak.

"Kendra, you are having a bit of extra bleeding. Robin will give you an injection to tone up your uterus."

Robin, of course, had the medication ready and swiftly administered it. I saw that Maddie was doing bimanual compression or squeezing the uterus with both hands. She had placed one hand in Kendra's vagina and one on her abdomen. She was now compressing the uterus between both hands to stop the bleeding.

Maddie and Robin exchanged glances. I saw Maddie nod, and Robin left the room quietly.

I looked at Haley. Her eyes were wide. "Haley, would you get a chair for Miguel, please?" I asked. Miguel needed to sit, but I also needed to distract Haley's focus for a few minutes.

In less than a minute, Maddie said, "Your uterus is firming up now. The medications are working."

Dr. John Armstrong, the Director of Maternal Fetal Medicine, followed Robin into the labor room.

"Hello, I'm Dr. Armstrong. Maddie asked me to check in."

Maddie smiled at him. "Everything is under control now. Kendra's bleeding is fine. Her uterus is nice and firm."

"Excellent." He moved to see the baby. "And who is this beautiful human?"

"This is Valentina," Miguel said proudly.

"What a lovely name," Dr. Armstrong replied.

"Am I okay, Maddie?" Kendra asked.

"You are fine. You had some extra bleeding, but that has stopped now. It can happen with a bigger baby and a long labor. You become tired, and your uterus also gets tired. But you're fine now, and we'll watch you closely."

Kendra smiled.

"You're in great hands," Dr. Armstrong said as he departed.

"Let's get you cleaned up and get Valentina back to you, Mama," Robin said.

Robin, Haley, and I changed the linens, got Kendra a clean hospital gown, and ensured the new family was cozy. Then I sent Haley to take a break and told her I would meet her to debrief in the lounge.

After saying goodbye to Robin, I met Maddie at the main desk.

"Nice birth," I said.

"Thanks for your help. I always love a postpartum hemorrhage first thing in the morning."

"You were cool as a cucumber, as usual," I pointed out.

"That's because Robin had the meds ready, and you were there for backup. And, as usual, Dr. Armstrong was a stone's throw away and so supportive. It always reminds me how lucky I am to work here."

"Now," I laughed.

"Yes, thank goodness."

We both vividly remember a time in the not-so-distant past when Creighton Memorial was not so friendly to midwives.

After checking on the other nursing students, I met Haley in the lounge to discuss Kendra's birth in detail. She had many questions and marveled at Maddie's calmness when presented with a potential emergency.

"Maddie is a great clinician and very experienced. In obstetrics, you must always be prepared for emergencies," I said. "Today, you saw how important judgment and experience can be when something unexpected happens."

"It was a great day. I saw my first birth and a midwife in action! Thanks, Maeve."

When the day ended, I said goodbye to the nursing students as we changed in the locker room.

"Have a nice night," I said.

"Ugh, I'm off to wait tables at the Rosemont College faculty dining room," Haley said, making a face.

"And I'm off to babysit Professor Kellogg's wild brood," Jenna, a tall brunette, added.

"That makes for a long day," I said.

"Wish we all could be Spirit Girls," Haley sang, mimicking the classic Beach Boys ode to California.

What was the deal with the Spirit scholarships? Did she think the selection process was unfair? I wondered which nursing students were Spirit recipients. I really wanted to investigate that issue further.

"Come on, Haley. I'll buy you one of those red velvet cupcakes you love," Helene said. With this, the group filed out.

I knew first-hand what it was like to be a "have-not." I had been both a campus tour guide and a library assistant at UMass Amherst and secured loans, grants, and a few scholarships to complete my undergraduate degree. I was always amazed that some students didn't need to work. It must be refreshing to know that you would not have a giant loan upon graduation.

Further education only increased the money worry. To this day, I was still making loan payments for my graduate studies. I had sworn I would never consume another microwaved cup of ramen noodles once I was working. Something needed to change with higher education costs, but I wouldn't solve that issue today.

Mentally, I moved researching the Spirit scholarships to the top of my ever-growing agenda. But did I have time to investigate the scholarships on top of helping find Theo's murderer? No sooner had the question formed in my mind than my phone rang. It was Meg—sister ESP at work again.

"What are you doing Saturday morning? Can you join me for a spa date?"

A glance at my tired face and very messy hair bun in the locker room mirror confirmed that I could certainly use a spa day. "Will is working, but I can see if Kate can cover."

"Wonderful! The owner of Opulent Oasis called and offered a courtesy day of beauty for me and a guest—I met her when she was looking for retail space."

I knew a five-star review and positive word-of-mouth from Meg would be priceless.

"But you're a regular at Pretty Nails," I objected. "What will Jasmine think?"

"Never fear, my dear. I'm not leaving Jasmine. She is the best. We talked all about the new spa. I told her that I would be her spy and report back."

"Well, you do have some detective experience," I stated.

"Exactly—and, speaking of detective experience, I hear the Mariner Heights residents frequent the place. We might pick up some scuttlebutt."

"So, a working spa date then," I said, laughing.

"You've got it. And, Maeve, try to dress up a little, okay? The Opulent Oasis is on a whole new level."

Special clothes for a spa? What could I possibly wear? Ugh, this would call for a deep dive into my closet.

CHAPTER SEVENTEEN

———

The thick muscle layer of the uterus is called the myometrium.

On Saturday morning, Will left at the crack of dawn to help with the morning rush at a Thyme for All Seasons Café, which, shortly after opening, had become *the* place to have breakfast in Langford. Although Will's staff was second to none, he liked to lend a hand on busy weekend mornings.

Kate was feeding Rowan and Sloane scrambled eggs and blackberries in our kitchen. I'd miss my time with the girls, but the spa visit was a generous gift and an opportunity to learn more about the Mariner Heights world.

At precisely 8:59 a.m., Meg pulled up in her new Portofino Blue Jaguar coupe. She changed vehicles every few years and loved luxury models. I slid into the passenger seat after stopping to say goodbye to Kate, the girls, and Fenway. I checked my image in the mirror, hoping that I would pass muster. Black slacks, a relatively new rose cowl neck tunic, and black leather ankle boots were the best I could do.

"Good morning, Meg," I said as I closed the car door. "I'm excited for this."

Okay, excited might be a stretch. But it was better than doing laundry or vacuuming, both of which awaited me later.

"I see you upgraded from your usual jeans and turtleneck. You look ready for prime time."

A fashion compliment from Meg? I better mark this date down.

Meg, I saw, was wearing chestnut hued gabardine pants paired with a white and camel-striped silk shirt. A matching shawl rested on the seat behind her. As always, ready for the paparazzi.

The Opulent Oasis was located a few blocks from the main downtown shopping area of Langford. Most of the businesses in Langford were red brick or white clapboard, in keeping with the New England village atmosphere. The new spa, however, resembled a sizeable silver fortress with lilac-tinted windows. More than one resident had pointed out its resemblance to a Las Vegas casino.

As we pulled into the driveway, a twenty-something valet in a sequined silver vest started towards Meg's door.

"Looks like a low-budget Disney production," Meg muttered.

The foyer of the Opulent Oasis was done in shades of white and silver. In contrast, the interior décor relied heavily on purple orchids—some real and many in photographs on the wall. All the chairs were upholstered in a deep mulberry linen fabric to enhance the color scheme. The walls glowed with a shimmery lilac pigment. Prince would have loved this place.

We walked up to the reception desk, and two platinum blondes with waist-length ponytails in matching sleeveless violet jersey sheath dresses leaped up to welcome us.

"We're Tina and Adina. So happy to have you join us. Are you ready for your adventure to begin?" asked the slighter, taller of the two young women.

Adventure? At a spa? I merely wanted a relaxing few hours.

Before we could respond, a middle-aged woman with a cap of slicked-back black hair, large gold hoop earrings, bright burgundy lipstick, wearing an ankle length flowing amethyst dress appeared at Meg's elbow.

"I am Donata. My name means gift, and I am yours. Come and be enchanted and changed in both body and mind at the Opulent Oasis."

Do not look at Meg. Do not start laughing. Bite your bottom lip. Control yourself.

Donata led us to a changing area decorated with a thick white rug, lilac leather chairs, and bright purple and silver lockers. There were luxurious, thick white terrycloth robes and slippers for us to wear. Once ready, we were seated in a warm room with deep violet leather recliners and offered drinks.

"Please try our signature Purple Passion libation. It contains elderberry and chamomile and is very calming," said Donata, not giving us a chance to decline.

"If they start talking religion, I'm pulling a fire alarm," Meg whispered. "Do you think Tina and Adina are twins or clones?"

I bit my lip to suppress a giggle. Meg could fire off one-liners all day.

"Donata, if that's her real name, has had some work, but clearly by an excellent plastic surgeon." Finally, Meg leaned back in her chair and shrugged. She was taking in the entire experience, so I decided to go along, too.

A striking woman in a pristine white lab coat approached us as we sat there. Her pale skin was glowing.

"I am Lola, the esthetician. Please allow me to place a soothing, warm eye mask and a seaweed wrap on your face. It will center you and ready you for the day."

We both nodded our assent. A mummy wrap was placed over our faces, and our hair was covered in a glaze before being wrapped in a towel. I nestled even farther back and cleared my thoughts. I might as well try to decompress and enjoy the pampering. It was free, after all.

"Tubular Bells" by Mike Oldfield quietly played in the background. As I started drifting off, I heard other clients enter the room.

"Poppy, here's a chair beside me. Bianca, please sit across from us with Victoria so we can all chat comfortably."

I heard shuffling and rustling as the women took their places. Just what I needed, ridiculous small talk. But I was trapped. I wished I had my earbuds.

"So, Poppy, how is Savannah doing? Have you spoken with her?"

"I called her yesterday, Arianna," the woman answered, her voice an unpleasant high-pitched squeak. "Her sister is coming to be with her next week. She's still in shock over Theo's murder. I mean, they were divorcing, but they had been together for such a long time, and their kids are still so young. Such a tragedy."

Wait a minute, they were discussing Savannah Archer!

"Is she still going to sell the house?"

Suddenly, I felt the seaweed wrap creep into my mouth. Gross! I couldn't spit it out without causing a scene. Okay, Maeve, breathe through your nose. Try hard not to swallow.

"Yes, she met with a new high-powered real estate agent."

I felt my body tense. That would be Meg! Thank goodness our faces were covered.

"Arianna, do you know anything about the funeral arrangements?"

"Well, now that it's officially a murder case, the interment may take a while."

"Imagine discovering Theo was both unfaithful and poisoned." I could tell by the voice that the speaker was Poppy.

"Poor Savannah, he was cavorting with the nanny right under her nose, and...she may be a killer."

"Oh, Bianca, can you just imagine her shock? I also heard that Theo's brother is an RN at Creighton Memorial and was on duty when Theo was brought in. That poor family."

"His name is Jeremy. As you know, I am an expert on grief, but without seeing him, I can only guess at what is going on internally. He must be suffering from PTSD."

"Well, you would know, Arianna," Poppy commented again.

Silence again enveloped the room for a few minutes before the chitchat continued.

"Victoria, how is your new nanny? I hear she's from the Bloomsby School."

"Well, it's early days. She does seem adequate. However, Maximilian and I really wanted someone bilingual in Mandarin to give the twins an edge."

"Bloomsby nannies have a great reputation. Thank goodness Savannah was able to get a replacement so quickly."

Why did it sound like she was employing a robot?

"Yes, so lucky for her. For us, there is a dilemma. The twins are two now, and we want them to speak Mandarin, Spanish, and English fluently by age five. It's possible to put them in a private group, but with our travel schedule, they'll miss a lot of precious class time. I'm trying to be optimistic. The nanny has color-coded their wardrobes and so far has correctly rotated the classical music settings during their naps. We'll just have to see how things unfold."

Oh, my goodness. These women were intense. I shook my head slightly, but more seaweed flooded my mouth. I was trapped. I felt like a beached fish.

"Do you and Maximilian speak Mandarin?" asked Poppy.

"We don't, but Maximilian's executive assistant does, and he has seen how invaluable her linguistic skill is in brokering deals. The girls will absolutely need it in the future. They'll go to Princeton and then Wharton. Their careers will be in finance, and as we all know, Asian markets are vitally important. They will turn three soon, and I hope their language window is still open."

Nothing like having a life plan mapped out.

"I'm having my Ian's Halloween costume created by Taffy Brio in Manhattan," Bianca said, changing the subject. "This year, he wants to be a paleontologist. Taffy does so many Broadway productions, but she's squeezing me in as a personal favor."

"Oh, that's just perfection," Poppy exclaimed. "Oliver used his connections to get Annalise's ensemble done by a rather famous LA designer. I'm sworn to secrecy, but you might recognize his work if you watch any BRAVO reality shows. Hint, hint," she tittered.

Gasps and giggling were heard as the foursome digested this news.

"Ladies, please join me in your private dining area. The Pinot Grigio and Cobb salads are waiting," Donata said, addressing the group.

As the footsteps receded, Meg took off her seaweed wrap and looked at me.

"Mariner mummies at their finest."

"Going off to eat their yummy lunch."

"The Yummy Mummies," we both blurted out together and then succumbed to a fit of laughter.

"That's the perfect name for them. They make me feel like a delinquent mother," I said, catching my breath.

"Oh, please. It's all for show. I feel sorry for those kids."

"It's a whole different universe," I replied, spitting seaweed into a towel.

We didn't see or hear from the Mariner Heights group again. After being scrubbed, painted, and blown out, we bade Donata farewell after Meg left a generous tip.

As we were leaving, Meg glanced at Adina—or was it Tina?—and whispered, "To be continued."

CHAPTER EIGHTEEN

———

Human Chorionic Gonadotropin (HCG) is a hormone produced by the placenta. The level rises with pregnancy.

We had not been able to debrief in the spa. It was a case of too many ears, too many treatments, too little time.

Meg revved up the Jag and drove to the nearest Dunkin' drive-through. Armed with iced coffees and jelly sticks, our order of choice, she went to our special spot overlooking Langford Harbor.

"Well, the Mariner Heights women are a fascinating group," I began.

"Mandarin at age two. Those poor kids," Meg commented.

"Kate tells me that the Bloomsby nannies keep to themselves," I said.

"They're probably busy writing lesson plans every night for the following day's schedule," Meg said.

"It seems the children's futures are all planned out. We know how that goes."

My thoughts turned inward, to my father-in-law, William Kensington. He was Oyster Cove Financial Service's founder and CEO, and he insisted that his sons follow his path. And even though his daughter had been free to choose art history, her spouse was happily ensconced in the Kensington family business.

Will, however, had always dreamt of a culinary career and rejected the path his father had laid out for him. He flourished in his chosen field after gracefully enduring numerous thinly veiled put-downs from the Kensington patriarch. I was aware of the heartache that rigid expectations could cause and realized that some of Mariner Heights' offspring could be headed down a rocky road.

As I studied the calm ocean, my thoughts turned to family, and I asked Meg how Henry was doing.

Henry was Meg's wonderfully adjusted teenage son. He was a junior at Langford High, a promising wrestler, and just beginning to explore colleges and career options.

"He's great. He's busy with school, sports, chess club, and volunteering at the homeless shelter."

"Henry's such a great kid, Meg."

A huge smile crossed her face. Whenever Meg talked about Henry, I recalled Shel Silverstein's book, *The Giving Tree.* Meg did love Henry very, very much. He was her life. She steadfastly refused to date anyone until he graduated from high school, although in the past year she had met Josh at Henry's wrestling meets. Josh had been a college wrestler and still loved watching the sport at all levels.

I took the smile as an opportunity to press a little further. "And how's Josh?"

Meg had been very reluctant to admit her interest in the relationship. She acted as if he was in the friend zone, but I knew my sister. She really liked him.

"He's good," she said, her smile still wide. "We've had a few dinners together, but only when Henry is busy. You know my rule." She looked out at the harbor for a moment before turning back to me. "I can't lie. It's been nice to have Josh in my life. We're taking it slow. The last two years of high school are a big deal, and I want to give Henry my full attention."

"I was happy to see him at Tom and Mike's dinner party. He's such a nice guy."

Meg gave me a small grin but was silent. I decided to move on to another topic. I knew when not to push Meg. "Well, the Yummy Mummies know who the premier real estate agent in Langford is."

Meg ignored that. "I need to show you Savannah Archer's social media presence. She has a huge legion of followers on Facebook, Instagram, TikTok, you name it. She's a lifestyle maven who posts everything—and I do mean everything. Her décor, clothing, makeup, fragrance choices, and meals are included. Even her two young kids are like props. Here, let me show you."

Meg scrolled through her phone and pulled up some photos. A very attractive woman with long flowing brunette locks was in shot after shot. Many showed her modeling designer outfits by the pool, at the shore, and in a very well-appointed home. Other posts were displays of luxury linens, glassware, and home goods. I noticed that every one of them included a link for purchase.

"That's not a good look, Maeve."

I didn't realize that my mouth was hanging open.

I recovered by taking a large sip of iced coffee. "I'm always amazed that people can make a living posting photos and getting sponsors."

"Her photos are very carefully, not to say craftily, curated. She makes people believe that buying a robe or lamp will make them happy, and they strive to create her supposed lifestyle in their homes. I mean, QVC does it all the time. You can practically smell the cookies and feel the softness of the sweaters through the television screen. She makes a good living, but remember, Theo bankrolled the bulk of it."

Hmm...she wouldn't want to give up that lifestyle. Maybe Jeremy is on to something.

When Meg dropped me off at Primrose Cottage, I found Kate folding baby clothes in the den.

"Hello there, Maeve. Your sweet angels have had a fine walk, lunch, and just went down. Fenway is in the nursery, guarding them as usual."

"Thanks so much for today, Kate."

"Ah, no problem. I'm meeting Bridie in an hour, and we're going to the Boston Athenaeum. She loves libraries and has been so looking forward to the visit. Then we're off for a ride on the Boston Duck Tours."

"What a great plan. Bridie will love the Athenaeum. It's a fascinating destination for a writer, and you'll get a great look at the city on the boats."

I sat down beside her on the couch to help her with the folding. "I got an earful of a few of the Mariner Heights women's expectations of their nannies today."

"Those kids are programmed at birth. They can't step off the path," Kate said.

"I had no idea."

Kate continued to smooth out a onesie and then turned to me, "Well, they all have Bloomsby nannies now."

"All of the other nannies are gone?"

"Every last one. They were all given different reasons, but truthfully, all the women in Mariner Heights want Bloomsby nannies."

"The women certainly are a different breed."

Kate burst out laughing. "A different breed, you say. They sure are. I could never be a nanny there. But they wouldn't choose me. They want multilingual nannies, as well as someone who is very posh and sets strict schedules."

"That's the impression I got, too. At least from the group of Yummies Meg and I overheard."

"The Yummies?"

I could feel a blush rise in my cheeks. "Meg and I christened them the Yummy Mummies."

Kate laughed out loud again. "Oh, that's brilliant. Wait until I tell Bridie and Fiona, too. It will give that poor girl a laugh. It's the best name for those women. We referred to them as Stepford Wives, but your name takes the cake. They spend hours in the gym in their colorful spandex outfits and have stylists and beauty advisors. Mariner Heights is nothing if not a keep up with the Joneses type of place."

"Are the Bloomsby nannies fitting in well?"

"I assume so, but I don't know. Like I said, they keep to themselves. Honestly, Maeve, I think some of the mothers are intimidated by them. Those women won't admit it, but I think they're often uncertain about how to raise their kids. And on top of that, they usually don't want to change their lifestyle to accommodate their children's needs. So, in the end, they often defer to the nanny's way of caring for them. Luckily for the Yummies, as you call them, Bloomsby nannies are excellent at what they do."

"I'm sure they are, Kate, but the right fit is the most important aspect to me and Will." I wanted a nanny who loved my girls and agreed on my child-raising techniques. I could not imagine having a nanny who dictated everything.

Kate still looked troubled. I knew Fiona was front and center in her thoughts. "You do know that Meg is working on a position for Fiona, right?"

"I know, and that's fantastic. I just hope the police leave her alone now. She did not have a fling with Theo Archer and had nothing to do with his murder." Kate crossed her arms tightly as if warding off evil.

"Indigo is a brilliant attorney. The truth will prevail," I said.

I mean, I hoped it would.

"Those Yummy Mummies are like a pack of hungry wolves. I'm afraid they'll turn on Fiona like she was helpless prey," Kate said, her mouth pulled in a thin line.

Kate might be correct about the Mariner women. Meg and I had to find the killer…and soon.

"I may be wrong, Maeve, but it's what I see." She neatened the stack of colorful baby clothes and rose to leave. "Well, I'm off now. Have a grand weekend."

As I watched her leave, anxiety gripped me. Could Meg and I really find Theo's killer before the wolves ran Fiona to the ground?

After Kate left, I prepped toppings for pizza. I wanted time this evening to relax with my family, but also to review all the suspects. I must have overlooked a vital clue. Someone was hiding something. The M&M's were in the thick of it now.

CHAPTER NINETEEN

———

The inner and outer folds of skin around the vaginal opening are called the labia.

I enjoyed the clinical and teaching mix as my days alternated between Rosemont and Creighton Memorial. I was beginning to get into a rhythm with this dual appointment.

Today was my first scheduled day at the college health center, and I was interested to see if I would get any takers since I wasn't sure how familiar the community was with midwives. Part of my concern came from knowing that many women were unaware that midwives provided both obstetrical and gynecological care. In fact, in the past there had been many heated discussions at the national level regarding abandoning our beloved name for something more universal. But the word midwife means "with women," which was our finest description.

I cherished the title.

Rowan was playing with pastel-colored wooden blocks, and Sloane was gnawing on a board book when Kate arrived. Rowan started clapping when she spied her, and Sloane put her arms up for a hug. Not to be left out, Fenway also began to cry with joy.

"Morning, Maeve. And my three beauties," she said, kissing each in turn.

Saying quick goodbyes so I wouldn't be late, I gathered my tote and headed to Rosemont College. As I drove along Main Street, I saw signs advertising the Langford Home Tour, which was taking place in a few weeks. Meg was coordinating the entire event, and I had promised to help. Eight historic and contemporary homes would be open to the ticketed public from noon to five on a Saturday in late October. Tickets were priced at $100 apiece, and all proceeds would benefit the Langford Animal

Shelter. A Thyme for All Seasons, Will's catering company, would provide a savory boxed lunch for the attendees at the Talcott House, one of the Langford Historical Society's beautifully restored properties.

A quick stop for a hazelnut coffee was necessary for beginning my day, and I didn't resist the pull. Luckily, the drive-through line wasn't painfully long today, and I was as close to being in and out as I could expect on a weekday morning.

As I pulled into Rosemont College, the beauty of the green still amazed me. The fall colors framed the space majestically.

Entering the health center, I noticed the gleaming end tables with neatly stacked brochures and magazines, the pots of pink sedum, red asters, yellow calla lilies, and the pale-gray leather chairs, and I couldn't help but smile. Someone went out of their way to make this a very comforting space.

"Good morning, Maeve," Kristin said. "Let me show you to your office and have you meet Dr. Tim."

I followed her down a long corridor into a light-filled office on the right. A small walnut desk held a computer workstation and a small red and yellow pepper plant.

"What a pretty plant."

"Just a little welcome gift from me," Kristin said.

"Thanks so much, Kristin. The waiting area looks so welcoming. Did you have a hand in that?"

"I wanted our patients to feel that the health center is a warm, welcoming space. Plus, I'm an amateur gardener. I dream of having a greenhouse one day."

We continued to the back of the clinic, and Kristin gently knocked on the open office door.

"Hi, Dr. Norris. This is Maeve O'Reilly Kensington, the new midwife."

A tall, stately gentleman in his late fifties stood up from his desk. "Welcome, Maeve. Come in and take a seat, and please call me Tim."

Tim's desk was very neat, and I saw a print copy of the *New York Times* open to the daily crossword. Putting his pen down, he chuckled softly.

"I've been doing the daily puzzle for years. I know one can access it online, but I like tackling it the old-fashioned way."

What I specifically noticed was him doing the *Times* crossword in pen. Very impressive. I only attempted it online, where one could erase endlessly.

Dr. Tim leaned back in his seat and smiled. "I'm so glad you've joined us at Rosemont. It will be excellent to have a provider solely for GYN care. I'm an orthopedist and maintain a private practice but come here twice weekly. An internal medicine specialist covers the other three days. We provide annual physicals and follow-ups for sports injuries and surgeries, and see urgent visits for colds, flu, or any other health-related issues. Rosemont College has a great mental health referral service, too. In case of accidents or injuries, we provide initial emergency care and use Creighton Memorial for backup. For a small facility, we do strive to cover all the bases. However, we have always lacked dedicated GYN services. I know the female faculty and students will welcome you with open arms."

Dr. Tim filled me in on his background, which included a stint in Afghanistan courtesy of the National Guard. Then, he asked some questions about my experience and was very happy to hear that nurse midwives were involved with medical student training at Creighton Memorial.

"That's how it should be," he observed. "Medicine, midwifery, and nursing should learn from each other. Combining all those different perspectives enhances the patient's care."

Kristin interrupted us to say that we both had patients checking in. I returned to my office with great enthusiasm, knowing that I had a supportive physician in Tim.

Pulling up my schedule, I saw that I had four patients booked. It was a slow start, but that was fine. The first two patients needed yearly physical exams, Pap smears, and birth control prescriptions renewed. The third was the thirty-two-year-old head soccer coach, who wanted to talk about pre-pregnancy concerns. This would be a very relaxed morning, which was good because it gave me time to read and complete all the yearly continuing education modules for health providers at Rosemont.

I finished charting on my first three visits and then saw my final patient's name was Bella Taylor. She was a senior and had told Kristin that she believed she had a urinary tract infection. I knocked on the exam room door and opened it to find a five-foot-eight-inch-tall brunette with arresting deep green eyes. Her makeup and hair were impeccable. Her fingernails were manicured works of art embellished with navy and white stripes.

"Hello, Ms. Taylor. I'm Maeve, a nurse midwife."

"That's so cool. I've read about midwives. Oh, and please call me Bella. Did you take that lovely photo of the Pont des Arts in Paris?"

The Pont des Arts was a bridge over the Seine where lovers attached padlocks with their initials. Due to the crushing weight, the custom was no longer allowed at the site but love locks could still be found all over Paris.

"No. Dr. Norris, who works here, took it. He captured it with a truly magnificent sunset. Have you been there?"

She gave me a tiny smile, but her eyes were cloudy and sad. Remembering a lost love?

"Once for a quick weekend. Paris is like a dream."

Pricey trip for a weekend. Okay, I needed to get back to business.

Bella began by telling me that she was captain of the cheerleading squad, a biology major, and hoped to attend medical school to become a pediatric oncologist. Her younger sister had childhood leukemia but was now in remission. Interacting with her sister's care team and seeing her journey made Bella set her sights on this career path. Then she talked about her scholarship at Rosemont and her fondness for the college. Finally, we got around to the problem that brought her to the clinic.

"Tell me your symptoms," I said.

"I have urinary frequency, burning, and I'm voiding small amounts. I've had a urinary tract infection before, and this feels the same."

As I listened and typed, I realized Bella had become quiet. I looked up. "Is there something else, Bella?"

She looked down at her lap.

"Bella, nothing we talk about gets repeated. And trust me, there is nothing that you can tell me that I have not heard before. I'm here to help you."

Bella drew in a deep breath. She didn't respond but gathered her long hair into an elastic tie. As I watched her pull the band tight, it struck me that her nail art featured Rosemont's school colors. I needed to become more observant to keep up with the student fashion trends. I would never be considered hip, but I needed to be aware.

I was quiet and hoped Bella would tell me what was on her mind. Finally, she said, "Can these symptoms be a sign of a sexually transmitted infection?"

"Yes, that is a possibility," I said.

With that, a torrent of words flooded out. Bella told me about her worries about STIs, her partner, and her sexual activity. She asked a lot of questions about various infections and how long the testing results took to process. She visibly relaxed as I answered each inquiry and went over the protocol I would follow.

After calling in Kristin to chaperone, I performed a pelvic exam and gathered samples.

"The results will be posted on the health center site under your name," I said. "I'll check them daily."

"Will anyone else at the health center see them?"

"Kristin checks all the labs daily, but please remember, Bella, we are all bound by HIPAA. We cannot discuss your care with anyone. You have complete privacy."

A weak smile appeared on her face.

"From the urine sample you gave before your visit, I believe that you have a urinary tract infection. Since you have no drug allergies, I'll start you on a broad-spectrum antibiotic. The final culture results will be back in a day or so."

"Thanks so much, Maeve. It was great meeting you."

Back in my office, I printed out a list of pending lab work I wanted to discuss with Kristin. As I rounded the corner on my way to the main desk, I saw her talking with a slender Asian woman neatly dressed in a light beige skirt and vest, holding a clipboard.

"Maeve, this is Aoki, our resident computer whiz. She keeps Rosemont connected and humming. Aoki, Maeve is our new practitioner."

Aoki's long bangs almost obscured her eyes as she barely nodded and held more tightly to her notes. Her Rosemont ID hanging squarely in the center of her chest read: *Aoki Yoshida— Computer Services*.

"Nice to meet you," I called after her as she swiftly bade Kristin goodbye and headed for the door.

Watching her retreat, I briefly wondered why her name seemed so familiar. Wait a minute—Aoki Yoshida was the person who'd helped develop Theo Archer's app. She claimed that after she wrote the app, he reneged on making her a partner. She, too, worked for Rosemont College?

"I hope I didn't interrupt your conversation, Kristin."

"No worries, Maeve. Aoki is a true introvert. It takes her time to warm up to people."

"Has she worked here long?"

"I believe she worked for some startup in the past but now maintains several computer systems in the area. She's quite talented and does most of her work remotely. I was having a glitch with the electronic medical records, and, as usual, she came right in and corrected the issue. We are lucky to have her."

Hmm, Aoki might be more than a highly skilled programmer. Perhaps she had added killer to her resume. If she'd gone from creating an app and being promised untold riches to servicing mundane operating systems, she must be harboring some sort of resentment. What a betrayal.

Yes, Aoki was definitely vying for prime suspect on my list, I thought as I walked out the door.

CHAPTER TWENTY

The endometrium is the lining of the uterus.

The morning of the Meet and Greet at The Country Club, I dressed Rowan and Sloane in matching Hanna Andersson navy rompers and blue and white striped jerseys. They looked charming, if I did say so myself. To complete their outfits, I zipped up their lilac hooded sweaters, which Winnie, my midwife colleague and dear friend, had knit. Their cuteness factor was over the top today. It's too bad their mother was not as coordinated.

I wore my best black slacks, a soft maroon wraparound sweater, and new black Hoka sneakers. I was going for a sporty but pulled-together look. But as I buckled Sloane in the van, I noticed my headband listing slightly to the left. Oh well, I could always just wear my hair loose if needed.

Amazingly, I had roped my big sister into attending with me under the guise of gathering info for the M&M Detective Agency, especially now that our suspect list was growing.

Meg texted me her parking spot at The Country Club, and I pulled in beside her.

"Good morning, angels," she called out to the girls.

Meg was dressed in fitted navy slacks, a crisp crimson Lafayette 148 linen jacket, and navy leather flats. She was a perfect model of the chic suburban mother.

"Doting aunt reporting for duty," she said as we transferred our charges from car seat to stroller and wheeled them toward the main entrance.

The Mommy Meet and Greet was being held in the Abigail Sawyer Suite. As we entered, a fortyish woman dressed in an aquamarine linen shirtwaist dress and heels took our names and explained that a group of sixteen Bloomsby nannies would entertain the children while we mingled. I surveyed the baby playroom and saw it was immaculate and well-equipped with toys. Mothers could watch their children through a glass wall. I thought Rowan would be excited to check out the offerings, but Sloane would probably opt to stay with Meg and me.

On the buffet table, beverage choices consisted of kale smoothies, coffee, and tea. Next to that were bowls of blueberries, blackberries, strawberries, and plain Greek yogurt. Obviously, carbs were not allowed with this crowd. But still, it was a very lovely Meet and Greet, I thought.

Much to my surprise, Rowan and Sloane settled into the playroom, each with a uniformed Bloomsby nanny.

"Mary Poppins, on steroids," Meg whispered to me.

"Looks more like a scene from a Margaret Atwood novel," I replied, taking note of the apparel.

I saw my sister-in-law, Eloise, sitting with her friend group, and stopped briefly to chat. I was happy her table was full. We had a lovely relationship, but I wasn't sure how Meg and I would fit in with her squad, and I was already a bit edgy about this event.

We got coffee and settled in at a table near the back. The centerpieces were large Nantucket baskets filled almost to overflowing with flowers, candles, tinned nuts, and gift cards.

Could we please have one of these?

The crowd was beginning to take their seats. A quartet of apparent friends joined our table. Nodding hello, I began introducing myself when a very toned woman clad in a hot pink sweater set, matching knife-pleated skirt, and a choker of iridescent green marble-sized Tahitian pearls stood in the center of the suite and addressed the gathering.

"Welcome to the first annual Mother's Meet and Greet. I'm Muffy Riggs, the chair of the Women's Groups here. The Country Club has many family functions, women's luncheons, and golf events, but the Board realized we didn't have anything solely for mothers with children ranging in age from newborns to high school seniors. I know that most of you have nannies for your young ones, but today, courtesy of the Mariner Heights contingent, we have a remarkable group watching your children for the morning."

A round of applause went up from the guests.

"Thank you. The nannies are from the Bloomsby Nanny School in Devonshire, England. They are of the highest caliber. The Country Club is ever so grateful to the Mariner Heights ladies." She paused for a moment, and her long, French tipped manicured nails casually brushed her bangs to the side of her face. "I mean, if Bloomsby nannies are good enough for William and Kate, then I suppose they'll do for our brilliant children."

Giggling ensued as Meg lightly tapped my shin with her shoe.

"Let's all settle in and have a bite to eat before the program gets started. I know we're all watching our waistlines, but today's fare is healthy and light on carbs, so enjoy it with no guilt."

Meg sat back with a slight pout. She would have plenty to say about the breakfast choices—or non-choices.

Our table companions resumed the introductions, picking up where I'd been cut off.

"I'm Arianna Gladstone," said a striking woman with coal-black hair and dramatic eye makeup. "And this is Poppy Rothschild," she said, motioning to a petite woman with a warm brown complexion sitting to her right. Poppy gave Meg and me a quick smile. "And next to her is Victoria Bamford." She motioned to a platinum blonde with chiseled cheekbones and a firm, wrinkle-free face. Botox was clearly Victoria's dearest friend. "And, of course, the lovely Bianca Chamberlain." She motioned to a reed-thin woman with a very full gold charm bracelet dangling on her child-sized wrist. Bianca gave Meg and me the slightest nod of acknowledgment.

Before Arianna was even finished with the introductions, I'd recognized their names. They were the group we overheard at the Opulent Oasis! Little did they know, we had already had a glimpse, so to speak, into their chummy little foursome. Although we knew they had heard of Meg, because of her stature in the real estate business, we introduced ourselves. As we did, I decided that Meg could quickly adapt to this setting, but it was out of my league. These women spent hours at the spa and hair salon.

"We seem to have an empty place at the table," Meg pointed out, tilting her head toward the unoccupied chair.

"The last member of our group is absent today," explained Arianna. "It's Savannah Archer. I heard that you recently met her, Meg. She was planning on coming, but as you know, she recently has had tragedy enter her life." Arianna closed her eyes and folded her hands.

Following suit, the rest of the group looked solemnly at the table and shared a moment of silence.

"But we know that Arianna will spend extra time with her and assist her on the road to healing soon," Poppy piped up while checking her lipstick in a jeweled compact. Gosh, her high-pitched squeak was like nails on a chalkboard to me.

Was Arianna a minister? From the exchange I overheard at the Opulent Oasis, I thought she was a therapist.

Before Meg or I could ask, Arianna sat up straighter in her chair and said, "You may have seen me on the morning shows. I am the Grief Whisperer."

She paused as Bianca, Poppy, and Victoria looked at her adoringly. Did I hear correctly? A *grief* whisperer?

"Sadly, I also lost my devoted spouse a short time ago. I was bereft for a time but had an extensive organization and supply chain management background. Using that expertise, I devised a foolproof system for powering through grief and emerging as your best self quickly."

And *she* had diagnosed Jeremy with PTSD?

"When life gives you lemons," Victoria commented before taking a tiny sip of her smoothie.

I could not believe what I was hearing. Grief took time. Everyone progressed on their own schedule. But on the other hand, I'd never heard of applying supply chain principles to the grieving process. Later, I'd have to ask Meg if she'd ever heard of this method.

"My system is foolproof for those courageous souls willing to embrace it fully. You can also follow me on Instagram and TikTok."

As she spoke, she handed us cards emblazoned with a golden sunrise.

Arianna Gladstone,
The Grief Whisperer
Power through your grief with me!

This was too much. I decided I needed to find out more about her system. It sounded far-fetched. However, before I could ask her anything specific, the table conversation had turned to nannies.

"Thank goodness Savannah has reliable help now. In fact, all the Mariner Heights families have Bloomsby nannies now. Savannah was the last one to come onboard." Bianca beamed, nibbling on the lone strawberry she'd put on her plate. I wondered if it exceeded her daily calorie count.

"Was she using a different agency?" Meg asked.

I realized she was trying to find out why they thought Fiona was dismissed.

"She had an Irish girl, but there were unsavory issues." Arianna grimaced as if she had bitten into a ripe lemon. "And, of course, no mere agency nanny can hold a candle to a Bloomsby nanny. They are educated in every aspect of childcare and family relations. Savannah will be very happy with the change."

She turned to Meg and me and asked, "Do you employ nannies?"

Meg leaned forward in her seat. *Buckle up, Arianna.*

"My son had an outstanding local woman who has become part of our family. I could not have asked for better childcare. Maeve has a terrific young Irish woman for her girls. Again, what could be better?"

Arianna and Meg locked eyes—clash of the Titans. I'd put my money on Meg any day.

Arianna blinked. "Well, every mother knows what is best for her children. Quality always wins, though."

"Exactly," Meg said as Arianna winced.

Before anyone else could respond, Muffy Riggs returned to the floor. "Is everyone having a fantastic time? Get ready to switch tables. The women with red dots under your saucers, please move to the table to your right and mingle. We'll switch again in fifteen minutes. Remember, those sumptuous centerpieces will be going home with some lucky winners. We'll have the drawing very soon."

"Oh look, a red dot!" exclaimed Bianca as she lifted her bone china teacup.

"Arianna, Poppy, and I have them, too. How terrific. We get to stay together." Victoria looked as if all she needed was a pompom to wave.

Meg made no move to look under her saucer. "So nice to meet you," she said, smiling at the foursome as they left.

"You never even looked for a dot, did you?" I asked.

"I'm not playing musical chairs with this crowd."

We were joined by four more women and engaged in some small talk. They were primarily interested in makeup trends, upcoming social events at The Country Club, holiday vacation plans, Botox providers, and the pros and cons of diamond hoop earrings versus studs. Meg took her phone out and began scrolling when Muffy stepped to the microphone.

"And now, for the moment you've all been waiting for…the raffle results." She began to call out the names of the lucky winners, and the last one was Meg O'Reilly.

"You won!" one of the women at our table cheered while clapping her hands.

Meg nodded and raised one hand in a show of thanks.

"What a phenomenal day. Congratulations to our winners," Muffy said as the crowd dispersed.

Meg picked up the overflowing basket a bit reluctantly, and we headed out. Finally, we got to my van and buckled Rowan and Sloane into their car seats, where they promptly fell asleep.

"Winner, winner, chicken dinner," I said.

Meg gave me a frosty look from behind her oversized black Gucci sunglasses. "You know I hate to win prizes," she said.

Meg always wanted to be the giver, never the receiver, of gifts. It had been that way all our lives. Buying her a birthday present was almost impossible unless it was a frame for a photo of Henry.

"I know, but there's a lot of goodies in there," I pointed out.

We were standing shoulder to shoulder, leaning on her car. The windows of my van were open, and we watched the girls.

"I can't get enough of this pair, Maeve."

"I know. Sometimes I need to pinch myself. They are my miracle babies."

After a moment, Meg turned to me. "The Grief Whisperer? I need to read up on her program." She sighed and continued, "It sounds ludicrous. But still, she obviously has strong support from her Mariner Heights friends."

"It sounds like she'll have Savannah enlisted in the bereavement cult very soon," I observed.

Meg pulled her keys from her purse. "Well, I'm off. Call me. Love you a lot. Maybe not enough to do another Yummy Mummy teatime, but a lot."

Later, when unpacking the girls at Primrose Cottage, I saw the Nantucket basket on the car's floor. My sister…

CHAPTER TWENTY-ONE

Females have two X chromosomes. A woman always gives an X chromosome to the fetus.

My jaw dropped when I entered Olivia and Patrick's Cape Cod style home in West Langford. Gone were the lace curtains and heavy satin drapes. The deep jewel walls and plaid sofas had also vanished.

Now, the entire house was redone in creamy off-white. A wrought iron chandelier took pride of place over the dining table. Full-length linen-tinted, raw silk drapes graced the windows. Black and white toile slipcovers had transformed the sofa. Was I in Paris? Provence? However you looked at it, there was no denying that Olivia continuously poured her heart and soul into her transformations.

"Bonjour, Maeve! So happy to see you," Olivia said, beaming. She was dressed in maroon wool slacks and a blush silk blouse. A pearl pink scarf was tied jauntily at her neck. She would have been right at home in any arrondissement in Paris.

"Your home looks beautiful, Olivia. It's so serene."

Her smile deepened. I handed her the white hydrangeas I had purchased on my way.

"Ah, merci beaucoup, Maeve. *De si belles fleurs.*"

I knew Olivia was thanking me, but I would have to do a deep dive into my French dictionary if this phase continued for a while.

"Go say bonjour to *la famille.* Dinner will be out *tout de suite.*"

Everyone was gathered in the living room listening to Penelope, Abigail, Becca, and Cassie, all dressed in matching black and white houndstooth pinafores, belt out their rendition of

"Frere Jacques." When they finished, a sustained applause went up from the family.

I caught Meg's eye, and she gave me a shrug with a smile. What could we say? Olivia was a phenomenal mother, wife, and sister-in-law, and life was never dull with her.

"*Le diner est servi*," Olivia called, carrying a large soup tureen to the table.

Each place setting had a white card with a detailed menu.

Dîner de Famille

Bisque de homard
Poulet à l'estragon
Purée de pommes de terre à l'ail
Asperges
Carottes glacées
Mousse au chocolat

"What does this say?" Mom asked, holding the card close to her eyes and squinting. Tonight, she was dressed in bright red slacks and a silver sequined cardigan with a matching tank top.

"It's in French, Mom," Meg explained.

"Are we eating French food like crêpes or french fries?" Mom asked. "I love french fries."

"Allow me," Sebi intervened. He picked up his card. "This gourmet dinner will start with lobster bisque, followed by chicken with tarragon, garlic mashed potatoes, asparagus, and glazed carrots. But the pièce de resistance might be the chocolate mousse."

"You went all out, Olivia," Will said. "I can't wait to sample this masterpiece. I feel like I'm a guest at Julia Child's."

Will was proven right, as everyone enjoyed the meal. Maybe it was the variety of cuisines that Olivia had perfected, but there was no denying she was a very skilled cook.

As the meal wound down, Olivia said, "*Mes enfants*, you may play until dessert is served." While most of the family decamped for the living room, Meg, Patrick, and I met in the sunroom.

"Faithful deputies reporting for duty," Meg said.

Patrick gave her a weary half-smile. "Please don't make me regret this."

"Well, we know Fiona did not kill Theo," I said.

Patrick gave me a solemn look, and Meg quickly stepped in with our newfound information.

"Maeve and I had dinner with some Rosemont College faculty and have a new list of suspects for you."

She proceeded to tell Pat what we had heard about Carter Morrison, Philippe Duval, and Aoki Yoshida.

"We knew about Carter Morrison from the lawsuit," Pat said in return, "but I had not heard the chatter about Theo's app. The Langford PD will get right on that."

He raked his long fingers through his short hair and looked like he was struggling with a decision. Finally, he said, "The tetrahydrozoline was in Theo's water bottles. That finding will be released to the news outlets tomorrow. Now, there's something else I need the two of you to do."

Meg and I gave him our undivided attention, still astonished that Patrick included us in the investigation. What a change from the inquiry into the first murder that Meg and I had witnessed.

"Here's what we know so far. Theo Archer always used the same water bottles. They were designed to fit into his custom-made running shirt and were inscribed with his initials. Theo filled them at his house with a special blend of vitamin water and supplements but always worked out at his gym prior to his run. He kept them refrigerated. We were told Theo was very methodical and only drank from them after coming down the stairs at First Light. His workout mates said he never deviated from this routine."

"That means the eye drops were either added at his home or the gym." Meg crossed her arms as she pondered this fact.

"And Fiona and Savannah were both at the house that day, right?" I asked, my voice full of worry.

Patrick nodded. "Meg, I know you are a member of The Art of Wellness on Blanton Avenue. I was hoping that you and Maeve could spend some time at the gym and watch how the Ironman competitors work out, store their gear, and mingle with the rest of the exercise crowd."

"Oh Pat, I only became a member for the contacts. You know I hate to sweat."

"Come on, Meg. I'll even go with you," I said, grinning as I pantomimed lifting arm weights. "I'll be a prospective member, and you can show me all the areas."

"As if I know my way around. All right. But I'll have to get us color-coordinated workout outfits, or the Yummies won't spill any gossip."

"The Yummies?" Patrick asked.

"The Yummy Mummies. The Mariner Heights crowd. They are charter members of the gym. You don't think they'd be caught dead at Planet Fitness, do you?"

Patrick shut his eyes briefly. Then a tiny smile appeared and just as quickly vanished. "Remember, don't ask a multitude of questions. I don't want the two of you put in harm's way. Just observe and let me know. And thanks for the info on Theo's app."

"*Le chocolat est prêt,*" Olivia called out.

We returned to find that the chocolate mousse topped with homemade whipped cream was worth every calorie. It was clearly destined to become a family favorite.

"Well, Olivia, I can't read your menu, but I love your food," Mom said.

The entire table applauded.

"All I can say is, *vive la France!*" Will cheered, raising a glass to toast our hostess.

CHAPTER TWENTY-TWO

———

Males have both X and Y chromosomes. They can contribute either one to the egg and thus determine the baby's gender.

After grabbing a large French roast, I checked into the labor unit for my twelve-hour shift. I had left Will at home making cinnamon waffles for Rowan, Sloane, and, of course, Fenway. He was not going to work until later because he was catering a dinner graduation ceremony for newly minted firefighters in nearby Norberg. Kate had adjusted her schedule to accommodate us, and I hoped to use the opportunity to have a quick chat with her when I got home.

I dropped my carryall in the midwifery call room, where I ran into Winnie. She was a very skilled, British-educated, Montserrat-born midwife and the unofficial mother of the group. She was also a wise, gentle woman who could channel her inner Olivia Pope when needed, which is perhaps why we had forged a very close bond during the births of my daughters. Winnie was there for me through all the ups and downs of Rowan's adoption and also for Sloane's dramatic entrance into the world.

"Good morning, Maeve. How are my girls?"

"They're fine, Winnie. You should come by and see them this week."

"Auntie Winnie will. And how is the charming husband?"

"He's doing well. In fact, why don't you come for dinner soon? It will be something good. Will usually brings dinner home from the café."

"That sounds right up my alley. Count me in. We'll coordinate later."

"How was your night?"

"It was quiet. We currently have no one in labor, but Geena Sheehan will be in at 8:30 for an induction."

"I gather Geena is being induced because of cholestasis?"

"Yes, she is now thirty-seven weeks, and Dr. Wu did some fetal testing last night. Her amniotic fluid is a bit low, and her other fetal testing was not totally reassuring. It's time."

Cholestasis could cause severe fetal complications, which is why patients with this condition were monitored so closely.

"Okay, I'll get her started as soon as she arrives."

"You know, I think we need to have a midwife get-together soon," Winnie said.

"I agree. We've been like ships passing in the night lately. It's time we caught up on our lives without any shoptalk."

"I'll float a few dates to the group. Someone will need to stay on the labor unit, so I'll speak to Maddie. Maybe one of the per diem midwives can cover."

After Winnie left, I changed into scrubs, finished my coffee, and logged into the Rosemont College provider area. I saw that Bella Taylor's results were posted. She indeed had a urinary tract infection but all her other testing was negative. I also saw a note by Kristin saying that a follow up call found that she felt better and she was continuing the antibiotics. Kristin, as I suspected, was right on top of everything.

I went on to the unit to start my day, only to find that the floor was eerily quiet. Even Triage was quiet. I ran into Val, the labor and delivery nurse manager, and we looked at the empty labor board with no comment. A long-held belief of labor personnel was that you never acknowledged a lack of patients. That would be tempting fate, and the labor gods would surely rain down their fury.

"How are you feeling, Val?" I asked.

Last winter, one of the medical students discovered a few nodules on Val's thyroid. She'd had a thyroidectomy for early cancer, which had been confirmed by a biopsy soon after the exam.

"I'm doing well, Maeve. My thyroid supplement is finally at the correct dosage, and I am back to biking."

Val and her husband were avid mountain bikers.

"That's great, Val."

"I'm forever thankful you were doing thyroid checks that day. I see the specialist every few months, but all my exams and lab tests are normal."

"I'm happy the medical student was having trouble feeling thyroids. I saw her a few months ago. She asked about you and said she is considering specializing in endocrinology."

Strange how serendipitous life could be.

While waiting for my patient, I got a text from Jeremy Archer: *Morning, Maeve. Any time for a chat?*

I texted back that I was available now, and I buzzed Jeremy into the unit when he arrived.

He was a handsome guy, but the newly formed bags under his eyes were taking away from his appearance. I doubted he was sleeping much, if at all.

"Hey, Maeve, thanks for meeting me."

"Of course, Jeremy. Let's go sit in the midwifery call room for some privacy."

As we entered the warm, comforting space, I saw Jeremy smile for the first time. He whistled softly as he took in the comfy couch, soft throws, framed artwork by Jonathan Green, and numerous small vases of colorful flowers courtesy of Winnie.

"I love this. What an oasis!"

"It truly is. It's great to take a break in here. It's such a comfortable cocoon."

We settled on opposite ends of the couch, and I waited for him to start speaking.

"I'm sure you saw the press release early this morning stating that the tetrahydrozoline was found in Theo's water bottles."

I hadn't, but I already knew that information from Patrick.

"Maeve, I still have this terrible suspicion that Savannah killed Theo."

I had a million questions but stayed silent to avoid interrupting his thoughts.

"It's like I told you and Meg—Theo and Savannah had an iron-clad prenup. I didn't want to tell you this before, but he had evidence that she was cheating on him. Theo swore me to secrecy. To keep from hurting his kids, Theo was holding back information he had gathered. Sorry for not coming clean." He paused before going on. "But think about it. Savannah was very bitter and had access to the water bottles. Plus, she knew his routine."

"Jeremy, I don't know Savannah. Do you believe she would be capable of killing the father of her children?"

"She's changed, Maeve. No one knows what happens in a marriage. I'm aware that I'm team Theo, but it appears to me that she is the most likely candidate."

I wrestled with my thoughts. I didn't want to alienate Jeremy, but I needed to address my own concerns as well. Finally I said, "I heard through the grapevine that some additional people may have harbored grudges against Theo."

His eyebrows arched up sharply, and his shoulders and jaw tensed. "Please don't tell me that wingnut Carter still says Theo stole his book. I have been a beta reader for Theo since he began writing. It was his work."

I nodded slowly. Jeremy was so distraught that I was a bit nervous about pressing on. But I was a deputy, right? Police business could be painful, but so was murder.

"There also may have been some issues with his company's app."

Jeremy stood and began pacing. The midwifery call room wasn't very big, but I could see that in his current state sitting was out of the question.

"My brother was brilliant. People were so jealous of him. What did you hear?"

I needed to tread carefully. "I heard in passing that Philippe Duval was unhappy with sales after he purchased the company."

Jeremy shook his head. "That's due to poor management on his part. Philippe is no Theo. It's a ridiculous claim."

Clearly, Theo was Jeremy's hero. I didn't bother bringing up Aoki Yoshida. I knew that I would be met with another massive denial.

"Maeve, I came to warn you again about Savannah. As the evidence mounts, she'll strike harder at the nanny. What better way to throw the police off her trail? Please be wary of Savannah."

I walked Jeremy to the elevator and hugged him goodbye. Then I returned to the labor floor and put myself in Jeremy's shoes. What would I be thinking if one of my siblings had been murdered? Would I try to find the killer and defend my family no matter what? Undoubtedly.

And were his feelings about Savannah the result of his brother's pending divorce or based in reality? Whichever, it was a good reminder of the need to protect Fiona at all costs.

I didn't notice Robin catching up to me until she spoke. "Maeve, your patient is in room six," she said, breaking me out of investigative mode.

Upon entering room six, I saw Geena Sheehan and her partner waiting expectantly.

"Good morning, Geena."

"Hi, Maida."

Should I correct her? Since she was about to be induced I let it pass.

I extended my hand to the tall, sandy-haired guy sitting by the head of the bed. "Nice to meet you."

He awkwardly pulled his hand from his pocket, and I noticed his fingers shook a bit. "I'm Paul." He was obviously very anxious.

"So, I know that you saw Dr. Wu last evening, and the plan was made to get this little one born."

"Yes, and it's a little scary. Are you sure it's not too early, Maida?"

To Geena, I would always be Maida. It must have been what she heard the first time we met. Oh well, I'd been called worse.

"Your baby is now thirty-seven weeks. That is considered a full-term baby. With a diagnosis of cholestasis, we monitor you closely, and Dr. Wu began to see a few signs that it's time for him to be born."

"I've heard terrible things about inductions. I'm scared." Geena's knuckles had turned white from clutching the sheet so tightly.

"Geena, let me reassure you. Dr. Wu noted that your cervix is nice and soft and is already one centimeter dilated. That's great. Your baby is about eight pounds, which is a nice size."

At that point, Robin, the nurse assigned to Geena, entered the room and introduced herself.

"Everything will start very slowly. Robin will draw some blood and start an IV. You will have a fetal heartbeat and contraction monitor attached to your abdomen. We'll begin the medication at a very low dose. As always, there is pain medication if you desire it. We are going to be with you all the way, Geena."

Geena visibly relaxed, and Paul reached for her hand.

"I know this isn't what either of you imagined, but we will try to make it as nonfrightening and calm as possible."

At that moment, Dr. Wu walked in. "Good morning, everyone. What a beautiful day to have a baby," she said, motioning to the brilliant blue sky over the harbor outside. As always, she put a positive spin on the moment.

Dr. Wu and I reviewed Geena's chart, answered a few questions, and told the couple we would check on them.

"I'm here for twenty-four, Maeve. Hopefully, she'll deliver by midnight or shortly after," Maiya told me as we reached the main labor desk.

"Well, I'm on until seven, and then Bev will relieve me."

"Sounds good."

Looking around the unit, I saw that we only had two patients. This did not bode well for the night shift. At some point, we would pay.

I checked Geena's pre-induction tracing on the labor desk monitor. Her baby looked great. After I entered a few comments on the workspace computer, my mind drifted back to likely suspects. I turned over a lab requisition sheet and began to make a list.

Savannah?

Philippe Duval?

Carter Morrison?

Aoki Yoshida?

Fiona? I crossed Fiona's name out yet again.

How many others?

How many people knew tetrahydrozoline in huge amounts could kill?

Who wanted Theo dead?

Who profited?

I folded the list and put it in the top pocket of my scrubs. As we said in the medical trade, "Follow-up needed."

CHAPTER TWENTY-THREE

The XY chromosome denotes a biologic male. The XX chromosome denotes a biologic female.

Geena Sheehan was six centimeters dilated and very comfortable with an epidural when my shift was done. True to form, the night would be epic. Eight patients were already on the unit in labor, and thirty-three-week preemie twins whose mother's membranes had ruptured were due in shortly. Triage was packed to the gills, and I wished the staff "Godspeed" as I left Creighton Memorial. Not for the first time in my career, I wondered what it would be like to work in a specialty where admissions were scheduled.

I arrived home to find intoxicating smells filling my kitchen and a place set for me at the table.

"Welcome home, Maeve. The angels are asleep. Fenway is in his bed, and I did the girls' laundry. It's all put away."

"Kate, a million thanks. How was the day?"

"Sit here, and I'll tell you. I've made Guinness pot roast and colcannon. There are some soft rolls from Murray's bakery, too."

"You know, if you decide law is not for you, a Michelin star might be in the offing," I said, savoring my first bite.

Shaking her head, Kate said, "Just some Irish home cooking."

She sat down opposite me with a large mug of tea, her bright blue eyes anticipating my questions.

"Tell me what you hear from Fiona. Is she doing okay?" I began.

"She's up and down. She feels very betrayed by Mrs. Archer. Maeve, that girl tried so hard even though her work situation was crazy."

"How did she get along with Mr. Archer?"

"Fiona was fine with him, but her final pay was late by two weeks. She says Mrs. Archer lied and told Mr. Archer she had paid her."

"How did she get her wages? Check? Venmo?"

Kate momentarily looked down at the table. Her bright red fingernail circled the rim of her mug.

"Well, Maeve. After the first month, the Archers asked if they could pay her off the books in cash. The Archers said she could avoid taxes and would come out ahead. The rest of us get paid through the nanny agency. Somehow, the Archers got them to dissolve the contract. I'm sure it involved a large sum of money, but Fiona didn't ask any of us for advice. Once the nanny group found out, though, we all told her not to do it. But Fiona doesn't like to rock the boat. She trusts everyone. Well, she used to."

"So, Mr. Archer believed Mrs. Archer when she said she paid Fiona?"

Kate nodded.

"I hate to bring this up again but tell me about the accusations of an affair."

Kate's face turned crimson, and she frowned deeply. "That vicious woman. Fiona was most upset about that. Maeve, Fiona is a quiet, very shy girl. She's young and has never even had a boyfriend. This is her year before uni. She wanted to come to the States, be a nanny, and save some money. That part about an affair is just all too much. If Fiona was looking for a mate, it would be with a much younger guy. And now, the wife saying Fiona killed her husband! What a tangle of lies. I think Mrs. Archer is pure evil."

Well, that was the second time today I was hearing that.

"Mrs. Archer needed to get rid of Fiona with no muss, no fuss."

"But why accuse her of murder?"

Kate got up and placed her mug in the dishwasher. She put her hands on the top rung of the ladder-back chair.

"Maeve, Fiona told Bridie and me that Mrs. Archer had bottles of those eye drops everywhere. Maybe she wanted to take any suspicion off herself."

Well, that certainly put an interesting spin on things.

After Kate departed, I called Meg. Maybe it all came down to Savannah Archer. Maybe money did trump all.

"Hey, Maeve, how was the day?"

I debriefed her on Jeremy's visit and what I had heard from Kate.

"Savannah is certainly staying in first place," was Meg's only comment.

"I know."

"I feel bad for Jeremy. It sounds like he won't see any chinks in Theo's armor."

"I know. Well, now we're aware that Savannah frequently uses eye drops. But then again, so do many people."

"Yours truly included," Meg pointed out.

"To the consternation of Mom," I said. "Luckily, that's not an automatic ticket to the suspect list."

"It figures Mom would know that they could be used as poison."

"She truly missed her calling as an FBI agent," I agreed.

"Hey, Maeve, do you have time to inspect the show houses quickly with me? I need to get the lay of the land before the Home Tour. I'm in charge of the entire event so I need precise details for the volunteers. It will also be a good opportunity to delve further into the Mariner Heights community since four houses are there."

"Yes, I'll be done early tomorrow. I'll be at Rosemont, but I only have patients in the morning, and I'm not lecturing. I caught up with grading this weekend, so I can leave after office hours."

"That development still bugs me. Being shut out when they were being built and watching clients overpay still stings. That's probably why I'm determined to do as many of the resales as possible." She paused and added, "Come to my office when you're done. I'll drive us."

I took a quick shower and then snuggled under our feathery white comforter, waiting for Will. I scrolled through Instagram, searching for Savannah's profile. Seven Savannah Archers were listed, but I remembered that her handle was @Savannahsworld, and I finally located it. Her most recent post was a rearview shot of a tall, thin young woman in a gray uniform holding the hands of two small girls.

"Bloomsby nannies are the best!" read the caption. Wow, she had one million followers, and that post already had 400,000 likes. I suspected the Bloomsby school was overrun with requests for nannies with a mention like this. I wondered if Savannah got some type of kickback or just liked showing that she could afford elite, high-priced help. It's too bad her posting wouldn't help childcare pay, in general, to rise.

I must have fallen asleep, because I was dreaming of eye drops, nannies, and Yummy Mummies when I was startled awake by my alarm.

"Morning, honey," Will said, enveloping me in a side hug. "You were fast asleep with the laptop open when I got in last night."

"I was checking out social media sites. Isn't it crazy that people are so drawn to them?"

"It's the way of the world, Maeve. The smartphone is king. Ella convinced me to open an account for A Thyme for All Seasons. She started posting our daily lunch specials and a few of Malia's mouthwatering desserts, and now we've sold out six weeks in a row."

"That's great. I guess I need to get with it," I said, laughing.

"In my line of work, I see too many people addicted to their screens, but I can't fight Ella's marketing plans. She's been a godsend."

"I hear you. Hey, you never know, Will—I might become an influencer, too. How about *A Midwife's Guide to Pregnancy* or something catchy? Maybe companies would send us some baby swag."

We chuckled, but I decided to bring up starting a social media site with the midwifery group at our next meeting. Why not get in on the act?

On the way to Rosemont College, I stopped for a lemon ginger tea and a toasted raisin bagel with cream cheese. Six patients were scheduled to see me today, and I was glad that the bookings were picking up slightly.

Pulling into the faculty lot, I realized I was beginning to feel at home here. How lucky was I? To be both a practicing midwife and a member of a college nursing faculty was turning out to be a great fit. Plus, it was a step forward for the Creighton

Memorial midwifery group to be involved in both medical student and nursing student education.

Dr. Tim held the health center door open for me as I approached.

"Good morning, Maeve. What a beautiful morning."

"Yes, it is. It's such a pretty campus, too."

As we walked down the hall to our respective offices, Kristin, dressed today in a teal mock turtleneck under her white scrubs, called out, "There's a fresh sour cream Bundt cake in the break room."

Kristin, as usual, took care of the staff.

My first patient was a fifty-three-year-old professor of philosophy who was here for an annual visit. After reviewing her chart, I knocked on the exam room door and entered.

I didn't have time to close the door when Kristin called, "Dr. Tim, Maeve...I need you in exam one, now." Her voice sounded urgent.

CHAPTER TWENTY-FOUR

———

Premenstrual syndrome (PMS) usually starts before the onset of a woman's monthly menses. Symptoms may include headache, breast tenderness, fatigue, irritability, anxiety, insomnia, or sadness.

Telling my patient that I would return as soon as possible, I hurried to room one. A young woman was lying on the exam table. Her long hair was tangled, her pink sweats were ripped and bloody, and she was shaking and crying.

"This is Bella Taylor, a senior, who says she was attacked in the tunnel going to the main dining area," Kristin briskly reported. "Two students somehow got her out and carried her here. Her right arm appears to be fractured, and her right ankle will need an X-ray. She has a few facial lacerations. I've called 911 for transport to Creighton Memorial."

I recognized her as the same Bella Taylor I had seen for a urinary tract infection. But tunnels? What tunnels? Clearly, they were left out of my Rosemont orientation.

Dr. Tim joined us at the bedside. Bella's breathing was fine but she was obviously distressed. One cut on her forehead was significant and would need sutures, and Kristin was applying pressure to stop the bleeding. Luckily, the others were small and contained. Her right arm was bent at an odd angle. It certainly looked fractured to me. The ankle on that side was red and incredibly swollen.

I took her uninjured hand in mine and gently rubbed her left shoulder.

"Can you tell us what happened, Bella?" Dr. Tim asked in a calm reassuring voice while starting his exam. Kristin motioned a medium-height female campus police officer with precision-cut black bangs to come into the room.

Shuddering, Bella took a shallow breath, and tears ran down her cheeks.

"Easy breaths, Bella," Kristin soothed her.

"I…I was leaving my microbiology lecture and wanted to grab some breakfast. I decided to use the tunnels to save time. I had earbuds in and was walking fast. As I got to the stairway to Camden Dining Hall, someone shoved me from behind, and I flew down the flight of stairs."

Again, a flood of tears spilled from her green eyes. "I was shocked. I couldn't straighten my arm, and the pain was so bad in my ankle that I was afraid to try to stand. I heard someone running. I realized they were running away but I was afraid to call out. I didn't know what was happening. I thought someone was trying to kill me. I stayed very still and prayed that someone would come along to help me. A few minutes later, two sophomores I knew found me and brought me here."

At that moment, two paramedics entered the room. The health center staff stepped back to let them assess Bella. In a matter of minutes, they were transporting her to Creighton Memorial ED.

After they left, Dr. Tim said, "Let's meet and discuss this incident after seeing our patients."

"I'll be back at noon," the campus police officer said.

The excitement over, I went back to see my first patient again.

After that, the morning flew by. I tried to give each patient my full attention, but my mind kept returning to Bella. How was she doing? Who had wanted to hurt her? And why did I not know about the tunnels under Rosemont College?

Finishing up, I added my last note and headed to the staff lounge. Kristin was setting up a tray of sandwiches and drinks, and I helped her by putting out paper plates. Dr. Tim and two campus police officers were at the door.

"Come, sit," Kristin said. "We can go over this morning's events while we eat."

"Maeve, this is Commander Louis Peters, the chief of campus security, and Sergeant Angel Gleason, who you met this morning. Maeve O'Reilly Kensington is a nurse midwife. This is her first year at Rosemont. She teaches in the nursing department and sees patients here one day a week."

As we shook hands, Kristin continued, "There's turkey and Swiss, BLTs, roast beef and Brie, and toasted veggie wraps."

What a tasty lunch. Kristin went out of her way to order this assortment. I was realizing that she always saw to every detail and was chiefly responsible for the sense of family that emanated from the health center.

"Thanks so much," Dr. Tim said. "Why don't you begin, Kristin? We'll start from the top."

Angel took out a small notebook and pen after she unwrapped her sandwich.

"About 8:40 this morning, two male students, Jordan Henning and Dante Campbell, carried Bella Taylor into the front lobby. They said they found her in the north tunnel. They thought she fell down the flight of stairs leading to Camden Dining Hall. I had them put her in exam room one and called out to Dr. Tim and Maeve as I quickly assessed her condition. Seeing the extent of her injuries, I called 911 for transport to Creighton Memorial," Kristin said.

Dr. Tim nodded and looked at me to continue.

"I entered the exam room and saw it was Bella Taylor. I had met her last week at the health center. Her right arm appeared to be fractured, she had a large facial laceration. Her right ankle was badly swollen and needed imaging."

Dr. Tim continued, "I agree with Kristin and Maeve's assessments. The paramedics quickly followed my arrival."

"We all heard Bella say that she was shoved down some stairs in the tunnel on the way to Camden Dining Hall. Have there been any other incidents like this?" Dr. Tim asked.

Commander Peters shook his head vigorously. "We pride ourselves on how safe the campus is. I mean, sometimes, on a weekend, there can be an incident, but it's usually involving alcohol and poor judgment. We've never had an assault like this at Rosemont."

"Tell me more about the tunnels. I didn't even know they existed," I said.

Kristin and Dr. Tim deferred to the officers. Commander Peters nodded to Sergeant Gleason to fill me in. "There are tunnels connecting almost all of Rosemont College. They are mostly used in the winter, so your department may have forgotten to tell you about them. And they're typically utilized by students, although some faculty do find them handy during a snowstorm.

At this time of year, though, foot traffic is light. They're always kept well lit and we patrol them a few times daily."

"I'll have to check them out," I said.

"Maeve, you're the only one of us who knew Bella, even briefly. And, of course, I don't want you to violate HIPAA, but were you at all concerned for her welfare after her prior visit?" Dr. Tim queried.

"Not at all," I said, shaking my head vigorously. "If so, I would have contacted the proper authorities."

"Of course, Maeve, I know you would have. Forgive me, I'm just grasping at straws," Dr. Tim said.

"We'll talk to Ms. Taylor when she's stable," Commander Peters said. "Also, we'll interview her dormmates and friends."

"She is a cheerleader and quite popular, I believe," Kristin said.

"Obviously, not everyone seems to be a fan," Dr. Tim added. "Will the campus police tell the student body to avoid the tunnels while you investigate, Louis?"

"I've talked to President Saunders. We'll report the incident and urge caution, but we don't intend to limit tunnel access currently."

There wasn't much more to say, so the group finished lunch and broke up. As everyone went to leave, Kristin put out a tray of jumbo-sized chocolate chip cookies.

Saying goodbye, I took two for the road. "I'll check on Bella at Creighton Memorial," I said as I left.

Tunnels at Rosemont? What other secrets were buried here? Why was Bella attacked? Jealousy? Scholarship envy? Just like with the daily online word puzzles that often left me mystified, I was stuck with a feeling that I'd missed some vital clues.

CHAPTER TWENTY-FIVE

———

Oocyte cryopreservation, or egg freezing, is a process that involves hormonal stimulation and oocyte retrieval to freeze eggs for later use.

On my way to Meg's office, several questions vied for my attention. Had Bella recently spurned a suitor? At her visit, she was concerned about sexually transmitted diseases. Did she have a traumatic breakup over a cheating partner? Maybe a jealous cheerleader wanted to sideline her?

All right, that last thought did cut a little too close to a Lifetime script.

I entered Meg's office through the rear door and found her deep in conversation with a striking woman with long, platinum curls. Dressed in a deep navy pencil skirt and a matching silk jacket with silver buttons, she gave off an air of elegance and sophistication.

"Hi, Maeve. Great timing. I want you to meet Diane Coblyn, our loan officer. Diane, this is my sister, Maeve."

We exchanged hellos, and I noticed that Diane had a warm, engaging smile.

Diane straightened her jacket and prepared to leave. "I'll let you two get going. Good luck with the final touches on the Home Tour, Meg. As always, you'll do a fantastic job."

Waving goodbye, Diane headed off to the front of the agency.

"Is Diane new?" I asked.

"She is. And we were so lucky to get her. She's smart, personable, and a dream to work with. Clients love her. We also recruited two new rental agents."

I knew that all hiring decisions were Meg's call.

"It seems that you are running the show here. Any thoughts of buying the business when Jeff Sizemore retires and sells the business?"

"I'll think about it. Jeff is encouraging me to take over. We'll see."

No matter what she said, one day, I could see my big sister owning Langford Realty.

Meg grabbed her bag, and we started off towards the Mariner Heights neighborhood. As we pulled onto Harmony Drive, she asked, "What's up, Maeve? You look distracted. College life too taxing?"

Without mentioning names, I told her that a female student had been attacked. I didn't know if Bella's name had been released to the press yet.

"Oof. That sounds awful. Any ideas who did it?"

"None. Although the circumstances seem too odd to be a random attack," I said.

"Hmmm. Tunnels under Rosemont College. I've heard of them at some schools, especially in northern climates."

They were an interesting feature, but I was still fixated on Bella. "The college seems too bucolic for such an attack."

"Everything and everyone has a dark side, Maeve."

As always, Meg made me face reality.

Like everything else about Mariner Heights, the entrance left no room for subtlety. The road was flanked on both sides by stretches of red brick wall at least six feet high. Each wall carried a bronze sign declaring *Mariner Heights* in foot-tall letters. Imposing seemed to be a theme here.

As we came closer, I saw a cornucopia of pumpkins filling the ground in front of the walls. Corn sheaves were neatly tied together to frame each side. An assortment of bronze lanterns of varying heights lined the grassy area. Naturally, the Yummy Mummies put their stamp on things, and I imagined that the décor would change with the seasons.

Meg pulled to the side of the red brick drive leading to the clubhouse. Its stone frontage and expansive wings made it resemble a palatial manor, fit for a Gatsby.

"Okay, Maeve. Four of the homes on the tour are in this development. We're about to come face to face with the Yummy

Mummy contingent again. I need to note everything about their homes, particularly any areas they don't want to show, special rules, etc."

"Meg, let me be your assistant. That way, I can look around and scope things out. You are better at asking questions and getting people to open up."

Meg looked at me dubiously.

"What?" I asked. I knew Meg's sarcastic look too well.

"Legibility. You. Does everyone in the medical field have terrible handwriting? Is it a prerequisite for entering the profession?"

"You are so hilarious. Don't worry. I'll print it, or even better, I'll take notes on your iPad. I can also take photos."

Meg handed over her device with a bit of a smirk.

"Please be worth more than I'm paying you. Okay, the first home is that of Hillary and Sterling Forrester. He owns a hedge fund. I mean, who doesn't? Hillary is from Greenwich, Connecticut, and is to the manor born. Sterling hails from Atherton, California, which is an equally wealthy town. They have one daughter, Isabella Marguerite, who is two years old."

"Does Hillary work outside the home?"

"Dearest Maeve, Hillary is a full-time mother with a nanny, chef, and house manager. In her free time, she helps coordinate A Newborn's Nest, a charity that provides clothing, toys, and infant paraphernalia to families in need."

"Well, that's a worthwhile endeavor. I'll have to get the information for Creighton Memorial. Maybe it could assist some of our new mothers. I'm not familiar with that organization."

"Let's do her home first. I hope she is friends with Savannah Archer and can spill some dirt," Meg said, parking in front of Hillary's home.

The "home" was a sprawling custom-designed colonial of white brick with black shutters situated on well over an acre of lawn. Meg rang the bell on the glossy red front door. Within a few seconds, a fifty-ish petite woman in a black rayon uniform answered. She had close-cropped brown hair and white Chloé platform sneakers on her feet.

"Good afternoon, I'm Geneva, the Forresters' house manager. I assume that you are the advance team for the Home Tour?"

Meg introduced us, and Geneva continued, "Please come in, and cover your shoes with paper booties. You will see an assortment on your left."

Meg and I sat on an onyx metal bench and covered our footwear.

"On the day of the Home Tour, we'll have plenty of disposable slippers, which participants will be asked to use. This is of utmost importance. The Forresters cannot tolerate dust or dirt being tracked throughout their abode."

Truthfully, I thought taking off shoes when entering a home was a great idea, especially with children, but this decree felt a bit like being scolded.

We traversed the expansive foyer, passing a sweeping bridal staircase on the left, and were led into a formal living room. The entire space was done in shades of white and light gray. An ornate white marble fireplace was at the far end, and floor-to-ceiling windows overlooked the side garden.

"Mrs. Forrester has the specifics on the furnishings. She will meet us in the sunroom. The fireplace was imported from a villa in Tuscany."

French glass doors revealed a dining room with a gleaming mahogany table and matching chairs for sixteen. Scarlet floral wallpaper adorned the walls, and a white Persian rug graced the floor.

I wondered if children were allowed to eat in here. My two would require plastic sheeting around their chairs plus spreading out six feet in all directions to protect the furnishings.

Geneva narrated the provenance of each item as we passed. "Mrs. Forrester commissioned the wallcovering to commemorate her grandmother's summer garden in the Hamptons. The carpet is hand-knotted and was purchased on a trip to Iran many years ago by Mr. Forrester's father, a diplomat at the time."

Hmm…it certainly was not bought with a government salary.

We passed through two dens and a library and entered a gleaming white kitchen. The scent of lemons filled the area. White Carrara marble graced every countertop. The island was about the size of a real island. Three oversized white ranunculus arrangements in tall Simon Pearce glass vases were placed around the room.

Tastefully, of course.

"The kitchen was a collaboration between the Forresters and Malcolm Graham, the award-winning designer," Geneva said, continuing without a hiccup or a pause.

I was typing notes as fast as I could.

We were ushered into a vaulted ceiling sunroom decorated like a Lily Pulitzer showroom. A burst of fuchsia and green enveloped us. Bonsai plants were on every flat surface. Tall glass vases held bountiful bouquets of dusty rose peonies. Forest green wicker furniture with hot pink printed cushions completed the look.

"Mrs. Forrester, let me introduce Meg O'Reilly, the Home Tour organizer, and her assistant," Geneva said.

Gee, I didn't even rate a first name.

A very chic-looking woman with jet black hair in a tight chignon was seated at a glass-topped wooden desk. She looked up from her laptop.

"Good morning. Please allow me a moment to finish up. A dear neighbor's husband recently passed on, and I need to finalize the family's dinner menu."

Meg and I exchanged looks.

Bingo!

CHAPTER TWENTY-SIX

———

An ovarian cyst is a fluid-filled or solid sac that develops in or on an ovary.

Not one to be told to wait, Meg strolled around the room on her own, much to the consternation of Geneva. I used the time to pull the house up on Zillow. It was 7,500 square feet with five bedrooms, six bathrooms, a pool, a four-car garage, and a tennis court. I wondered how they fit everything in until I noticed the lot was three acres.

Hillary finally closed her laptop and stood to shake our hands.

"So sorry for your loss," Meg said, reaching her hand out.

"Yes, it's so tragic. The meals are for Savannah Archer. I know that you are providing her with your selling expertise, Meg. She certainly can use a better real estate agent. That house should have sold immediately. But poor Savannah is just at sixes and sevens right now." Barely taking a breath, Hillary continued in a whisper, "Theo was murdered. I just can't believe it. I thought Langford was so safe." She shivered.

"I only met Savannah briefly, and we focused on her house. How is the family coping?" Meg asked with a concerned look.

Hillary looked to the garden, then turned back to us. Her long lashes were a bit wet.

"Savannah is strong. Luckily, she has our brilliant friend Arianna Gladstone to guide her journey. Savannah also has a new British live-in nanny for the girls, thank goodness. Her last nanny was a horror show. In fact,"—her voice dropped conspiratorially—"she may have killed Theo in a jealous rage."

"How terrible," Meg said, keeping a straight face.

I found myself clasping the iPad very tightly. What rubbish! But I had to stay in character as the lowly right-hand person without a name or an opinion.

"It's been a real trial, but our friend group is trying to care for her. I ordered meals from Chez Hans in Boston from Sterling and me."

The price of an average entrée at Chez Hans was about seventy-five dollars. Their food was elegant, but I doubted anyone would want it every day. And it decidedly was not for children.

"That's so thoughtful," Meg said, sounding completely sincere.

I was amazed at her ability to empathize with Hillary. I knew she must be seething inside.

"Sterling and I use their services whenever a friend or one of our staff is in need. It's such a little thing but so helpful. We believe in showing love for our people. After Geneva, our devoted house manager, had hand surgery, we sent her to Turks and Caicos to recover for two weeks."

I loved a good, humble brag. That last comment wasn't so much a show of TLC as it was letting us know she was oh-so-wealthy. On the other hand, with perks like that, if Hillary ever murdered someone, she could probably count on Geneva to dispose of the body.

"What a supportive friend group. Savannah is fortunate to have you."

Hillary beamed. "Yes, we will pamper her and the girls, and Arianna will get her started on the road to recovery soon."

"I'm not familiar with Arianna's methods," Meg ventured.

"Oh, she is cutting-edge," Hillary gushed. "Her approach is radically different but has proven successful. Here, let me pull up her latest speaking tour." She went to her laptop and turned to us with a big smile. "You're in luck. She's speaking at the Langford Library next week. You need to see her in action, but you must register early. I'm sure it will be a packed house. Geneva, I sent Arianna's schedule to the library printer. Please give it to Meg when she departs."

Hillary showed us the primary suite with his and hers baths and matching walk-in closets. But was a closet still called a walk-in if it had a sitting area, hair station, and three-way mirrors?

Isabella's room was awash in sky blue and daisy yellow. Hillary thoroughly detailed the story of every custom piece made for her daughter, from the canopied little-girl bed to the antique dollhouse. The second floor also contained a playroom stocked to make FAO Schwarz green with envy, a laundry room with a double sink and a separate table for sorting and folding, and a few guest bedrooms—en suite, of course.

The lower level housed a movie theater, game room, and climate-controlled wine cellar.

"Our staff have their suites over the garage. Naturally, they are off-limits. The pool house will be available for viewing, though."

"Wonderful," Meg said warmly. "I think we will need twelve volunteers to man the house. They'll be briefed on the furnishings and will watch over your belongings. But, as with any public event, small valuables should be stored away."

"Geneva will make sure that everything is secure. She also has a list of dos and don'ts for you."

"That will be very helpful. Thank you for your time, Hillary. It's very kind of you to lend your home to the tour. The Langford Animal Shelter is very grateful."

"We love to interact with the community. Our fur babies are family to us. We had to get them from breeders because Sterling had his heart set on Cavalier King Charles spaniel puppies. Besides, shelter pets often have behavioral issues and can cause allergies, but of course we fully support the Langford Animal Shelter's mission. It's such a great low-cost option. It's a shame our girls are out for a walk with their handler right now because I know you'd positively adore them. Well, so nice to meet you, Meg. Oh, and be sure to hear Arianna speak. She is life-changing."

Meg and I didn't say a word until we were back in her Jag and headed to the next home on our list. Meg pulled out the list Geneva gave us as we left.

"Here," she said. "You better read it because I'm on the verge of gagging. This would likely push me over the edge."

I took the list from her and read it aloud:

No photos

No uncovered street shoes— please use disposable booties
No food or drink in the home
No leaning against walls
No sitting on the furniture
Maximum of 30 guests at a time
Do enjoy our home
Do place used booties in the recycling containers
Do give generously to the Langford Animal Shelter

"That's not as bad as I expected," Meg decided. "Some people might think the shoe coverings are a bit much, but, you know, it's a smart move with a large volume of spectators."

"I agree. I didn't love the belief that pound puppies are inferior to her precious purebreds, though." That remark had pushed my buttons because Fenway had come to us as a rescue from a shelter when she was five months old.

"Well, Yummy Mummies are a different species. Hillary's life has been a very privileged one of live-in staff, enormous wealth, opulent homes, and luxury travel. It's all she's ever known."

"She does live in a bit of a cocoon. I wonder if she's ever had a job," I mused.

"Her 'job' is maintaining staff, looking beautiful, attending luncheons with her friends, and keeping up with her social circle. At most, after college and before marriage, she had some type of unpaid 'intern' position at a glossy fashion magazine. But remember, her charity does a lot of good."

"I'm sure it does. I'm just thankful my Will chose a different path."

My spouse, Will Kensington III, had also been born with a silver spoon in his mouth but had managed to take it out and worked hard to run a community-based catering business.

"Will is a peach," Meg agreed. "He's humble, gracious, kind, a fantastic uncle, and a devoted dad. Not to mention, he's a terrific brother-in-law, and, ah yes, he loves my sister. A lot. Sometimes, I don't know how he escaped Lydia and William's clutches."

"I believe it was due to a wonderful nanny. And Grand, of course."

Will's grandmother thought his life choices were flawless and had encouraged him at every turn.

As much as I liked praising Will's character, we needed to get back to the murder at hand. "We should attend Arianna Gladstone's presentation. I'm curious about her methods," I said.

Meg was scrolling on her phone. "I've already registered us for her talk."

"Meg, I know Patrick wanted us to get the skinny on the Yummy Mummies, but do you really think that one of them killed Theo? I mean, murder is messy, and they live very contained lives."

"Oh, come on, Maeve. You are getting rusty. Poisoning, especially in Theo's case, was simple. Add a large dosage of eye drops to his water and, since he was so regimented about his exercise routine, he dies on his run."

"I guess you're right. The Yummies' lives are so unfettered, though. Why kill him? Just subtly axe him out of the group."

"That's an excellent point. So, there must be something sinister buried beneath the layers. Theo, as we know, had many enemies, plus a nasty ongoing divorce. Let's see if we hear anything at the next three homes."

"Three more?"

"Five more—three in this neighborhood. But look what I have." She pulled out two water bottles, a large bag of orange slice candies, and another of bite-sized Snickers.

Taking a handful of candy, I grudgingly settled for another foray into McMansion land.

The following two homes were very similar to Hillary's, complete with house managers, nannies, gardeners, chefs, and dog walkers. Conspicuous consumption of luxury goods was the recurring theme. I took copious notes and collected additional lists of restrictions.

The last home was Arianna Gladstone's abode. She was not home, but Miri, her personal assistant, gave us the tour. She added a publicity sheet, which included a very flattering headshot. In Arianna's den, I was stopped in my tracks by an expansive wall of exquisite handblown glass paperweights. There were flowers of every color, millefiori patterns, and female profiles resembling cameos. Miri explained that the profiles were called sulfides. They were breathtaking. What a stellar collection.

Miri explained that some of the paperweights were one-of-a-kind antique French works of art, and others were from contemporary artists around the world. Arianna's collection rivaled many museum offerings. Meg assured her that she would station three volunteers in the room to make sure that the display was viewed but not touched.

After finishing the last Mariner Heights home, we gratefully left the neighborhood to its own devices. Arriving at the next stop, we found a refreshingly charming red brick antique on a high cliff overlooking the Atlantic. Sheila Gillespie, the owner, had three rescue pups and a garden complete with multicolored wooden gates and birdhouses of every description. Her vintage kitchen made one want to sit and have tea and a scone. The primary bedroom was done in restful shades of Wedgewood blue and cream and had stellar views of the Atlantic below. She laughed when we asked about restrictions for the viewing public and handed us a small basket of molasses cookies as we left.

"I want to live there," I said, munching a chewy cookie as Meg drove.

"She is so warm, and her décor is unique. Her home will be a favorite."

The last stop featured a rather odd, cold, modern structure with a distant ocean view. Meg used the lockbox to enter, and I made notes as she reeled off a long list.

"It needs bright flowers, at least four arrangements. We need a wreath on the door, potted plants, and some colorful throw pillows. Also, the air is stale. We need some diffusers, maybe jasmine or chamomile. I'll send over the staging expert from my office to take a look. Okay, let's hit the road. Thanks so much for your help, Maeve."

"It was eye-opening. I'll give it that."

"I don't know if we discovered much, but we still have the gym to explore."

Leaving her office, I headed straight to Creighton Memorial. How was Bella Taylor doing?

CHAPTER TWENTY-SEVEN

Endometriosis is a condition where tissue similar to the type that lines the uterus grows on other organs. Often extremely painful, endometriosis can also develop outside the pelvic area.

The emergency department was busy but not at capacity when I arrived. I asked if MJ was on duty and was immediately directed to the staff lounge.

A few medical students were reading journals in one corner. On the bulletin board, I saw the typical staff listings about shift potlucks, apartments for rent, and sign-up sheets for various school fundraisers.

"Just couldn't stay away, could you?" MJ said, entering the lounge from the women's locker room.

Her eyes took in the group of medical students. "We could use help admitting a few patients if you have some downtime," she said to them. The foursome looked up expectantly. "Tell Amelia, the nurse with short, spiky black hair and purple glasses at the admissions desk, that MJ said to assign you to patients. When the chief resident is finished in the procedure room, I'll tell her where to find you."

They eagerly filed out.

"So, Maeve, just visiting?" MJ asked.

I filled MJ in on Bella Taylor's accident at Rosemont College.

"I didn't know the midwives taught there."

"This is the first year. The new president of Rosemont wanted to strengthen ties to Creighton and see if a mix of nursing faculty would benefit the students."

"Sounds like a win-win to me. Is Ms. Taylor one of your nursing students?"

"No, she's premed, but I met her on campus."

HIPAA was so ingrained in me I would never disclose that Bella was my GYN patient.

"It appears that someone pushed her down a flight of stairs. The results were rather nasty," MJ reported. "She has a fractured right arm and a severely sprained right ankle."

"How is her facial laceration?"

"I called in one of the plastic surgeons. Bella will have a swollen face and two shiners from the fall, but that laceration will be difficult to find in a few months."

"That's awesome. Bella will be so grateful."

"I'm also having one of our social workers see her. She claims she didn't see anyone, but it's hard to believe that it was a random attack. The staff wondered if a relationship gone wrong was to blame."

Not desiring to get into a deeper discussion of Bella's history, I said, "I didn't even know there were tunnels under the college. Next time I'm there, I plan to walk through them."

"Better bring pepper spray," MJ said as she motioned me to follow her. "I assume you want to say hello. You have a few minutes before Janey, our social worker, can see her."

She left me at Bella's bay in the admitted patient area.

Gathering the curtain to open it, I said, "Knock, knock. Bella, it's Maeve from Rosemont College."

"Come in."

The hours had let her injuries show themselves. Bella's forehead laceration was bandaged, but both eyes were black and blue, and some blood was crusted on her face from three other cuts. Her right arm was casted, and her right ankle was wrapped and taped. Bella was leaning back on the pillow. Her eyes met mine.

"Maeve," she said quietly as tears started flowing. Her narrow shoulders shook, and I smoothed her hair and gently rubbed her left shoulder.

After a minute or two, she took a shaky breath and smiled at me weakly.

"Are you having any pain?"

"Just when I move quickly. The nurse gave me medication."

I nodded.

"The doctors want me to stay in observation overnight because I hit my head, but I want to get back to campus."

"I think it's a good idea to stay. Did you call your parents yet?"

"It's just my mom. She's in New Jersey with my two younger siblings. She wanted to come, but I told her I was okay. She's a schoolteacher, and I know it would be difficult for her to get away. My dad was a captain in the Army. He was killed while on deployment in Iraq. My aunt helps, but I know how hectic my mom's life is."

This family had certainly had their share of tragedy.

"My mom wants me to stay overnight, too."

"Bella, here you have a hospital bed and someone to help you get up. Trust me, hospitals don't keep you if it's unnecessary."

Bella gave me a half smile. "You're right. I'm being silly."

Pulling a chair up beside her bed, I took her hand. "I know you already answered many questions, but are you positive that the attack was random?"

Her eyes widened, and she looked at me questioningly. "I think so."

"I just wanted to make sure that there wasn't a jilted boyfriend or a jealous cheerleader in the mix."

Bella laughed a little but then looked very serious. "I just had a tough breakup, but I'm sure it wasn't him. As for an evil cheerleader, I don't think so."

She was very quiet for a few minutes, and her brow furrowed. "I… I think some students are envious that I have a Spirit scholarship."

"Tell me more about that." Maybe I would get some detailed information.

"It's a scholarship for women at Rosemont. I was so worried about taking out a huge loan for college but shortly after I received my admission letter, I was notified that I was awarded a Spirit scholarship. I was given instructions to meet an older woman in downtown Boston, and she explained the terms, and I signed some documents. It pays for all my expenses if I maintain a 3.0 GPA."

"Who provides the funds?"

"The woman said that wealthy alums wanted to help women flourish in college, but desired to remain anonymous. She said no application was necessary and that it was based on financial need. She stressed that the recipients were hand-picked by the alums as very likely to succeed."

Bella looked down at her hands and seemed a bit uneasy. Maybe she was uncomfortable about the fact that she needed substantial monetary help. I decided to ease up with the questioning. She had been through a traumatic experience.

"Hello, Bella Taylor?" A tall woman with a deep brown complexion wearing a silk blouse with a striking black and white abstract design peeked through the curtain. "I'm Janey Barker, the social worker for the emergency department. I wanted to meet you and tell you about our services."

I stood, introduced myself to Janey, and said goodbye to Bella. On my way to the staff lot, several thoughts troubled me. Maybe Bella's ex-partner was more jealous than she thought. And why did other female students at Rosemont seem to look askance at certain financial aid? It became clear that I needed to delve more deeply into the Spirit scholarships.

As I drove home, I called Will, but his phone went straight to voicemail.

Then he quickly texted back: *Staff meeting. Kate making dinner. Be home at 6. Love you.*

Kate! How fortunate we were to have her!

As I opened the door to Primrose Cottage, I saw Kate on the playmat with Sloane, Rowan, and Fenway. Rowan happily banged on a toy piano, to Sloane's unbridled joy and Fenway's consternation. I went to the sink and washed my hands. When I joined them, I was immediately covered in two girls and a wily dachshund, all vying for my attention. Laughing, I pulled Sloane into my lap and let Rowan crawl on my legs. Not to be left out, Fenway wormed her way under my right arm.

"Mama's home," Kate said, laughing. "You're a lucky woman, Maeve."

A huge smile crossed my face. I knew I was. "What is that tantalizing aroma?" I asked.

"Ah, it's my mom's recipe for meatloaf with mashed potatoes, carrots, broccoli, and brown gravy. I also made a tea cake for dessert. You can serve it with some berries."

"Kate, how many ways can I say thank you?"

"No need. I did it while the girls were napping. I love to cook and made extra to bring home for Bridie, Fiona, and me. We need a taste of Ireland. I hope that's okay."

"That sounds great. I told you that you're always welcome to cook for you and your roommates."

"Thanks, Maeve. Bridie usually is the chef, but I told her today was my treat."

As Rowan reached over to hand Sloane a small stuffed duck, Kate smiled and said, "Sisters, nothing like it. You are so lucky to live close to Meg."

As a wistful look crossed her face, I realized Kate was undoubtedly missing her sisters in Galway.

"I *am* so fortunate," I agreed. "I helped Meg get ready for the Langford House Tour today. She's running the entire outing. We walked through some Mariner Heights homes. It's quite the place."

Kate frowned as she said, "I've been in a few myself, and you practically need a map to get around. But like I told you before, there are no Irish nannies there now—only Bloomsby graduates for those women."

"What does your agency say? It's crazy that all these nannies were dismissed."

"The head of the agency is not saying anything beyond, 'Sometimes placements don't work out.' You know what they say—money talks. Bridie recently overheard that the Mariner Heights families who break the contract with the agency without cause pay a considerable fee. But those families are so wealthy it doesn't bother them."

"How many nannies are still jobless?"

"Well, Fiona, but Meg is taking care of her. And there's Orla and Quinn, who need to find placements soon."

"Let me put the word out at Creighton Memorial and Rosemont College about their availability. This is so wrong."

"Thanks, Maeve." As she packed up, she said, "Fiona said that Theo and Savannah had many fights about money."

"They were probably arguing about the divorce. You know, dividing assets is always a nightmare."

"She also said the house manager told her some angry person kept calling the house, but Theo ripped up all the messages. Well, I'm off now. Have a nice family dinner. Goodbye, my sweeties."

Messages from who? Carter? Aoki? Philippe?

The dinner was comforting, just what I needed. Afterward, Will and I put the girls to bed and snuggled on the couch. I filled him in on my day, the lifestyles of the women we had met, and the Irish nannies' situation.

"I was raised under very similar circumstances to the Mariner Heights children. Now I'm so happy we live as we do." He was pensive for a moment and then continued, "Mariner Heights may look idyllic from the outside, but there's often a lot of underlying stress in those homes."

I rubbed Will's arm. I wanted him aware that he had my full attention.

He stretched his large frame out and drew me in even closer. "My parents gave me and my siblings the best of everything. Whatever money could buy. But as you can tell, daily childcare is not in their wheelhouse. They subscribed to the belief that children should be seen, usually twice daily for about ten minutes total, and not heard. Luckily for me, I had Grand. I spent countless hours at her house. She encouraged all my dreams and let me be a carefree little boy. My Nanny Beatrice, or Nanny B as I called her, comforted me when I was hurt, taught me to read, clapped when I made a soccer goal, and basically"—he paused, a bit choked up—"saved my life."

I put my head on Will's chest. I'd heard snippets of his childhood before. Even though he was such a wonderful father, husband, and business owner now, childhood neglect can always resurface and cause sadness.

"If not for Grand and Nanny B, who knows how I would have turned out. It's tough to have parents who are not engaged."

We were silent for a long time, and then Will hugged me and picked up the latest Grisham to read.

Will was soon asleep, and, not wanting to disturb him, I went into our bedroom to call Meg and fill her in on Orla and Quinn's job search.

"Mariner Heights sounds like a 'No Irish Need Apply' zone," Meg said. "It's disgusting."

I agreed. Then we went over the murder again. We had no leads. We said goodnight after agreeing we needed to infiltrate the gym.

I picked up *Murder at the Vicarage*, one of my favorites. Jane Marple could have solved Theo's murder without even trying. St. Mary Mead might not be Mariner Heights, but observation, questioning, and identifying suspects was the key to solving crimes. Like a wordplay game, everything must fit.

CHAPTER TWENTY-EIGHT

———

Perimenopause is the time period before a woman's body makes the full transition to menopause.

Meg and I stopped by Hanville Grove on our way to Arianna's presentation at the Langford Library. A newly hired security guard watched us sign in as we entered. After the events of last winter, the administration had tightened access considerably.

As soon as we passed muster, Louella, Ethel, and Gaby, Mom's best friends, who were also known as the Ladies of the Lobby, greeted us warmly. We had been through a near-death experience with them in this very building and, as a result, had bonded closely. They had shown themselves to be fearless warriors; Meg and I agreed they were our role models. Per usual, Louella was in yellow, today a bright canary from head to toe; Ethel had a navy and white polka-dot cardigan over red corduroy slacks; and Gaby wore a saffron midi skirt and a cobalt blue blouse with a huge bow. Fearless in spirit, brave, and loving, they never disappointed. I longed to have their flair.

"Hey, girls, your mom told us you might be up for a trip to Ireland," Ethel said.

"Ah, oh, maybe," I choked out, blushing to my roots.

"We're learning a lot of Irish songs to prepare," Louella said, beaming.

"It's definitely something to think about," Meg said, ushering me down the hall toward the elevators.

"Tell Mary I'll be up to get her for Bingo," Gaby called out.

"I love those women, but a trip to the Emerald Isle? I get a headache just thinking about the logistics," Meg said, pressing the up button impatiently as we entered the elevator.

"I know. When this is over we are going to need a sibling conclave to see what we can do. I mean, they are the Golden Girls personified."

Mom's door was wide open, as always. Security rules obviously did not pertain to her.

"Hi, Mom," I said, kissing her as she sat in her chambray faux leather electric recliner.

"I saw you and the girls talking in the lobby."

Mom never watched cable stations but instead tuned in to the Hanville Grove camera feed at the front door and lobby. Since she had once solved a mystery because of this practice, I never said a disparaging word about it.

"Meg, are those gardenias?" Mom asked, glancing at the bouquet Meg carried.

"They are, Mom. I got them at A Bloom of One's Own. I know they are one of your favorites."

"Thank you so much. That's such an enchanting shop, and Amber is an angel."

"She certainly is. Her gift to me helped me through a rough labor."

"Rough labor? I'll say." Meg threw her hands in the air.

"The girls and I could have delivered Sloane if it came to that. Remember, Ethel was a Navy nurse, and Gaby and I are devotees of *Call the Midwife*," Mom replied smugly.

If I had a white flag, I would have raised it. Sometimes, it was futile to defy Mom's warped logic.

"Put the kettle on, Meg. Let's have tea," Mom commanded.

This was our usual routine, and I loved it.

Meg brought out apple cinnamon scones, maple hazelnut muffins, pumpkin chocolate chip bread, and tea.

"Gee, Meg, did you empty the bakery case?" I teased.

"Malia is such a superb pastry chef that I wanted to try everything."

"She is very talented. Speaking of the café, does Will plan on having a food truck at the Autumn Fest?" Mom asked.

"Yes, he will. He is making a special menu."

"Great! The girls and I will meet you there. We're leaving Hanville Grove at nine sharp."

The Autumn Fest was held every October on the town green. Arts and crafts of every description were available for sale. Various bands played, and all manner of voice and dance clubs performed. Food trucks filled the municipal parking lot. It was an event that brought out all the citizenry.

As we drank our tea, Mom went through a litany of who was ill, who had died, and all the latest gossip from Hanville Grove.

"Is the new maintenance guy working out?" I asked. The last one had been a nightmare for all of us.

"Maintenance woman," Mom said proudly. "April is the best. She can fix anything and is always so cheerful. We just love her."

"Sounds like a match made in heaven," Meg said.

"And guess what? Aidan and Sebi are taking me to Manhattan next month to see *Wicked*. I can't wait. It will be so much fun."

Mom loved all musicals and plays. She circled all the shows she wanted to see in the *New York Times* Arts section at the beginning of each new season. Aidan favored sports, but Sebi and Mom were constant companions in the Dress Circle box.

"Will and I saw that in Boston," I said.

"The touring companies are good, but nothing beats an NYC cast and theater."

Meg gave a dramatic bow as she bit into a scone. Mom could quote entire lines from her favorite productions, and although she happily attended community theater, Broadway held her heart.

"So, tell me, what's new?" Mom asked. "What's happening with the murder investigation?"

"You'd have to ask Patrick," Meg said.

I suddenly found my mug very interesting.

"Oh, come on, you two. Give me a break. I saw you talking with Patrick in his sunroom. I know that you were going over the investigation. Even Patrick has figured out that my M&M's can solve any case. Now, take it from the top."

Meg put her head in her hands, and I started chuckling. Nothing escaped Mom.

"Mom, this is top secret. We are merely checking out the Mariner Heights social scene for Patrick. Please keep it quiet," I told her.

"Well, he finally realized what he has in the two of you. I'm glad." She took a long look at us over her teacup. "Run down the list of suspects."

Move over Sherlock Holmes. Mom had this covered.

"Okay, Mom, but remember this is highly confidential," Meg said.

Mom glared at us and drummed her fingers on the end table expectantly.

We filled her in on Savannah, Aoki, Carter, and Philippe and their grievances with Theo. She was already aware that Savannah had tried to cast blame on Fiona.

"That man certainly had a lot of enemies. They say that poisoning is usually done by women, but Putin uses it, too. So, you never know," Mom said, pursing her lips.

"Theo always left from his gym, The Art of Wellness, to go on his run to First Light. Meg and I will check that out next."

"The Art of Wellness sounds like some New Age nonsense, and I bet it costs a pretty penny," Mom said with a chuckle.

"We'll let you know. Anyone can purchase eye drops. It will be hard to find the killer," Meg said.

"Look for the motive. The more I hear about Theo, the more revenge seems likely. Was he stepping out on his wife?" Mom asked.

"Well, the wife claims he was with the nanny," I said.

"The young nanny from Ireland? That's pure foolishness. Why, the wife was probably cheating on him."

Mom always went right to the heart of the matter.

"Come talk to me after the gym outing. Maybe we can piece this together," Mom said.

I suddenly felt like Archie Goodwin trapped in a Nero Wolfe universe.

After exchanging assurances we'd meet at the Autumn Fest, Meg and I headed to the Langford Library and Arianna.

"Good thing we didn't tell Mom about the Grief Whisperer. She would have wanted to come, and there might have been an incident," Meg said.

Just as Hillary predicted, the library lot was full. "I'm glad that we registered," I said.

As we entered, I saw our friend Swati welcoming guests. Swati was now the director of Langford Library, replacing the much-loved Ingrid Olson after her untimely death.

"Welcome, Maeve and Meg. We're full tonight. There's quite a lot of interest in this intriguing take on how to handle grief."

"Congratulations on your new position," Meg said.

A wave of sadness passed over Swati's face, and then she smiled. "Thank you. I am trying to honor Ingrid's legacy."

"She would be so proud that you are steering the library," I said, giving Swati a hug.

"I heard that Crosby moved away," Meg said.

Swati nodded slowly. "Crosby felt that she needed a fresh start. She became a library director in Bend, Oregon."

"That's a big change," Meg said.

"She has family there. She's very happy."

We heard introductions being made in the Bancroft room. It was our signal to say a quick goodbye and hurry to find seats. We were lucky to find two in the back row just as the woman on stage began speaking.

"Good evening, I'm Arianna Gladstone, the Grief Whisperer." Arianna had pulled out all the stops. Her shoulder-length hair was blown out to perfection. A scarlet silk pantsuit with fitted pants and a shawl-collared jacket showcased her figure. An intricate silver necklace complemented the look. Black patent leather shoes with two-inch heels enhanced her height and made her look more in command.

"Thank you for attending. Tonight, I will share my groundbreaking method to mourn and move on. It's radical, but remember, life is short. Grieve and get over it."

"Elisabeth Kübler-Ross apparently wasted her time," Meg whispered.

CHAPTER TWENTY-NINE

———

A cone biopsy is performed to remove abnormal tissue from a woman's cervix.

"Let me begin by telling you my story. My beloved husband died tragically in an unfortunate hiking accident. He was only thirty-six years old." She paused and looked at the ceiling as if for dramatic effect before continuing. "We had been married two years, had just built our dream home, and were looking forward to starting a family. As you can imagine, I was totally devastated. Somehow, I muddled through the wake and funeral and then began to go to support groups. After a few meetings, though, I realized that some people had been attending for years. After a few weeks, I realized that I did not want to waste what was left of my life grieving. One day, I saw an article about a new way to handle loss. It led me to a retreat at Big Sur with Jackson Lewis, the world-renowned guru who teaches the art of rapidly recovering from the death of a significant other. It was life-changing. Applying his principles, I must say I am thriving. Of course, I remember my husband dearly, but I have moved on as he would have wanted me to."

The crowd stirred, waiting to hear the secret of grieving quickly. Arianna had the lights dimmed and started a slide show. A beautiful ocean scene at sunset came up first. New Age music featuring a sitar began to play softly.

"Now close your eyes and picture your loved one passing on into the universe."

"Get the hankies out," Meg said.

The next twenty or so slides featured exquisite flower gardens, rolling hills, and crystal-clear lakes. Suddenly, the lights came on, up-tempo Muzak played, and the slides pictured men and women of all ages skiing, dancing, biking, and singing. They all wore large, beatific smiles.

Arianna swayed with the tune and then waved her hand to silence the room. She smiled widely and, grasping the handheld mic, said, "It's a new day. Time to put on a new face and *live*! We only go around once, and time is not for wasting. Follow my plan, and you'll move on in no time."

The following slide appeared with a list of starred items:
Have a ceremony to say farewell
Immediately clean out the person's belongings
Refresh your home—use sage–or move to a new abode
Develop hobbies—take classes
Make dates with friends
Use dating apps
Develop a daily mantra
Avoid sad movies—try comedies
Remember, life is precious—carpe diem
Hire a grief coach—my number is 555-222-6866

A few gasps were heard from the audience. The last slide showed an almost blinding sunrise, with Arianna's website prominently featured.

Arianna scanned the audience. "I know this goes against all the old clichés you've heard. Wait a year before any major decisions. Don't sell your house. Take time to grieve. But I'm here to tell you that is what makes people stuck. It's best to remember the one who passed and then move right on."

"What witchcraft is she peddling?" I asked incredulously.

"Therapists must love her. Their caseloads probably increase after people try her method," Meg said with a look of disgust.

Arianna fielded several questions from the audience. Some were dubious about her process, but others asked about her results.

"I loved my husband, but I can honestly say I have never felt more fulfilled. I went from heartbroken and barely able to get dressed to a new career as a bestselling author. I travel worldwide, holding seminars. I have legions of followers, and you can check my online reviews. My success rate is extremely high."

"Those were probably paid reviews," Meg grumbled.

"Her program is dangerous," I said.

"If she starts passing out Kool-Aid, don't drink any," Meg said.

Arianna had clearly recruited some of her followers to be in the audience, and we listened as they gave glowing tributes to her method. As soon as they finished, and before anyone could present another view, Arianna announced that her book was available for purchase and she would be signing copies. Meg insisted that we get one.

The line was long, and we were close to the end. Some people grasped Arianna's hands and thanked her when they reached the front of the line. She obviously relished her role as a grief guru and hugged a few followers as she passed out her business card. Finally, we reached Arianna and said hello.

"You were at my home today."

Meg responded immediately. "Yes. Your assistant showed us around. It's stellar."

"I hope the Home Tour does well. The Langford Animal Shelter is such a worthy cause."

"Your presentation was fascinating. There is so much heartache over loss," I said.

A look of concern came over Arianna's face. She totally ignored me, the lowly aide, as if I hadn't spoken but turned immediately to my big sister. "Have you had a recent loss, Meg?"

"Not me. I believe Maeve was thinking of Savannah Archer."

Arianna gave me a long, appraising look. "I am guiding Savannah," she finally said. "She will overcome this. I'll steer her ship."

Captain Ahab was alive and well.

"So tough that she was going through a divorce. I'm sure that only adds to her grief," I said.

That seemed to get her attention. She turned to me and asked, "Are you a psychiatrist, Maeve?"

No, but I play one on TV.

Meg, sensing my irritation, stepped in. "Maeve is a midwife at Creighton Memorial and is on the faculty at Rosemont College. She's also my sister."

Arianna froze briefly but then drew her head back with a haughty glare. A formidable sneer began to cross her face, but she quickly composed herself.

"That's so interesting, dear. You and I are at the opposite ends of the life spectrum. Birth and death, life's continuum."

She signed our book without even asking about a dedication. Then she waved us on and turned to greet her next adoring subject.

Meg and I left the room and found Swati standing in the hall. We said goodbye to her, and Meg drove me home.

"Arianna's a piece of work," Meg said.

"But her books sell," I countered. "It just goes to show grief is powerful, and people are always looking for answers."

"Talk about ripping the Band-Aid off. Well, it worked for her."

We were both quiet for a moment. I was reminded of our father's untimely passing years ago. Mom had four children and carried on, but our dad was always remembered and loved. We talked about him often, and Mom still wore his maroon cardigan on occasion. We all still mourned his passing in various ways.

"Are you at Creighton Memorial or Rosemont College tomorrow?" Meg asked, breaking into my reminiscences.

"Rosemont. I'm giving the lecture on labor and delivery."

"That shouldn't be too difficult for a midwife."

"Surprisingly, it is. I have ninety minutes, and while I want to get the information across, I also need to set the right tone. I don't want to overwhelm them with facts, but I still need to cover the basics. I think I'll bring in a patient scenario and make it a bit interactive. I hope that makes it more real."

"They should like that."

"I hope so. I need to go over it again."

And again, and again...

The following day, the auditorium was full as I began my lecture. Last night, I'd rewritten the entire talk and was going to present it from the point of view of a woman in early labor who was progressing through birth.

"Good morning. Today, we will explore the labor and delivery experience through the eyes of a first-time mother, also known as a primigravida. Anita Smith, who is not a real patient, is twenty-nine years old and thirty-eight weeks pregnant. Her prenatal course has been uneventful, and her baby is believed to weigh seven and a half to eight pounds. She had occasional contractions in the early hours of the morning, and as the hours progressed, she began to leak amniotic fluid."

Looking around, I saw that most students seemed to be paying attention. A few were discreetly texting, but that was the way of the world today. I continued, discussing the stages of labor. Along the way, Anita experienced a few bumps in the road but had a nice labor overall. Pushing and birth were discussed, along with comfort measures. Finally, my fictitious patient's baby daughter was born healthy.

I asked for questions at various points of the talk, and a flock of hands flew in the air, one of which was a beaming Haley. Along with their questions, a few of the students described situations or techniques they had encountered at their clinical placements.

When the bell rang for the next class, I felt exhilarated. To my surprise, the lecture had been fun. I hoped the students enjoyed it as much as I did. I wanted them to perform well on the exam material that my lectures covered.

After class, I noticed a navy baseball cap peeking out from under one of the front-row seats. *Haywood* was printed on the back, and *Rosemont Spirit Scholarship* was written on the side. I didn't know where lost and found items went, and with classes currently in session, there was no one around to ask, so I held onto the hat.

With my presentation over, I decided to use my free time to visit the underground tunnels. As I stepped out onto the green, the sun was blazing. To shield my eyes, I decided to wear my newfound headgear. I'd drop it off to Trudy Delchamps when I returned, and she could make sure it got back to its rightful owner.

Asking directions, I entered the north tunnel where Bella was attacked. Immediately, I saw that, as the campus police had reported, the tunnels were very well-lit. There was not much foot traffic, probably because of the good weather and because classes were in session.

Walking down the long cement corridor, I passed bulletin boards with numerous postings for rideshares, tutoring, and upcoming events. When the brick walkway forked, I decided to head to the Camden Dining Hall, just as Bella had. As I walked, I noticed there were many offshoots in the tunnel. It was obvious that anyone traveling away from the main thoroughfare needed either a map or familiarity to get around.

After a few steps, I heard rustling behind me. I turned but saw no one, and the noise stopped. When I kept going, though, I heard it again. I quickly pivoted, but once more no one was there.

Was I imagining things? And how far was I from my destination? I took out my phone, but found I had no reception down here. I thought for a moment about how long I'd been walking and decided that the dining hall could not be far off. I sped up as much as I could and quickly turned the next corner.

That was when the rustling became a scraping sound. Someone was definitely following me.

"Hello?" No answer. Total silence. I started walking again, and the footsteps followed.

"Who's there?" I demanded. No one answered, but I could feel a presence.

Up ahead, I could see the exit to Camden Dining Hall. Throwing caution to the wind, I did an all-out sprint to the staircase. I was not going down without a fight, not when I saw my exit just ahead. I flew down the stairs, wrenched the door handle open, and practically fell into the seating area. A uniformed security guard gave me the once-over.

"Do you need help, ma'am?"

"Someone was following me," I gasped as I briefly fell forward.

He stiffened immediately and spoke rapidly into a radio attached to his collar. Then he helped me to a seat at an empty table and said, "Stay here, please."

Almost immediately, four more security officers appeared. Three of them went into the tunnel while the other had me retell my story. When she was done, some of the students in the dining hall left their trays to come and ask me questions.

"Is there a deranged person in the tunnels?" inquired one.

"Is someone out to get Rosemont students and faculty?"

The officer asked the students to step back and give me space, for which I was very grateful.

Just then, the door to the tunnel flew open, and the security guards came out holding a squirming man.

"I wasn't doing anything wrong. I am on the faculty. Let go of me!"

Carter Morrison!

CHAPTER THIRTY

———

Premature menopause is defined as menstrual cycles ending before the age of forty.

Sitting in the security office, I repeated my story of being followed. I grudgingly had to admit that nothing happened. I was not attacked. Commander Louis Peters informed me that Carter insisted he was innocent. He claimed he was listening to a podcast and didn't hear me call out.

"I understand, but I know what I heard. Do you think there was anyone else in the tunnel?"

"My staff searched the entire area. There is no one else down there now. I don't know what you heard, but there is nothing to charge Carter with since you did not suffer any harm."

"There are so many twists and turns in the tunnels. Anyone could disappear quickly if they were familiar with them." I paused momentarily. "Do you think this has any relation to Bella Taylor?"

Commander Peters frowned. "I don't think so, but we still don't know what really happened with her. We want everyone to be safe and call us if necessary, but the bottom line is that we don't believe there is some crazed attacker on campus."

But someone followed me...and it wasn't to say hello.

"By the way, Carter wants to speak with you. I'll be present, of course. If that's okay with you?"

Carter had seemed harmless at Mike and Tom's for the short time I met him. Inebriated but harmless.

"That's fine," I said. "You can bring him in."

Carter came in with his shirt partially untucked, his hair standing upright in places, and red blotches on his wan skin. One of the officers stood close by.

"Maeve, we met at Professor Grantham's dinner party. You know I would never attack anyone. I had my earbuds in. I didn't see you or hear you."

I knew nothing about Carter apart from his claim that Theo Archer stole his manuscript.

"Did you see anyone else in the tunnels, Carter?" I asked.

"No one, but that's not unusual at this time of day. I'm sorry something scared you, but it wasn't me. Please, may I buy you lunch?"

Although I still felt unsure about Carter, I wanted to hear more about his manuscript. If we ate in the campus dining hall, I knew I would feel safe enough to converse with him.

I thanked the campus security officers and selected a table set off by the large side window while Carter went to get our sandwiches. Our seats were far enough from other people for privacy but still in plain sight.

Over chicken salad wraps and raspberry lime seltzers, Carter seemed to relax. He again apologized.

"Let's put this behind us, Carter," I said to reassure him.

"Thanks, Maeve. I don't need anything untoward on my record. I'm up for a promotion at Rosemont this year. The position will come with more money and benefits, and I will be able to cut down or perhaps eliminate my part-time job."

"I was there when Theo collapsed. I didn't know him, but I heard he was a retired tech bigwig. I also heard about his bestselling book and movie deal. I had no idea of your claim until the dinner."

Carter lowered his head and stopped eating.

"Look, if you don't want to talk about it, I understand," I said.

But I also wanted to hear the story from the horse's mouth. Maybe it would help solve the murder.

Carter took a shaky breath. A look of defeat overcame him. "I want to talk about it. I want people to know what he did to me. I realize my case was thrown out of court, but I'm not giving up." He looked out at the tall pines for a moment, gathering his thoughts. "I've been writing nonfiction for years. Finally, I came up with a brilliant idea for a thriller. I was a teaching assistant here, and Theo Archer and I were in an evening writing class. One of the faculty perks is that you can audit classes with permission." He paused and folded his hands. "Theo and I became friendly and went for beers now and then after class. I felt very comfortable with him, and we decided to critique each other's work in progress."

Carter began to bite his bottom lip. "Theo told me he liked my plot but not my setting. He suggested I rewrite it and place it in the Pacific Northwest instead of New England. I fooled around with it for a few months, but it just didn't ring true to me. After the class ended, Theo became very distant. He told me he was selling his company and had no time to meet. I missed him, but I understood."

He hung his head.

"A short time later, I saw an article in *The Financial Times* reporting that Theo had sold his app for millions, written a best seller, and sold the film rights. In the interview, he said that his book was a thriller set in Maine."

Carter's eyes glazed over. "The paper featured an excerpt, and it was my manuscript. Word for word."

We were both silent for a few minutes.

"I called him repeatedly, but he never answered, and finally, he blocked my number. I took him to court, but he had a fleet of prestigious, high-priced lawyers who filed motion after motion until it was impossible for me to fight. The judge had no choice but to dismiss the case. Maeve, it wasn't so much that I lost but that I never got my day in court. Theo didn't even bother to show up."

He hung his head again.

Instinctively, I patted his hand. He looked up with tears in his eyes. "I lost my life's work and a lot of money, I started drinking too much, and I've come close to sabotaging my marriage. It's been hard to accept, and sometimes despair gets the best of me, as you saw at the dinner."

"You went through a very painful time."

"My wife says I have another thriller in me, and I hope she's correct. Right now, though, I'm trying to get promoted here at Rosemont, and we're thinking of trying for a baby. I really do need to put this behind me and move on."

"Good for you, Carter."

"Oops, look at the time. I need to run." He began gathering our plates for the bin.

"Got a class?" I asked.

"I have a second job at The Art of Wellness. I work in the equipment room. Usually, I work in the early mornings, but I'm covering for a coworker today. See you later, Maeve."

The Art of Wellness—Theo's gym. Carter worked early mornings. Motive and opportunity. Meg, I need you.

CHAPTER THIRTY-ONE

———

A fibroid is a benign tumor that develops in the uterus.

Meg's phone went directly to voicemail. Ugh. She must be with a client. I knew she would call me back when she could.

While waiting, I decided to learn more about Rosemont's history. I needed to check out the Spirit scholarship details and also get a quick overview of the college's past. I figured the best place to start was the administration building, Shelton Hall. It had a gracious red brick façade that would look at home on any New England college campus. I went up the stairs to the main office and was immediately welcomed by Xiomara Cruz, President Saunders's administrative assistant, whom I had met at my interview.

"Hello, Maeve. So nice to see you again. We're all excited about you joining the faculty. Your background will add a lot to the students' learning experience. Also, I know several women who are looking forward to scheduling a visit with you at the health center."

"Thank you," I said, smiling. "That's so flattering. I feel very welcome. I hope I can live up to everyone's expectations."

Maybe Xiomara needed to have a one-on-one with Professor Prudence Owens.

"Don't worry. I can tell you are going to do just fine. Just remember one thing. In academics, it's not a sprint. What counts is how you inspire and the knowledge you impart to the students in the end. That's the prize you keep your eye on."

"Thank you, Xiomara. I need all the advice I can get and I will remember yours," I said.

"Great." She gave me a bright smile. "But tell me, what brought you here today?"

"I realized that I don't know much about the college in general, and I'd like to learn more. I know I can use the internet, but I wanted to see if there were any yearbooks, journals, or historical records the college keeps in its collections."

"You know, not many people go for that approach anymore. It's refreshing. All right, let's have you start in the Reading Room." Xiomara glided her wheelchair around her desk, and we went down the long hallway and turned toward the back of the building. I was expecting the Reading Room to be in the main campus library, but it was part of Shelton Hall. It was a circular room with floor-to-ceiling bookshelves. Some shelves held books of different sizes, ages, and colors; others had entire sets of identical books. Leather club chairs with side tables sat in designated places around the room, while a couple of long black wooden tables with arched back chairs held a place in the center.

"This section contains the history of Rosemont College. The first few volumes were penned by the college's founder, Jacob Deering. His wife, Harriet, loved roses and thus the name." She pointed to several bound, hard-covered navy leather volumes. "As you can see, President Deering took notes on every aspect of the college. The next bookcase holds copies of the *Daily Bloom*, the college newspaper. Finally, we have the trustee meeting minutes and all our yearbooks. Feel free to look through anything. I'm so glad that you have an interest in Rosemont."

I thanked Xiomara, and she spun around and slipped out the door. I went to the first shelf, pulled out a few of Jacob Deering's volumes, and began rifling through the vellum pages. Jacob Deering was a wealthy visionary. Wanting to leave his mark on education, he purchased fifty acres of land in 1820, recruited leading scholars of the day, and Rosemont College was born. From the beginning, the school was open to all scholars, although it seemed women were few and far between until the 1960s.

I also found something that answered one of my more significant questions. It was Deering himself who had started the construction of tunnels under the campus. He saw them as a way to make travel quicker and more accessible for the students, particularly in winter. As I read his account, I realized he was talking about a time before snowblowers, plows, and down parkas. Suddenly, Deering's idea made a lot more sense.

I found another volume about the origin of the nursing college. Even though it took decades to get started, it was currently highly competitive, and its graduates were widely recruited.

As I read, I felt a renewed pride at having been asked to stake out a place for midwives in the faculty. But this was quickly tempered by my apprehension of not measuring up. After all, the history made clear to me that the full-time faculty was comprised of accomplished professionals. I realized anew that all eyes would be on me, and I needed to demonstrate how valuable nurse midwives were to the future of nursing education.

To put those thoughts out of my head, I set the nursing archives aside and thumbed through some of the trustee meeting notes. Was the college on sound financial footing? The summaries showed that Rosemont was well endowed into the future through wise investments, alumni support, and exceptional money management. Jacob Deering's work had indeed been carried on in grand fashion.

I checked my watch and realized I barely had enough time to get to Creighton Memorial for the weekly midwifery meeting. The yearbooks would have to wait for another time. I retraced my steps to thank Xiomara again and headed out.

I made it back to the hospital, but with only minutes to spare. On the way to the Hadley conference room, I caught up to Maddie as she walked down the corridor.

"Hey, Maddie. How's it going?"

"Great, Maeve. Hey, I thought you could update us on your Rosemont experience today. Everyone is interested to hear of your experience. The group is excited that we are involved in nursing education."

"Of course. What's new around Creighton Memorial?"

"Do you remember that terrific medical student, Maryn Scofield? Her mom is a well-known OB/GYN in NYC."

"Yes, of course. She was delightful and already had a great clinical mind."

"Well, she matched at New York-Presbyterian/Columbia Hospital and started a blog on pregnancy and women of color. You'll see the signup link in your Creighton Memorial email."

"Good for her. She is on a mission to decrease maternal mortality. I'll be very interested in reading it."

Settling into the conference room seat, I said hello to Winnie and Bev, my other closest friends in the practice. The three of us and Maddie were the original group of four, but now the midwifery practice numbered twelve. Maddie had the foresight to add part-time staff, and Dr. Patel, the current OB chief, had created new positions and expanded our reach to health centers and Rosemont College. What a difference new leadership and a few years made, from almost closing shop to flourishing.

I saw that Winnie had made her mouthwatering butterscotch cookies, and I had one while we chatted.

As we talked, Maddie took a place at the head of the table. She had notes in front of her and looked up to start the meeting.

"Strong week, everyone. Our stats look great, and our enrolled patients are up." Maddie paused and looked at the group. "Winnie posted the schedule for the next two months. Please remember to put any holiday vacation requests in early. If any part-timers want to pick up shifts, please email her."

After a few more housekeeping items, Maddie turned the group over to Bev, who reviewed the schedule for medical student small group teaching. When she was finished, Maddie turned to me and said, "Maeve, fill us in on the dual appointment, please."

Describing my weekly schedule, I also added in a few bits of newfound Rosemont College history. The group was very interested in how lectures were presented and received. I described adding clinical vignettes and slides to enhance the presentation.

When I was done, Maddie turned the meeting over for staff input. Renatta, one of our newer members, smiled and took the floor.

"I just saw Lynn Perry and Joe Belton for a postpartum appointment. Some of you might remember them. They were a couple who struggled with their twin diagnosis and were followed by the obstetric team. Lynn's pregnancy went well, but the babies were both breech, and she had a cesarean section. They were a bit overwhelmed at first, but they had been seeing Faye Martindale from social service, and she had worked hard to prepare them for postpartum life. Joe's mother will stay nearby for two months, and the Langford "Mothers of Multiples" group will provide a meal train. Lynn looks well, and she and Joe are very happy."

"What did they name the babies?" Bev asked.

"Arwen and Aragorn."

There was silence for a moment. Midwives heard a lot of unique names. Winnie even claimed she could often tell a person's age by their first name.

"They are avid *Lord of the Rings* fans," Renatta explained.

"Thankfully, they decided against Gollum," Winnie commented. She was partial to traditional names.

As the meeting broke up, I saw a text from Meg. Once the conference room emptied, I relaxed in my chair and returned the call. She answered on the first ring.

"Hey, Maeve."

"Hi, Meg. Well, I had an interesting morning." I filled her in on the tunnels, my conversation with Carter, and my foray into Rosemont College beginnings.

"Do you think Carter was telling the truth?"

"I believe him, although that means someone else was there."

"And he works at The Art of Wellness."

We were both silent.

"We have to get to that gym," Meg finally said.

"We're meeting Mom and the ladies at the Autumn Fest tomorrow. What about early the next morning?"

"Sounds good. I'll see you tomorrow. Oh, stay out of those tunnels, please."

On hearing those words, a shiver ran up my spine and my hands turned ice cold. I suddenly had the sense of someone following me all over again.

That night, I woke at 3:00 a.m. Aoki Yoshida worked at Rosemont, too. Had she been following me?

CHAPTER THIRTY-TWO

———

Menorrhagia is the term used for heavy or prolonged menses.

The following day, I dressed Rowan and Sloane in matching white turtlenecks with pumpkins. My beautiful girls. They looked adorable, if I did say so myself.

My selection was a bit simpler. I put my hair in a braid and slipped on a fitted navy fleece jacket over my favorite boyfriend jeans. We were ready to roll once I had the girls in their car seats.

Will had left early to help with his food trucks and would meet us at the Autumn Fest. Because of demand for the wares of his pastry chef, Malia Harris, he had a new truck featuring all manner of desserts.

I parked behind Meg's real estate office and transferred the girls to their double stroller.

"Hello, Rowan—hello, Sloane!" Meg came out the back door carrying two small bags adorned with a rainbow of ribbons. "It's just a little something for my girls," she explained.

Two small, fluffy, stuffed polar bears came out of the bags and were immediately scooped up by my daughters.

"Thank you, Aunt Meg," I said as I watched the girls play with their new toys.

"Please, they needed them," she said with a shrug.

"So where are we meeting Mom?" I asked.

"Do you really need to ask? You know they will make a beeline for the white elephant table."

I laughed. "They could contribute plenty of things to that sale."

The Langford Chamber of Commerce put on the Autumn Fest each year. Proceeds from this event were earmarked for the Langford Veterans Center. About forty stalls featured crafts, art, food, and personal businesses. The only requirement for having a booth was that a portion of sales be given to the Vets Center.

We arrived to find the town green awash in pumpkins, baskets of colorful mums, and cornstalks. The smell of popcorn, maple sausage, and candy apples wafted through the air. At the pavilion, a local band was playing "Turn! Turn! Turn!," made famous by the Byrds but written by Pete Seeger. The atmosphere was relaxed but with a festive vibe.

Meg stopped to buy two yellow balloons. She attached them to the stroller to the fascinated delight of Rowan and Sloane. They stared and reached for the balloons as Meg pushed the carriage over the grass. Finally she stopped in front of a large tent featuring a sign with no words, just a picture of a white elephant.

The tent was packed with patrons looking for hidden treasures. Other daughters may have had to call their mother's phone to locate them, but the ladies of the lobby were consistent, if not predictable.

Mom was decked out in a bright red boiled wool jacket with a gold sequined scarf. Louella, as usual, was in vibrant yellow. Her jacket may have been able to glow in the dark. Ethel was a bit more subdued in a navy cardigan, but her chartreuse pants more than balanced that out. Gaby's outfit was the most unique with a bright aqua wool blazer, a candy-apple red crocheted scarf, and a black and white polka dot midi skirt. They all thoroughly embraced their favorite colors and styles and wore them proudly. I already knew what an unbeatable group they were, and I had to admit, their wardrobes were fit for superheroes.

We said hello, and, after promising to meet later, Meg and I left the white elephant tent to explore all the booths. There were stands with impressive watercolors of the beach and various gardens by local artists, knitted goods of all types, hand-crafted jewelry, and many with honey, chocolates, and savories.

As we strolled up to the last aisle, we came upon the Mariner Heights exhibit, or rather, extravaganza. Designer wreaths of all sizes, each a work of art, were hung in the booth. Various plants graced the table, presented in everything from elegant teacups to large blue and white Asian vases. Unlike most other booths, where people mostly strolled by, this space was packed with customers vying for their favorite offering. Two women in matching lululemon black pants and red plaid fleece jackets staffed the booth. The pair stood out from the crowd by their crisp white embroidered aprons, which read, *Mariner Heights...a place to love*. They were doing their best to keep up with the demand.

"I'm sure they had real artisans make those wreaths and stage the plants, but you must hand it to them. They know what sells," Meg observed.

We neared the end of the last row, where The Art of Wellness had a sizeable booth. Peloton bikes had been set up in front of a large screen showing trails in the countryside, and two women were demonstrating a Pilates class. As Meg and I took in the scene, Patrice, a lean thirty-something woman in a sparkly turquoise spandex bodysuit, waved us over.

"Good morning. Welcome to the Art of Wellness outpost. Are you familiar with our health club?"

"We are," Meg nodded.

"Childcare is available daily," Patrice said, looking at me and my daughters. Without taking a breath, she continued, "The Art of Wellness is unlike any other facility. We are passionate about pampering our guests and respecting their visions. You can follow your own workout path, or we have private fitness trainers if you prefer that. Here, let me give you a brochure."

Meg gave me the look. Smile, be nice, and we'll talk later. We thanked Patrice with the requisite smiles and moved on.

"Well, that calls for apple cider donuts," Meg said, guiding us to a table where we could sit.

While she was gone, I got a snack out for the girls. They were mesmerized watching the crowd. Rowan even swayed to the music.

As we waited for Meg, Will found us and came over to the table. "Hello, my beauties," Will said, kissing me and the girls.

"Hi, honey. What a great day. Meg went to get us a bite to eat. How are the food trucks doing?"

"Great. The breakfast burritos were a great idea, and we sold out. Ella always has smart menu choices. Our dessert truck sold a ton of scones, muffins, and donuts."

"Luckily, Malia saved some apple cider ones for us," Meg said, returning with a harvest of festival snacks. She unloaded her tote onto the table and we each took a donut.

"Hey, Meg," Will said, kissing her on the cheek. "I'd say it's a great day for the town and the Vet Center."

"It's Langford at its best," Meg agreed between bites.

"We should check on Mom and the ladies soon," I said.

"How about I take the girls to the petting zoo, and we'll meet you for lunch?" Will asked.

"Okay, honey. They might need a diaper change soon."

"I'm all over it, Maeve." Will kissed me goodbye, then wheeled the girls off towards the pens holding animals from a local farm.

Meg and I finished our treats and headed out to find Mom and her pack of fellow bargain hunters. When a complete circuit of the white elephant tent left us empty-handed, we went to see if the lobby ladies had expanded their shopping radius to include neighboring booths. We rounded the middle row of stalls and saw a Day-Glo orange and red one with glittering moons and stars of all sizes. How did we miss this on our first pass?

A sign festooned with tiny colored lights boldly proclaimed *Zeena, Queen of Mystics*. And, front and center, Mom, Louella, Ethel, and Gaby were at the head of the line, waiting for the great and powerful seer to appear.

"Hi, girls." Mom waved as soon as she saw us. "Zeena had to take a break, but we're next! I already paid for the two of you so that you can join the line. Isn't this just fabulous!"

"Mom, we are good. We'll wait while the four of you see her," Meg said.

"Absolutely not. Zeena predicted that Maeve was going to be a mother of two. She has a window into the future, and I want to know what's in store for the both of you."

In the past, Zeena had said that she saw me surrounded by babies. I mean, she knew I was a midwife, so seeing me with infants was a safe bet. But then again, after fertility struggles, I now was the mother of two under two, so who was I to judge?

Bracelets jingling, tiny bells on her necklace ringing, Zeena appeared in a floor-length white velvet cape over a silver and purple floor-length gown. Today, her long, curly hair was dark chestnut with streaks of flaming apricot. Her dramatic makeup gave her rosy cheeks and bright red lips. Wearing a beatific smile, she motioned Mom behind her sapphire curtain to begin her session.

"I can't wait for my reading," Gaby said. "She's so accurate. There are a lot of pretenders out there, but not Zeena. She truly connects with the great beyond."

Mom came out all smiles as Louella took her place in the inner sanctum. Mom's wheelchair had a green ribbon tied around the armrests.

"Oh, girls, this is so exciting. Zeena says I am in for a year of travel and excitement. She says my most flattering color is green, and my lucky number is eight. I can't wait to hear what she says to everyone else."

"That's great, Mom. It sounds like an astonishing prediction," I said, trying not to chuckle.

"And it's so unique," Meg added.

"Go ahead and mock me, girls. You'll see who's right in the end." Mom flipped her sequined scarf over her shoulder.

Louella, Gaby, and Ethel were also promised a year of travel and adventure. Finally, it was my turn. With a bit of hesitation, I entered the back of the booth. Zeena motioned me to sit on a deep-seated, damask-upholstered chair that looked like it belonged in an old-time movie theater. Without saying a word, she reached for my hands, and immediately, her head fell forward. She was utterly still.

Was she sleeping? Should I shake her?

I simply could not be in the presence of another dead body. Patrick would never forgive me.

Suddenly, Zeena looked up, and her heavily mascaraed eyes locked on mine.

"Babies, lots of babies. Trouble, deceit, darkness."

I shivered a bit. Was she predicting problem births? More children for Will and I? Wait a minute, Zeena traded in mystery. None of this was real.

Or was it?

"Drinking game, Mraeve, be fearless."

Mraeve was what Zeena had always called me. Who was I to correct the psychic?

Drinking game? I wasn't in college. Without another word of explanation, I was dismissed. Meg entered as I left.

Mom and the ladies had gone to Will's truck for lunch, and I waited for Meg. I was surprised to see the line for Zeena stretched around her booth. Mom certainly wasn't alone in her opinion about the crystal gazer.

Meg came out, and we started off to find Will and the girls and lunch.

"Well," Meg said, "share with the class."

"More babies and some suggestion of more trouble. It was a bit daunting for a midwife."

Meg smirked. "Well, she knows my weaknesses, travel and food. She saw an airplane and scones for me."

"At least that sounds nice."

"She also saw crystal flowers and told me to be fearless."

"What? Me, too. And I think she warned me about drinking alcohol."

"Take it for what it's worth. It's Zeena," Meg pointed out. "Come on, it's lunchtime."

The wind had picked up a bit by the time we finished lunch, but it was still too nice a day to head for home. Mom and the Ladies of the Lobby sat at the pavilion with Meg, the girls, and me, listening to the Walrus Cove Chorus sing a medley of classic show tunes. Will had gone back to check on the food truck's inventory. To our right, Kate, Fiona, and Bridie also participated in the festivities. Across the way, two Bloomsby nannies were feeding infants while three toddlers played in the grass in front of them.

"Those nannies would never get time off to enjoy the Autumn Fest," Meg said.

A massive gust of wind suddenly blew up from the shore. It scooped up the large tin Autumn Fest sign from the pavilion and sent it airborne. As it sailed into the air, time seemed to stand still.

The Bloomsby nannies were frozen in place as if hypnotized, watching the sign fly up and then start down toward them. In contrast, I saw Kate, Fiona, and Bridie jump to their feet. As the sign began its descent, they raced over to where the other nannies sat. Each scooped up a toddler and ran toward the food tent with their precious cargo.

They were barely three steps away when the sign landed with a thud exactly where the children had been sitting. The music stopped, and no one moved for a few moments. Then, a scattered applause began. It crescendoed quickly as the crowd appreciated the nannies' quick reactions.

As the applause continued, the three women returned the children, unhurt but crying, to the Bloomsby minders. They took their charges with grateful looks but also appeared sheepish about their inaction. A group of Mariner Heights women who had been sitting in a circle talking rushed over to check on the babies. A Langford police officer picked up the sign and placed it under the pavilion. As Kate, Fiona, and Bridie returned to their seats, everyone applauded their heroism.

"Easy work for Irish women," Mom said, beaming with pride.

Meg and I hugged Kate, Fiona, and Bridie, who were slightly embarrassed by all the attention.

"Well, that's going to give the Yummy Mummies something to think about," Meg said.

Later that night, as I was cleaning out the top storage section of the stroller, I gathered up the flyers and brochures I had accumulated. The glossy Art of Wellness brochure stood out, reminding me how much I dreaded our visit. I had never been one for deluxe gyms, but I knew there was no escaping the upcoming visit to this one.

As I went to toss it out, a name caught my eye. It was Antoinette Duval, and she was listed as a personal fitness trainer.

Antoinette Duval? The wife of Philippe? After a quick Google search, I confirmed she was indeed his spouse.

That meant Carter and Antoinette were both employees at The Art of Wellness.

So many suspects! Wordles alone were challenging for me. Could I handle a Quordle?

CHAPTER THIRTY-THREE

———

Metrorrhagia is the term used to describe vaginal bleeding at irregular intervals between menstrual cycles.

That evening, I made Cobb salad and my unbeatable chocolate cake. Will knew it was made with a mix, but he didn't care. It was the dessert that had made me comfortable in the kitchen, and now that I had it down pat, I often served it warm with vanilla ice cream when I was craving comfort food.

After the girls were asleep, Will, Fenway, and I curled up on the couch.

"What a great day we had, Maeve. I have to say this town shines brightest at community events," Will said.

"It was such fun, and I am sure it raised a lot of money for the veterans. Rowan and Sloane loved the music and balloons and seeing the farm animals."

"Rowan was really mesmerized by the goats," Will commented. "She was still murmuring 'Baa' as she fell asleep. Did the lobby ladies have fun?"

"They did. They bought out the white elephant table and even had a reading by the mysterious Zeena."

"I hope she told your mother good news."

When didn't the Mystic to the Stars promise wealth and happiness to her biggest fans?

"Oh, yes, she gave her a lucky number and promised her a year of travel."

"Well, there you go. Ireland may be in her future…or at least a trip to Finnegan's for dinner! I can't imagine better news for her, short of hitting it big on a scratch ticket. And what, pray tell, did Zeena promise you?"

I was quiet for a few moments.

"Maeve, honey, it wasn't anything terrible, was it?" Will asked, hugging me close.

"No. Well, it's not completely terrible, anyway. She saw more babies in my life as she always does, but then she warned me of darkness and trouble." I pulled up the thick, beige throw closer to my neck.

"Well, she was correct about babies in the past, and it turned out just fine. But I don't like the danger warning."

"Of course, Meg and I had been talking about the murder just before I went into her booth. Zeena could have picked up on those vibes."

We were both silent as we watched Fenway open one big brown eye to monitor why the conversation had stopped.

"I know you are so careful, Maeve, but please walk with a partner you can trust in the tunnels at Rosemont. I can't bear the thought of anything happening to you."

"Don't worry, I have no plans to use them again. At least not as long as no one knows if someone is targeting students. Hopefully, Bella isn't hiding something."

Will moved Fenway to his lap so he could inch closer to me. "How is the investigation coming? Are you and Meg any closer to identifying a murderer?"

"It feels hopeless. There are too many suspects, and tetrahydrozoline is a very easy poison to obtain. It's doubly frustrating because Patrick finally gave us our big chance to assist him, and now we are not helping at all."

"I wouldn't worry about Pat. He knows as well as you do how difficult this is. I'm sure he'll be grateful for whatever you find. And he knows that you and Meg look under every stone."

After that, we were quiet, enjoying each other's company. Then Will took both of my hands in his and drew me closer.

"You know, Maeve, I am thrilled with our family, but I would be happy to have more children if that's our decision."

I laughed. "If we have more, we'll be outnumbered." I stroked Fenway's neck and smiled at Will. "Let's talk about this again after Sloane turns one. For now, I'm content and feel lucky we're parents."

We finished our cocoa and watched the fire until it was time for bed.

I woke the next morning to an existential dread centered around spandex and Lycra. The day had finally come when I would find out what outfits Meg had selected for our foray into the den of sweat and stretch.

Henry greeted me at his front door. "Hi, Aunt Maeve. I am so happy that you and Mom are going to work out. I know you row all the time, but my mom needs to get more exercise."

Henry was a high school wrestler and was very disciplined about physical conditioning.

"I heard that, sweetie," Meg called out as she entered the room. "Be careful what you wish for. Who knows, maybe I'll become a gym rat."

I was speechless when I saw her. Who was this woman, and what had she done to my sister?

"Cat got your tongue, Maeve?" Meg was decked out in hot pink lululemon leggings, a matching sleeveless top, and blush Hermès sneakers—a neon pink headband made for a crowning touch.

Olivia Newton-John 2.0!

"Uh, no," I finally said, trying my best to feign indifference. "I was just admiring your look."

"I know it's a bit much, but I want to blend in with the Yummy Mummies."

I wasn't sure that *blending in* was the correct term.

"Do you think they're this colorful?"

"Of course, Maeve. They are peacocks at heart. They positively adore color. You need to come up to my room now. I have your outfit all ready."

Before I could answer, a horn beeped outside.

"Mom, I'm off to the high school," Henry said. "The Chess Club meeting will run until one, and then we're going to Sal's for pizza. Is it okay to invite a few kids over for movies here tonight?"

"Of course, honey. Have a good day. And remember, seatbelts, please."

"Yes, Mom," Henry said, kissing Meg and me goodbye. He gave a quick pat to Brady, his black Lab, and was off.

We watched Henry walk to his friend's car. "He's growing up, Meg."

"I know. I just want to freeze him like this for a bit," she said, smiling.

We ascended the wide, curving staircase to the second floor when the car drove off. As usual, I marveled at Meg's décor. Her home blended gleaming hardwood floors, Palladian windows with ocean views, and walls painted a soft almond into a serenity-inducing cocoon. Meg's bedroom was in various shades of blush, and her bedding and chairs were covered with smooth, lush fabric. It gave me a sense of peace and calm.

These were very short-lived feelings, though, as my eyes were riveted to something bright, purple, and shiny on Meg's bed.

Oh, no. It was…"Ah, Meg, I brought some navy sweats that will do me just fine."

"Are you kidding me? Where we're going, you'd be like a novice undercover agent wearing a suit and tie to a dive bar. If we're going to get information, we must look the part. Go, try it on."

"That's easy for you to say—you have a model's figure. I'll look foolish."

"Don't give me that. You're beautiful and look like a fit athlete. Now get in that bathroom and change."

As I gathered the clothing, Meg held out a miniscule piece of lilac silk. "Here, you'll need a thong with those pants. Can't have lines."

What had I gotten myself into? Maybe I could wear a sweater over this thing?

I changed and realized the pants felt like the shapewear I had tried once. They also left nothing to the imagination. As I pulled on the top, though, I had to laugh. This clothing wasn't very different from the rowing unisuit I had worn in college. Still, though, I pretty much looked like a tall grape.

I walked back into the bedroom and twirled. "Tell me the truth."

"Excellent. I love that color on you. And we look like regular Yummies. Here, put these sneakers on."

"Meg, how much did these designer shoes cost?"

"Trust me, all the Yummies will have them. Come on now, we want to get there early."

Looking in the full-length mirror as we passed, I realized that Lucy and Ethel had nothing on us.

CHAPTER THIRTY-FOUR

Oligomenorrhea is the term used if a woman has infrequent menstrual periods.

The Art of Wellness was bustling, even at this early hour. The parking lot was filled with Teslas, Lexuses, Mercedes, Porsches, and BMWs. Luckily, we had taken Meg's Jaguar and passed our first potential inspection. My minivan might have been refused entry at the driveway.

Patrice, whom we had met at Autumn Fest, greeted us as we entered. "Good morning, ladies. I'm so pleased you decided to join us today. I love your outfits."

I didn't doubt that for a second, seeing her dressed in a shiny gold and tangerine ensemble.

"I'm a member," Meg said as she approached the reception desk. "But I've been away for a while, so I'll need to reorientate to the facility. My sister, Maeve, is my guest today."

"Welcome, Meg and Mavy. Let me get Sage to show you around. I'll be right back."

As she turned, Meg said, "Of course she's Sage. Are you ready for this, Mavy?"

"Lead on, my liege."

"We'll see how you feel after a few classes."

Sage was a lithesome, gorgeous twentyish woman with a light brown complexion. She easily could have graced a magazine cover or walked a runway. Flashing a quick, radiant smile, she began her spiel.

"The spin classes and instructors are listed here," she said, pointing to a bulletin board. "They fill up early, so if you're interested, reserve a bike now."

"Thank you. That's what we came for." Meg added our names to the sign-up sheet.

Was she serious? Did Meg know what these classes entailed? She was likely envisioning a leisurely ride along the banks of the Seine, not a climb up the Alps.

Sage showed us every area of the club, including the equipment room, where we saw a gym employee assisting an exasperated patron with her tennis racket.

"Why is it bent at the top?" The ponytailed woman pouted.

"It looks like there are bite marks on it. Where do you store it?" the employee asked.

It was Carter Morrison! I didn't want him to recognize Meg and me. Discreetly motioning Meg over to the weight section, I made sure that we were out of his line of vision.

"In the back of my Lexus SUV. It's safe there. Well, sometimes, Sweetie rides in back."

"Sweetie?"

"She's our Great Dane. She's very disciplined, though. I doubt she'd chew it. Sweetie has been to obedience school, and she's only allowed to play with her toys."

Sage looked slightly exasperated and swiftly moved us to the private fitness area. "Some members desire to have one-on-one instruction. To satisfy their needs, we have four fitness instructors. You can read about them online."

"Are any of them available in the early morning hours?" Meg asked.

"I'm glad you asked that. One of our finest, Antoinette Duval, is always available early in the day."

Meg merely nodded. I had already told her that Philippe's wife was on the payroll.

The tour continued with stops at the snack bar, childcare room, and the state-of-the-art kitchen available for members.

"This is so well-thought-out," I said.

"Yes, we have many runners, swimmers, tennis players, etcetera, who bring their own specific snacks and power drinks. We have three large refrigerators, so there is no overcrowding and plenty of space to store a day's worth of hydration and nutrition." She opened the first one to demonstrate, pointing out the rows of water pouches and bottles. Each was labeled with the appropriate member's name.

Oh, Theo, you never stood a chance.

"Well, that concludes the tour. Remember to have the monthly calendar sent to your email. Now I'll drop you at your spin class. It's about to start."

"I need to use the ladies' room first," Meg said.

"Me, too," I quickly echoed.

We checked inside the ecru and white striped bathroom to ensure we were alone.

"So, Carter and Antoinette both work here and easily had access to Theo's water bottles."

"Savannah could have added tetrahydrozoline to his equipment at their home, and Carter and Antoinette could have tampered with his water here. We have three strong potential suspects. I think we've found what we came for. Now we just need to get out of here before we get roped into some kind of physical torture," Meg said.

It was a good idea, but our execution fell short. As we opened the door, Patrice was waiting for us.

"Come on, ladies. Philippe is waiting for you."

We were trapped. We were being taken for a ride in more ways than one.

We must have been the last arrivals because the bike room was packed. The Mariner Heights contingent, consisting of Arianna, Bianca, Victoria, Savannah, and Poppy, took up the front row. They were dressed in different shades of neon spandex and looked like a row of psychedelic crayons together. They waved enthusiastically as Meg and I climbed onto the last open bikes.

I studied the rest of the class and saw how the term *riot of colors* might have started.

Couldn't anyone here just go with T-shirts and black bike shorts? Meg was right. This was not just exercise. It was a fashion show.

Meg smiled bravely as she settled onto her seat and adjusted to the pedals. She hated being told what to do, even in a class setting.

"Good morning. For those who don't know me, I'm Philippe Duval. Those of you who are regulars know that I am here every day and lead the spin class on occasion. Today, I'm filling in for Ginger, whose daughter is ill. I know that this class loves strenuous rides. So, let's saddle up and get this rodeo going."

Meg looked at me with wide eyes. Philippe Duval? The Art of Wellness was turning into a rogue's gallery of suspects.

Before we had a minute to process this, he started the class. I rowed a lot but knew that hard-core spinners prided themselves on their fitness. Meg, on the other hand, believed that walking briskly through open houses was exercise enough. Could we keep up? Or were we about to go out in a blaze of color, if not precisely glory?

The lights went down, and the massive screen in the front of the room showed a picture of a winding, paved road with lavender framing both sides. "Somewhere over the Rainbow" began to play. Meg looked at me and gave me a brief nod. She apparently had no idea of what was to come.

After a five-minute warm-up, we entered a nightmare of crushing climbs and spurts of speed. For forty-five minutes, we were sitting, we were standing, we were pedaling…and basically, we were flying.

Periodically, Philippe would call out encouraging chants. "You got this!"

"You bet we do," Meg muttered softly.

The entire class moved as one—well, except for Meg. She was definitely riding at a slower pace. Because of my frequent rowing, I was able to keep up.

"Keep going!"

"Can't he just shut up and pedal?" Meg was getting testy.

"Hang tough!"

Meg was leaning forward, jaw clenched, pedaling for her life.

"Up and over this hill!"

The large screen kept stalling and flipping from scenes of mountains to lakes to forests. Philippe was clearly annoyed but just kept shouting commands.

"Pretend this is a hill. Everyone stand up."

Meg shot up, and her entire body shook from the intense pumping.

"Come on now, no slacking!"

I purposely did not look at Meg. I was fearful of what I would see.

"Okay, grind those pedals. Feel the burn."

Meg looked slightly shocked, but her inner competitive spirit took hold. She pedaled as if her life depended on it, pushing along to a blaring rendition of "The Eye of the Tiger." Finally, mercifully, the tune became "We Are the Champions" as we came to the final downhill stretch.

And then it was over.

"Great piece," Philippe called out.

The class filed out after congratulating each other, but Meg did not move. I was exhausted but got off my bike to make sure she was okay.

"Don't touch me," Meg snapped.

"Meg, what's wrong?"

"I'm all sweaty."

I couldn't help chuckling, but she cut me off with an evil glare. "Also, I might fall on the floor when I try to stand up."

"I got you, Meg."

She slowly began to get off the bike. "Never again," she said once her second foot was firmly on the floor.

As we were getting ourselves together, Patrice bounced into the room and addressed Philippe.

"Any computer glitches?"

"I had to skip past some sections, but the system needs a total rehaul."

"I hear you. Aoki Yoshida hasn't been to this area yet. She comes in very early. I'll shoot her an email to start in this room tomorrow."

Aoki Yoshida? That meant she also had access to Theo's water!

Meg and I staggered to her car and then collapsed.

"Aoki, too? Was every potential suspect at The Art of Wellness on the day of Theo's murder? This is like *Murder on the Orient Express*," I sighed.

"Jelly sticks," Meg gasped as she started the car. "We need recovery food."

CHAPTER THIRTY-FIVE

———

Kegel or pelvic floor exercises help to strengthen muscles and support pelvic organs.

As we made our escape, we saw Arianna and Savannah talking in the parking lot. They were standing between two cars. The sleek black Tesla with the vanity plate that read *GRIEF1* was obviously Arianna's, and the *SWORLD* one had to be Savannah's.

Meg didn't seem to notice them. She was silent as we drove through town, saying nothing until we pulled into our favorite parking spot overlooking the harbor. Even then, she could only sit back and reach for her large, iced coffee.

I opened the bag of donuts and handed her one wrapped in a napkin. Then I watched seagulls cruising the beach while waiting for Meg to revive.

Finally, Meg found the strength to talk. "Spinning is intense. I feel like I ran a marathon. Why do it?"

I did not respond, knowing that citing health benefits would not go over well.

"Well, at least we looked like we fit in," Meg said.

"You were right," I ventured. "Chic exercise outfits were the way to go. Navy sweats would not have made the cut."

It must have been the right thing to say, because Meg's eyes finally took on some focus. "Okay," she said. "Let's review our newly revised suspect list. Philippe Duval, Aoki Yoshida, Antoinette Duval, Carter Morrison, Savannah Archer, and, of course, Fiona all had access to Theo's water bottles."

"And just to speculate, there could be more. Theo had so many people angry at him that collecting enemies seems to have been his career goal. Who knows if other gym members were holding a grudge?" I ventured.

"On top of that," Meg pointed out, "Patrick said that only Theo's fingerprints were found on the water bottles."

"Disposable gloves are easy to come by. I'm sure the Art of Wellness stocks them for cleaning."

"Well, we are sure that Fiona is innocent," Meg said, finishing her first jelly stick.

"I just hope the police do. Savannah needs to recant her accusations."

We were both quiet, realizing that would never happen.

Meg finally said, "Fiona should be fine. She has Indigo to defend her, and Savannah has no proof that Fiona had a dalliance with Theo or poisoned him. By the way, we're hiring Fiona at the real estate agency. We need an administrative assistant, and she'll be a tremendous help during the Home Tour since she knows the Mariner Heights neighborhood very well. Also, I think I might have placements for Orla and Quinn. They come with great recommendations, and good nannies are hard to find. Two young couples relocating to Langford in the next few weeks are very interested."

That was my sister, always using her connections to help the underdog.

"Where do we go from here, Meg?"

"To a hot bath and bed."

"First things first," I said, chuckling.

"I honestly don't know. We should talk with Patrick since we have more questions than answers."

Meg started the car, and we drove through downtown Langford to her house. When we stopped at a red light, I noticed the bumper sticker on the Jeep in front of us—*Adults on board! We want to live, too!*

Meg and I started laughing simultaneously. Then, as she turned down River Road, another car decal appeared front and center in my mind.

"Arianna Gladstone and Savannah Archer both went to Rosemont College," I blurted out.

"How do you know that?"

"Their cars. They both had Rosemont stickers on their back windows. I didn't realize it until now because Arianna's license plate got most of my attention."

"Well, it's a great school. I bet several locals went there."

"I wonder if they were in the same class."

"If not, I'll bet they were only a year or so apart."

"And now they are both young widows."

"Well, at least Arianna will get Savannah on the road to recovery fast."

"Or else send her into a tailspin," I pointed out.

On my way home from Meg's, I decided to quickly stop for a gallon of milk. As I neared the store, I froze when I realized it meant walking outside my car in this getup. But we needed the milk, so I rationalized that it was just one quick stop, and besides, who could I possibly meet?

I parked as close as possible to Jenny's Quick Mart and darted inside. Along with a gallon of milk, I also picked up some baby cheese puffs that Rowan and Sloane loved. No one was in line at the register. Yes! I would be in and out of here rapidly. I paid, spun around, and headed for the door.

"Maeve, is that you?"

I stopped in my tracks. It was MJ's voice.

"Um, hi, MJ. How are you doing?" I said, turning slowly back around.

Her eyes widened as she took in every inch of my purple catsuit. "Somehow, I didn't picture you like this, Maeve."

"Oh, just trying out a new gym," I waffled.

"Vibrant purple—and with Hermès sneakers, no less."

I smiled awkwardly. "Great to see you, MJ. I gotta run," I said, waving the cheese puffs like a hall pass.

Back in the car, I checked myself in the rearview mirror. My mascara had run, my pony was falling out, and my sweat soaked headband had slipped sideways. All in all, I made a scary advertisement for gym membership.

MJ was parked beside me. As I went to back out, she approached the car and motioned me to roll down my window.

Olivia Newton-John's "Physical" blared from her phone as she danced to the music.

I burst out laughing and waved goodbye. Inwardly, though, I cringed thinking about my next visit to the Creighton Memorial emergency department.

When I got home, Kate was in the kitchen with the girls and Fenway. I put the milk in the fridge, kissed my daughters, petted Fenway, and tried to act nonchalant.

But there was no escaping. Kate's eyes were like saucers. Her face was beet red, and I could see she was trying hard not to convulse in laughter. She finally burst out, "You're a Yummy!"

I laughed with her and explained that Meg was a member of The Art of Wellness and had taken me as a guest.

"And did she buy the outfit, as well?"

"Yes. She insisted we shouldn't look out of place."

"Just don't tell me you're going to move to Mariner Heights now, Maeve."

"Hardly. Let me get out of this getup, and we'll talk."

After a quick shower, I put on navy slacks, a blue and white pinstriped shirt, and my rose cardigan. Before my afternoon patient session, I was going to review our quarterly statistics with Maddie for presentation to Dr. Patel.

The girls, Fenway, and Kate were in the family room playing with a set of red plastic measuring cups. I loved that such an inexpensive toy was so well-loved.

"I really needed that shower. But I'm sticking to rowing. That's more my speed."

"I might have to borrow that suit for a Halloween party, Maeve," Kate said, still giggling.

I decided to try changing the subject. "Meg tells me that Fiona will help with the Home Tour. I wish Savannah Archer would tell the truth. Do you have any idea why she would accuse Fiona?"

Kate looked at me directly. "Maeve, I finally got Fiona to open up a bit." She hesitated and looked a bit sheepish. "Okay, I might have pushed."

"You interrogated her?"

"A bit, but it was needed. It turns out that Fiona believes Savannah is the one who broke the marriage vows. She overheard many conversations, and Savannah was often not where she told Fiona she was going."

"Did she have any idea who it was?"

"She hated to say it, but she thinks it was a married neighbor."

"Did she tell the police?"

"No, she wasn't sure and felt like she was gossiping. Fiona is just too nice, Maeve."

"Kate, do you know if Arianna Gladstone and Savannah Archer went to the same college?"

"It's funny you should ask. Fiona said there is a group of Yummy Mummies they call 'The Roses.' They all went to the uni where you teach. Fiona says they send each other white roses on their birthdays, and they make a big deal out of mentoring students at the college. I am sure they want to recruit more Yummies."

"And this group all live in Mariner Heights?"

"They do everything in lockstep. You know, marriage, babies, Bloomsby nannies, personal chefs, exotic vacations, and, um, fancy, colorful gym clothes." There was another suppressed giggle that I chose to ignore. "A lot of the husbands went to Rosemont, too."

I bade Kate and the girls goodbye and headed to Creighton Memorial. Had Savannah really been cheating on Theo? Were Savannah and Arianna in the same year at Rosemont College? And if they were, was that just a coincidence, or did it mean something?

As my thoughts buzzed, I realized I was humming the words to "Physical."

Catchy tune.

CHAPTER THIRTY-SIX

———

A Pap test examines cervical cells to look for cancer or precancerous lesions.

Maddie and I finished up the stats before lunch. I had texted Jeremy Archer earlier and asked if he was available for lunch. We decided to meet in the ED and grab a quick bite at Sami's Falafel, one of the nearby food trucks that Creighton Memorial personnel favored.

When I arrived at the ED, I asked for Jeremy to be called and looked around for MJ. I knew I was in for a little more ribbing and wanted to know when to expect it.

The admitting clerk directed me to the staff lounge to wait for Jeremy. About ten staff members were eating.

"Hey, Maeve," one of the RNs called out.

"Hi, good to see you."

MJ walked in carrying a salad and a large soft drink. "Maeve, why didn't you wear your exercise suit?"

I shook my head and chuckled.

"Sit down and take a load off, or do you do pushups instead of eating?"

Yeah, this was going to continue.

As I sat, MJ started humming the opening trumpet notes of "Gonna Fly Now," the theme from *Rocky*. The story of my venture into the store and my attire must have been told numerous times because soon the entire room joined in.

What could I do but laugh?

As they finished, Jeremy appeared and beckoned to me. Doing my best Rocky imitation, I sprinted to the door and raised my arms in victory. The staff applauded, and I took a bow. This crew was so much fun.

"I heard about the purple Lycra suit and headband," Jeremy said with a smile. "You know, the staff only teases people they like."

"Well, it was humorous, Jeremy. Not my usual outfit."

We ordered and sat at one of the picnic tables since it was a sunny autumn day.

Although Jeremy still had dark circles under his eyes, he looked more relaxed than the last time I had seen him.

"How are you holding up?"

He gave a small smile and said, "At least work is good. It gets my mind off the horror of Theo's death for hours at a time, and I have a deeper compassion for families with sudden loss."

"Do you have any more thoughts about who would want to harm your brother?"

"I've racked my brain, and I keep coming back to Savannah. Even though I don't want to think evil of her, she stood to lose a lot in the divorce."

"But Theo would provide for his kids, right?"

"Absolutely. Remember, he was petitioning for joint custody. One thing about Theo is that he was extremely fair. Still, the divorce meant Savannah would have to get a real job. Her access to fancy trips and luxury items would be limited, ending her influencer status."

"Jeremy, I have to ask you a delicate question."

He looked up at me with his large hazel eyes.

"Do you have any idea who Savannah was having a fling with?"

Jeremy gave a tight smile. "I've thought about this a lot, too. With her house staff, two kids, social media presence, and Theo's needs, I believe it was someone from the neighborhood."

There it was. Could Savannah and her secret beau have conspired to get rid of Theo?

Mariner Heights. It always came back to that enclave.

"Did Savannah go to Rosemont College?"

He looked a bit confused at the switch of topic. "Theo and Savannah both did. That's where they met, although they were a few years apart. But Theo didn't graduate. He dropped out to work on his app. The relationship held together despite that."

Jeremy was about to continue, but his phone beeped, and a message appeared: *Incoming trauma to bays 1 and 2. MVA. ETA: 5 minutes.*

Jeremy hurriedly got up and collected his food wrappers. "Sorry, Maeve. Duty calls. We should talk more about this later." And with that, he ducked back into the ED, leaving me with some firmer suspicions and even more questions.

I headed back to the ambulatory suite for my afternoon session, making a mental note to stop and check the yearbooks at Rosemont tomorrow. Today, my schedule was fully booked with obstetric patients, many of whom I knew. It felt like a homecoming, and I soon fell into the comfortable rhythm of midwifery care at Creighton Memorial.

As I got in my car at the end of the day, I was surrounded by an explosion of red, gold, and orange leaves from the tree-heavy hospital grounds. While looking at their splendor, my phone vibrated.

"Hey, Meg."

"Finished for the day?" she asked.

"Yes. I spoke to Jeremy Archer today." I quickly filled her in about Savannah, Theo, and the Rosemont connection.

"You need to check out those yearbooks. It's sounding more and more like Savannah could be our murderer," Meg said.

"I'll look at them tomorrow. I'm seeing patients in the morning, but I'll have time in the afternoon."

"Let me know what you find. Are you all set for the Home Tour?"

"I aim to serve," I responded.

"I'll text you the itinerary for the weekend. Kiss the girls for me."

I saw the mighty Atlantic rolling out to the horizon as I drove. Usually, it would have given me a sense of distance and perspective, but now I felt more of an outgoing tide bringing all sorts of things to light. The problem was that while the waves had brought the Yummy Mummies, gym aficionados, and tunnels to my feet, they had done nothing to show how they could be connected.

CHAPTER THIRTY-SEVEN

Oophorectomy is the surgical removal of one or both ovaries.

My Rosemont patient schedule was fully booked, so I said a quick hello to Dr. Tim and Kristin and started with the first patient, Priscilla Babbins. She was a thirty-two-year-old engineering professor with a history of abnormal Pap smears. About eighteen months ago, she had a LEEP procedure, which excises abnormal tissue on the cervix. Since then, her exams had been within normal limits. Still, Priscilla was a bit anxious about this Pap test, so we reviewed her file and plan, including the fact that the results could take a few weeks. After that, she seemed a bit more relaxed.

The more familiar I became with the health center routines, the faster my mornings moved along. This one was no different, and it didn't seem long before I was down to my last patient.

Bella Taylor.

I knew she had been discharged from Creighton Memorial, but I thought she might have gone home with her injuries. As I took a large sip from my water bottle, I wondered if she had another urinary tract infection or if it was something else. There was only one way to find out; I knocked on the exam room door.

Bella was wearing full makeup, with her glossy hair in curls. She had on peach colored sweats. Her forehead laceration was hidden by bangs, and her cast was covered by her sleeve. One would hardly know she'd been severely injured.

"Hello, Bella."

"Hi, Maeve," she replied, biting her bottom lip.

"How are you feeling?"

"So much better."

"That's great. What can I do for you today?"

Bella stared at the floor, leaving me to wonder what the problem could be. Was she pregnant? Was she worried again about a sexually transmitted disease? Did Bella remember something about the attack? Realizing that this could be a delicate moment, I sat on the exam room stool to be at her level.

Bella looked up with tears in her eyes. "Oh, Maeve, it's all such a mess."

"Tell me, Bella."

"I've been so dumb."

"Everyone makes questionable decisions."

She shook her head slowly, and the story began coming out. "You know I'm one of the scholarship girls. Well, what you don't know is all that entails." And with that, Bella broke down into full-blown crying mode. I grabbed a box of tissues and sat quietly with her until she could speak coherently.

"I told you that the Spirit scholarship recipients are only women, but I didn't tell you the reason why. The scholarship pays tuition, room and board, travel expenses, and a generous monthly stipend."

"That's very comprehensive," I agreed, nodding slowly.

Bella's brow creased, and she frowned deeply. "Yes, but we're expected to pay a steep price in return."

Maybe it was from watching too much *Law & Order: Special Victims Unit*, but I was suddenly suspicious about what was coming next. I said nothing, though, as Bella hung her head and continued.

"In order to get the scholarship, you must accept 'dates' from wealthy, older men."

"What?" Wait, was that shrill, indignant response coming from me? I needed to regain my composure fast if I wanted her to share with the class.

"I didn't tell you the entire story about meeting the older woman when I was awarded my Spirit scholarship. I just couldn't. But I trust you now."

She closed her eyes for a moment and seemed to center herself. Then she began again. "Here's what happened to me. First, I got a letter with a number to call to set up an interview in Boston. I remember I was so excited."

I began to get a very sick feeling.

"A woman met me for lunch in a private room at a swanky Back Bay hotel and explained everything the scholarship would cover. She even offered an advance to purchase new clothes for college. As I told you before, she told me that two wealthy alums wanted to provide financial means to worthy students so they could experience all that Rosemont offered without incurring huge debt. She said the scholarship was only awarded to women because they wanted to honor their mothers."

At this pronouncement, Bella burst into a fresh round of tears. I knew this tale was about to go down a very dark road.

Bella finally composed herself, clenched tissues in her fist, and continued, "Honor their mothers? What a joke." She pushed a lock of hair behind her ear and said, "I realize now that the woman was evaluating my personality. Was I a pushover? Would I go along with the plan? But at the time, all I could see was a magical free ride."

Her eyes steeled a bit.

"At the end of the interview, she told me that 'friends' of the wealthy donors liked to meet the recipients and treat them to dinner. She said the Spirit women could show their thanks in many ways."

I was getting goosebumps. Trafficked! Was Bella trafficked?

"I was so dumb. I didn't see the forest for the trees. She had me sign a nondisclosure form from the Cortes company, which manages the scholarship. It expressly prohibited mentioning anything we had discussed, and I didn't see anything odd about that. What could possibly go wrong?"

I was afraid of what would come next.

"In October of my freshman year, I was invited to a Spirit scholarship party off campus. Limos picked the new recipients up at Rosemont, and we were driven to a lavish private home in a wealthy suburb. Each girl was introduced to the gathered group to enthusiastic applause. It took me a while to realize that besides my fellow students, only older men were present. Drinks flowed, and as the night wore on, phone numbers were exchanged so the scholarship recipients could meet with 'mentors' later."

I had heard many exam room confessions, but none quite like this. "Is it an escort service?"

"It's what the men want it to be." She shivered. "Some simply want to take you to an overpriced restaurant for dinner and have a date night, while others desire an exclusive relationship with all the trimmings."

I continued to listen. I did not want to interrupt Bella.

"Most of us are in a relationship by sophomore year. Most of the men provide luxurious gifts and book trips to glamorous locales. That's how I went to Paris and London," she sobbed. "Well, for quick weekend trips. I could only sightsee when my date was in meetings."

"What if a student doesn't want to participate?"

"Well, we all signed the nondisclosure agreement with Cortes company before any funds were distributed. At that time, we were told in no uncertain terms what would happen if we broke the contract. The money would not only disappear, it would all have to be paid back with interest. Most of us would not be here without the scholarship. We are all the first in our families to attend college. It's a tough bargain, but it's very difficult to turn your back on a free ride…no matter the conditions."

My head was swimming. How could Rosemont College allow this?

As if reading my mind, Bella said, "The school has no idea of the terms of the scholarship. We are told that it is underwritten privately and that life could become challenging if we tell the powers that be."

Bella grimaced. "I'm telling you all this, Maeve, because I feel like I can trust you. I've been very vocal to my gentleman friend and another senior scholarship student about my unhappiness with the program. The other student feels the same way I do, and we met with one of the *Roses* to get advice."

"The Roses?" I asked. I wanted to see what she knew about this organization.

"'The Roses is a group of professional women who graduated from Rosemont and provide guidance to women students. The woman we confided in was appalled at the terms of the Spirit scholarship, and I believe she will help us." Her chin quivered. "But I'm scared now, and I keep thinking that my accident was actually an attack, as I thought."

"Did that member of the Roses say she would go to President Saunders? I am sure that would lead to a full investigation."

"The Rose that Emerson and I talked to said to keep it to ourselves, and she would get back to us." Suddenly, fresh tears ran down her face. "Oh, Maeve, please forget I said that name."

"Of course, Bella." I needed to calm her down, but the name Emerson was now firmly embedded in my brain.

"You need to tell the campus security and President Saunders about the terms of the Spirit scholarship."

She went very still. "If I say anything, I'll be on the hook to pay all the money back with interest. That will take me a lifetime. Also, I was told that compromising photos of me would be sent to my family."

If not trafficked, at least blackmailed.

"President Saunders would never want students to be part of this despicable business. She'll help you and all the women recipients."

"No, Maeve. I can't. Please, I'd be too embarrassed. My mother can never know. Maybe you can tell the Rosemont administration you suspect something without mentioning my name."

I could see why Bella refused to spill the beans. She was both frightened and worried about her future. The selection interviews had obviously been set up to weed out strong personalities who might expose everything despite the supposed consequences. If that were the case, it somehow missed picking up Bella as a late bloomer.

"Bella, I'll do what I can, but the scholarship recipients' names are public."

"Thank you, Maeve. Please be as discreet as possible."

I watched Bella leave, still limping slightly on her sprained ankle. Her vulnerability became painfully obvious, and my eyes narrowed as I realized how badly she had been victimized. This was like Meg's story but on steroids.

Pushing down a rising anger, I shut the office door and called the other half of the M&M's.

CHAPTER THIRTY-EIGHT

———

Salpingectomy is the surgical removal of a fallopian tube.

"What? That's outrageous!" Meg shouted, instantly in full battle mode.

"I must tread softly," I reminded her. "I promised Bella."

"All right." There was a pause and I could almost feel Meg's outrage. Finally she continued. "What about researching the Rosemont yearbooks to see when the Spirit scholarship started? Maybe older graduates would be willing to come forward."

"That's a good idea. I'll go to the administration building now and call you when I'm done."

After saying goodbye to Kristin and Tim, I headed across the green. It was cloudy overhead, but the rain had not started falling yet.

Xiomara was on the phone as I went by the president's office, but she waved to me as I passed. At the yearbook shelves, I quickly went back about fifteen years and then took down a few volumes to look for Savannah Archer. Since I didn't know her birth surname, I flipped through the senior class of the latest year I'd grabbed. No luck. Picking up the next volume, I again searched for dark-haired women, and there she was. Savannah Enders—Pep Club, Yearbook Crew, Drama Club. As I scanned the rest of the page, I saw that Arianna Gladstone, née Clarkson, was also part of the Pep Club, Yearbook Crew, and Drama Club. True besties, indeed. Also, noticeably, they were *not* Spirit scholarship women. In fact, there was no mention of the Spirit scholarship until their junior year.

Next, I found Theo Archer and David Gladstone, who I assumed was Arianna's late husband. As Jeremy said, Theo began

at Rosemont before Savannah but didn't finish all four years.
Finally, I pulled out the rest of the yearbook volumes up to the
present. Using my phone, I took photos of each scholarship
woman for future reference. As a group, I saw that they were
racially diverse and had various interests, but all were stunning
women.

As I was finishing the final book, my pulse quickened.
Under the photo of a smiling blonde-haired young woman the
caption read, *Emerson Haywood, College of Nursing.*

This was Bella's friend and confidant. And the owner of
the baseball cap I had worn in the tunnel.

As I was snapping away, Xiomara entered the room.
"Anything I can do to help?" she asked.

Sorry, Bella. I need to get some answers.

"Xiomara, I was curious about the Spirit scholarship.
Does Rosemont administer that?"

I knew from Bella they did not, but I wanted to hear the
administration's perspective.

"The Cortes firm in Manhattan manages the Spirit
scholarship. It's surrounded by a bit of secrecy. Some wealthy
alums are responsible for the scholarship. I know that it has
helped many young women succeed."

"Do you know how the women are chosen?"

"We send photos, bios, and financial aid forms for the
admitted first-year women, and the Cortes firm takes it from
there. The president may know more. I can make an appointment
with her if you'd like."

"That sounds good." I booked a slot for early next week,
partly to give me a chance to run all of this by Patrick.

Before I left Rosemont, I texted Meg and Patrick to
arrange a meeting. Patrick texted back: *Schooner Point. Twenty
minutes.*

Meg responded, too: S*ee you there.*

Schooner Point was a beautiful bluff overlooking Snail
Cove. It had a small parking area for four vehicles. I was parking
beside Patrick's cruiser as Meg pulled in. A chill wind came off
the brilliant blue ocean, hinting at the approaching winter. I
fastened my thick Aran knit sweater up to the neck and pulled the
hood up tight.

Pat, Meg, and I sat on the wooden bench and surveyed the fantastic vista. Multiple rocky jetties stretched out to the sea, and on the distant horizon, cargo ships made their way south. Meg had brought two pumpkin lattes for her and me and a large black coffee for Patrick.

Patrick's time could always be cut short, so I detailed the Spirit scholarship as soon as we got settled.

"That's very damning," Patrick said. "Those poor students. The college will face harsh scrutiny just for starters."

"How can it have gone on for years?" Meg asked.

"I think whoever is behind the scholarship uses every scare tactic imaginable against the women. And I'm sure the women did not want the scholarship conditions revealed out of shame or embarrassment," I said.

"Where does it go from here, Pat?" Meg asked.

"There needs to be a thorough investigation, and, hopefully, some women will tell their stories. I'll make some phone calls and turn this over to the correct agency."

We were silent for a bit, watching the surf.

"I also need to check on David Gladstone," I finally added. "He left Rosemont the same year as Theo Archer. He must be Arianna's deceased spouse."

"Allow me," Meg said, googling on her phone. "Here it is. David Gladstone, age thirty-six, died while hiking Mount Washington in the White Mountains of New Hampshire. David had recently sold Pinnacle Endeavors and was planning a new business venture. He leaves his wife, Arianna. David was a very experienced hiker, and in lieu of flowers, please donate to the Mountain Rescue Team of Milton, New Hampshire."

"Pinnacle Endeavors? Wasn't that Theo's company? Why didn't anyone at Mariner Heights mention that?"

"Maybe because Arianna got over him so quickly. I bet she discourages talk of him," Meg said.

"I'll ask Jeremy Archer if he knows about the connection," I said.

The wind was picking up, and we all stood. Meg said, "Well, Pat, we haven't done much to help you. So many people had access to Theo's water bottles at the gym and, of course, Savannah could have tampered with them at their house. I mean, Savannah won financially by having him die," Meg said.

"And it appears that Savannah was carrying on with someone outside of her marriage," I added.

"I appreciate your help. I do. Hopefully, something will break soon. We are reexamining every aspect of the case, trying to find some sort of opening."

"Who knew so many people used eye drops?" Meg asked.

Pat and I both looked at her. "I know, I know. But I just use them to look refreshed before an appointment."

After some family catch-up, Pat hugged us both. "Be careful now. There's still a killer on the loose."

"Don't worry. We're hanging up our badges this weekend to run the Langford House Tour," Meg said.

"And you know we'll tell you if we hear anything of interest," I said.

Pat saluted us goodbye. "No cuffs, no bail, no headlines, no injuries. That's all I ask."

CHAPTER THIRTY-NINE

———

Myomectomy is the surgical removal of uterine fibroids.

For the Langford Home Tour, Meg had instructed all the volunteers to dress in black from head to toe. My interpretation of her directions consisted of black slacks, a fitted black linen waist-length jacket, and black flats, with my hair in a French twist.

When I got to Meg's office, I made a final check of my lipstick in the car mirror. Feeling pleased and confident with my appearance, I went in thinking that, for once, I might impress my sister with my look.

Then I saw Meg.

She was outfitted in Chanel from head to toe, complete with three-inch heels. How she walked comfortably in them for hours was beyond me. As usual, she appeared chic and in total command.

I loved her look. Once again, she reminded me that my big sister never failed to make me proud of her. Okay, at times, she could be overbearing, but when I needed her, there was no one better to lead the charge, no matter what.

Meg looked up as I walked in. I'm pretty sure I saw a slight smile of approval, but then she was all business. "Maeve, at ten sharp the vans will circulate along the entire route, starting and ending at the high school parking lot. Right now, you and I will make the rounds of the venues, and then I'll leave you at Arianna Gladstone's home. I want you and Fiona to be in charge there since I'm sure it will garner the most interest due to her celebrity status."

Realizing I'd be at the Gladstone house all day, I ran back to my car to lock up my purse since I wouldn't need it. My Rosemont tote was in the backseat, and I lifted a few files to stash my handbag under them and cover it from sight. As I did, I saw Emerson Haywood's baseball cap still sitting in my car. I made a mental note to return it on my next day at the college.

We made our rounds, with Arianna's home as Meg's last stop. When she dropped me off, I found the house even more impressive than the first time I had seen it. For today's tour, luxuriant flower arrangements had been strategically placed to add to the overall décor, and soft classical music wafted through the air. In the main rooms, there was a delicate scent of sandalwood with a hint of vanilla, while the primary suite held the lingering fragrance of roses. The tall cherry chiffonier doors were left open to display a vase of snowy white sweetheart roses and a glass bottle of Rose Prick perfume by Tom Ford.

Apparently, the Roses took their identity very seriously. But I had to admit the fragrance was heavenly. It made me feel like I was in a freshly blooming summer rose garden.

I noticed that copies of *People* magazine featuring Arianna on the cover were prominently displayed in the living room. It seemed as if she had crafted this setting as a backdrop for her business. She clearly knew how to prosper and thrive, even as a relatively recent widow.

Ten in the morning until four in the afternoon stretched like an eternity, and I was exhausted as the event ended. Instructing people to wear foot coverings, safeguarding the magazines from being taken as souvenirs, and answering endless questions about appliances, furniture, and paint colors was more than a full-time job. One statuesque redhead in heavy makeup was incensed about wearing booties and requested a pair in crimson to match her outfit. Keeping a rigid smile and hopefully a cheerful tone, I disabused her of the notion. Much huffing took place until she noisily succumbed. Salespersons must dream of murder frequently.

Finally, to my relief, Meg returned and dismissed the other volunteers in the home. Fiona gave us a cheerful goodbye as she left. Just to make sure Arianna would have no complaints, I did a last sweep of the premises to ensure everything was in order.

Everything looked fine, except the *People* magazine count seemed short. Oh well, Arianna still had more than a few left, and maybe she'd chalk up the missing copies to good publicity.

"What a success, Meg," I told her when I returned to the kitchen. "You ran a magnificent tour. Now let's pack up. You know Arianna won't be pleased if any remnants of today are left."

Meg gave a slight shrug as she went down the long hall to the four-car garage. "You're right. I think apoplectic would be the word if anything from the Home Tour is left behind. Let me grab a box for the chocolate lollipops. Harbor Sweets was so nice to send them over. I think everyone loved getting a parting gift. We can drop the extras at Hanville Grove on the way home. Mom and the ladies will be thrilled."

I held the door for her and heard her heels click as she crossed the blue-speckled, epoxy-coated garage floor. Wire shelving ran along the back wall, and she reached up to the top shelf where we had temporarily stored the treat cartons.

"Darn, I broke a nail," Meg said as the boxes tumbled onto the floor. Along with them, another cardboard container came crashing down, spilling its contents.

Hundreds of tiny identical plastic bottles rolled all over the garage.

"What in the world?" asked Meg as she put her finger with the sheared nail in her mouth.

Picking up one of the bottles, I read the label and gasped. "Eye drops. They're all bottles of eye drops or, as Mom would say, 'killer eye drops.'"

Then, I took a closer look at the bottle's ingredients. "And it looks like they all had tetrahydrozoline in them. But does that mean Arianna is the killer? That makes no sense; she comforts people after someone dies."

"A flawless way to get more clients," Meg said wryly.

"Let's pick them up. Here, put these gardening gloves on. We must protect any DNA evidence," I said, shoveling the bottles into a white paper shopping bag. I quickly filled it to the brim.

"We need to call Patrick. We told him we suspected Savannah was the killer, but now it's looking a lot like Arianna's the real culprit," Meg said.

We looked at each other, realizing we'd unfortunately left our phones on the white marble island at the far end of the massive kitchen. I quickly scraped up the last of the bottles and put their original container and the gloves back on the shelf. Then we sprinted down the hallway to the foyer, intending to circle back to the kitchen for our phones. We got as far as the foyer and stopped.

The doorknob was turning, and we saw Arianna through the doorway window.

"Act normal," Meg hissed as she opened the foyer closet door. I whipped the bag of eyedrop bottles in as a few rolled to the closet floor. Meg shut the door as quickly as she could.

Arianna bustled in the front door with her usual take-charge attitude. Her eyes narrowed as she surveyed as much of the main floor as possible from the foyer.

"I assume the Home Tour went well."

"Yes, it was a very full day. Everyone loved your opulent home, Arianna," Meg said.

Arianna preened with a self-satisfied smirk. "Excellent. I hope at least a few of the visitors could appreciate what they saw here. And I'd like to think some discovered fresh decor ideas for their homes."

I bit my tongue, but luckily, Meg was quicker with hers.

"I'm sure there were, Arianna. Your home is a treasure trove of hidden gems. In fact, we just finished going over every inch of it to make sure nothing is out of place. We just need to grab our phones from the kitchen, and then we can leave you to enjoy all this in peace."

That's great, Meg. Flatter the beast and get us out of here so we can call Patrick.

"Just be quick about it," Arianna snapped. "I'm scheduled to start a European book junket tomorrow, and my chartered jet is waiting to take off."

Arianna was going to escape. She could easily be in the air by the time Patrick could do anything official. But what could we do? How to stop her? We needed time. And we needed that bag of evidence. We needed to stall her.

That was as far as I got in my thinking when Arianna said, "I just need to grab a heavier coat." She strode to the foyer closet and opened the door.

Time stopped. Maybe, just maybe, she wouldn't see the eye drops.

But my heart skipped a beat as Arianna turned around with deliberate slowness and pointed a pearl-handled revolver directly at us. In her other hand she had a fistful of empty eyedrop bottles.

Well, that bag didn't hide much!

Her face was stony as she looked at us with disgust. "Such a meddlesome duo. Well, now I'll have to deal with you. Let's go to the great room."

Meg and I exchanged terrified glances and walked through the foyer ahead of Arianna.

Arianna *had* poisoned Theo. That was clear now. But what did she have in mind for us?

"Sit down. Make yourselves at home," Arianna commanded.

We sat side by side on the white chintz divan beside the mirrored bookcases. I noticed they held dozens of charming family photos.

Could we distract and overpower Arianna? We could try, but she wouldn't miss both of us with the revolver. And with one person down, the other might be an easier target.

Arianna walked over to the imposing china cabinet and pulled out two Baccarat crystal martini glasses. She brought them to the side wet bar and began mixing drinks.

"Shaken, not stirred," Meg whispered to me.

Arianna raised one eyebrow menacingly, but she kept working on her concoction. She reached into her large Prada leather bag and pulled out several small bottles. When she emptied them into the martini glasses, her plan became apparent.

It would be death by eye drop for Meg and me!

CHAPTER FORTY

Menopause is the term used to describe the end of menstruation. It usually occurs around age fifty and is defined as twelve months without a menstrual period.

"Arianna, why are you doing this?" Meg asked.

"Seriously, do you think I'm going to tell all my darkest secrets to you? You think this is a tell-all?"

"Why not? Who can we tell if we're dead?" I pointed out.

We had to draw this out. We needed to think of a way to escape. I scanned the room looking for, well, I didn't know what. An escape hatch? Another pistol? But when my eyes fell again on the family photos, I found myself wondering how she had become so bitter.

Arianna placed the drinks in front of us, complete with olives. She had even added two matching stone coasters, no less. I could almost sense the inner Martha Stewart in her.

Almost.

There was an abrupt change in Arianna's mood as she stared at us. "Why did you have to poke your noses into my business?" she lamented.

"We didn't. The eye drops literally fell on us. It happened when we were straightening your garage. But they don't automatically make you the murderer," I ventured.

Unfortunately, that brought the hostile Arianna back to life. "Please don't insult my intelligence. I'm amazed you didn't already call the police."

Now, it was my turn to lament. If only we'd had time.

"Now, ladies, drink up. I really need to be on my way."

As I looked at the glass, something in my mind clicked. Turning to look at the shelves, I pointed and felt my jaw slacken.

"What?" Meg asked.

Arianna gave me a dead-eyed stare.

"Cortes. In the picture, your husband's boat is named Cortes."

"Did your husband David have something to do with the Spirit scholarship or the Cortes firm?" Meg asked.

Arianna said nothing.

"You do know that the Spirit scholarship is really an escort ring, right?" Meg pressed.

"Cortes, Cortes…" I repeated. "Escort? Yes, escort. Cortes. Cortes is an anagram."

For a brief moment, I felt like a winning *Jeopardy* contestant. But I quickly realized my penalty for not posing the answer as a question would be so much harsher than losing money.

Arianna lowered the pistol briefly, and her shoulders sank.

"Your husband was involved in the Spirit scholarship?" Meg asked incredulously.

Arianna looked up for a moment and then met our eyes. "David told me he felt like a conquistador when he developed such a successful app. He claimed that's why he named his boat Cortes." She paused and rubbed her temple. "But what does it matter if you know now? You'll be gone soon enough."

Arianna paused and then continued in a slow monotone, "David and Theo thought they were so brilliant, and I mean, in some ways they were. They had the idea for their app as college freshmen and left Rosemont to pursue it. Theo was always the frontman, and David was the silent partner. When they needed funding to bring the app to life, they decided not to give up control to some venture capital firm. Instead, they dreamt up the so-called Spirit scholarship. They recruited high-flying—and by that, I mean wealthy—clients who were interested in discreet escort services, specifically with college-aged women. To fulfill that request, David and Theo lured beautiful, financially needy students at Rosemont and kept them in line with treats and threats. The arrangement provided both funds for the startup and money for the scholarships."

She looked straight ahead, her eyes unfocused. "How was I in the dark for so long? I was as willfully blind to the obvious as one of their 'recruits.' But I never knew anything about it until after Pinnacle Endeavors was sold. That's when I saw an email from Theo to David asking if he wanted to continue with the Cortes Foundation. I didn't ask David about it, but I discovered the truth after digging through his laptop."

She got up and began pacing. "What pigs. Everyone thought Pinnacle Industries was so wholesome. The company gave money to food banks, built playgrounds, and helped the unhoused. No one knew about the business that got it off the ground—or that it was still going on. Those two were loathsome men."

"It was you!" I gasped.

Both Arianna and Meg stared at me.

"The tunnels. You attacked Bella Taylor, and then you followed me. You saw the baseball cap and thought I was Emerson Haywood. Your perfume...when I was in the tunnel, I got a whiff of something, but I couldn't identify it. I smelled it again in your bedroom today."

I started shivering. Arianna was ruthless.

Arianna got a wistful look on her face. "Those sweet young Roses-to-be. They came to me so upset about the Spirit scholarship. I felt for them, but the truth was that I needed to keep them quiet. An online presence can be delicate and easily destroyed if the internet turns on you. I couldn't risk the escort service coming to light and hurting my new career. I know Rosemont was their ivy-covered dream turned nightmare, but those girls needed to face the reality they agreed to when they signed the nondisclosure agreement. They took the money. They needed to shut up, graduate, and be done. When they came to me, I'd already done my part. Without Theo and David, the Spirit scholarship would end."

In an instant, her expression turned to a scowl, and the vindictive Arianna was back.

"I've got to get out of here," Arianna almost shrieked. "Come on now, bottoms up."

She waved the pistol menacingly.

Meg and I gingerly lifted the glasses. There was no way we were going to drink the poison. Would Arianna pull the trigger?

"I said drink!"

As we brought the glasses to our lips, my hopes dimmed. I tried to imagine what a bullet would feel like. Could we pretend to drink the poison? Would we survive?

CRACK!

Arianna staggered and then sank to the floor. Blood spurted from a head wound and seeped onto the thick white Persian rug.

Was she shot? Were the police here?

"Got her," Fiona said, walking boldly into the room and looking down at Arianna.

I jumped up and quickly assessed Arianna's condition. "Her pulse is thready. Meg, call 911 and get me some towels for this laceration."

"Fiona, what did you do?" Meg asked.

"I am a Sullivan. One of the champion Road Bowling Sullivans of Cork, in fact," Fiona said proudly. That didn't tell us much, but Fiona went on before Meg or I could ask what that meant.

"I forgot my sweater and came back for it. I'm used to having to go in the back door in this neighborhood and treading softly in the house. But as I came to the foyer, I overheard Arianna going on about having to kill the two of you. So, I looked around, and wouldn't you know it, those pretty paperweights were just sitting in the den there begging to be used." She bent down and picked up a glass object next to Arianna's head. She held it out for us to see. "And I picked out a very pretty flowered one, don't you think?"

Fiona had saved us! I decided not even Tom Brady could have made a better throw.

Police and an ambulance crew arrived one after the other. Patrick ran in the door, ordered Arianna to be placed under guard, grabbed Meg and me, and hugged us tightly.

"I should never have asked you to snoop for me. I unknowingly put you in harm's way," he said in a shaking voice.

"Patrick, we stumbled on the eye drops during my Home Tour," Meg said.

"This was not your fault, and look, we're fine," I agreed.

With one last look at both of us, Patrick smiled and returned to being the deputy chief of police. He and Detective Shayna Russell took Fiona's statement and began talking to a group of officers searching the home. They knew to look for eye drop bottles after we told them about the bag we'd already collected.

When the dust settled, Meg and I gave our statements individually. Then I headed home while Meg stopped by her real estate office.

I called Will on my ride home, slowly filling him in on the day's events. I repeatedly assured him that Meg and I were safe and sound. Only when he was convinced that no bodily harm had occurred, except to Arianna, and that a suspect was in custody did I finally hear a measure of relief come into his voice. Still, I knew that a long discussion about the M&M's dangerous habit of sleuthing would happen at a time in the not-too-distant future.

The concern from our loved ones, especially Will and Patrick, was the price Meg and I paid.

As I pulled into Primrose Cottage, Kate and Fenway stood sentry at the front door. Fiona had filled Kate in on her role in Arianna's apprehension.

"Come in, come in, Maeve. The girls are fine. They're napping, and the kettle is on. Now tell me everything."

I ran through the afternoon's events and told Kate of Fiona's dead-on throw.

Kate laughed. "Maeve, Irish Road Bowling is a huge sport in Cork, and Fiona's family are renowned champions. Teams compete by seeing who can take the fewest throws to advance a metal ball down country roads. A paperweight must have been easy for her. That gal can throw."

She started giggling, "I can't believe it. A Yummy felled by an Irish road bowling master. What will happen to Arianna now?"

"The police will question her when she's medically cleared. She'll need to answer for her whereabouts the morning of Theo's death, and they'll get a search warrant for her laptop and phone."

"Well, this was quite a day. I'll be off now, and I'll check on Fiona as well." She stopped and hugged me. "Thanks so much to you and Meg for all your help."

About twenty minutes later, Will came bustling in with salmon rice bowls, garden salad, and New England Cornmeal pudding. He kissed me and held me close for a very long time. Finally, he pulled out a bouquet of pink carnations.

"Maeve, I was rushing to get home to you. This was all I could find besides roses, and I was not bringing roses into our home tonight."

I laughed and inhaled deeply. I loved carnations. They were often the overlooked flower.

Will, the girls, and I had a quiet dinner. After the girls were asleep, Meg stopped by to review the day. I told Will and Meg everything I had learned about Fiona's sport.

"I'm shocked about Arianna. The Grief Whisperer…how crazy is that?" Meg said.

"You know, according to your story, finding out about the escort service unhinged her," Will said.

"No wonder she could move on from her grief so quickly," I said.

"Did you call Bella?" Will asked.

"I did. She's worried about what will happen now but relieved that the Spirit scholarship will stop."

We discussed the case into the night. Finally, Meg and I stood with our arms around each other for a long time when she went to depart.

"I'll never make fun of your love of word puzzles again," Meg said. Then she cackled, "Yeah, you know I will. They really are so odd."

Only one sister, and so little time.

CHAPTER FORTY-ONE

———

The decline in estrogen production after menopause can affect a woman's bone health.

I awoke to the tantalizing smell of maple sausage and the cheerful voices of my family in the kitchen.

Wrapped in my violet chenille robe, I walked in to find Rowan with a huge grin on her face, holding tightly to a buttermilk pancake. Sloane was banging her spoon on the highchair and letting out little squeals of joy. At floor level, Fenway was waltzing back and forth between them while jumping for each stray bit of flying food.

"Good morning, beautiful," said Will. "Welcome to the breakfast of champions."

I made my rounds, kissing and petting my pack.

Finally, I sat. Three pancakes and a large mug of coffee later, I stretched happily.

Will looked at me and read my mind. "Relax, Maeve. I'm going to get these lovebugs cleaned up for their day."

That prompted a second cup and time with my laptop. I turned it on and brought up the *Langford Times* website. A large headline ran across the top: *Breaking News—Arianna Gladstone Arrested for the Murder of Theo Archer—Ex-husband's Body Being Exhumed.*

My phone began ringing. Without looking, I knew who it was.

"Maeve, have you seen the paper?" Meg asked.

"I just started reading."

"Here's what I heard from Shelley." Shelley, as always, had her finger on Langford's pulse.

"Arianna is recovering and escaped with only a mild concussion. She refused to answer questions at first but changed her tune once she was told that the police already knew about the contents of her laptop. It seems that our stories, plus her googling *tetrahydrozoline poisoning*, gave the police ample grounds to hold her on suspicion of murder. Once she was backed into a corner, she became a songbird. I was told her mood still swings between deep sadness and combative bitterness. It seems once she got the idea about the eye drops, she decided to kill two birds with one stone. Goodbye, David and Theo."

"I thought her husband fell from a cliff while hiking," I said.

"He did, but undoubtedly after drinking Arianna's specialty electrolyte packs he carried."

"Tetrahydrozoline?" I asked.

"That's what she says. The authorities are digging him up as we speak."

"You know, I hate to admit this as an M&M, but I really didn't see this coming."

"Yeah, me neither. I can't wait to talk to Patrick for more details. That is, if he tells us the full story."

"He better. He owes us big time. We'll pry the details from him at family dinner this week."

Babies, Creighton Memorial, class preparation, and my growing college GYN practice filled my week. The Rosemont Health service had asked me to give a series of talks open to all students on various aspects of GYN care. I was thrilled that the administration saw midwives as an asset to the entire college. On top of that, the nursing exam scores were back, and the OB nursing students scored highest on the material I covered in my lectures. I knew that Prudence would notice. Hopefully, she would see that nursing education needed both traditional faculty and current practitioners.

After a full day at Rosemont, I closed my laptop and made my way to my car. Family dinner was at Meg's, which hopefully meant takeout from China Sky. Their cuisine was second to none. As I opened my car door, my phone rang—it was MJ.

"MJ, hello." I could hear monitors beeping, the overhead paging system blaring, and someone talking to an ambulance driver on the intercom. The ED was rocking.

"Hey, Maeve. I wanted you to know that Jeremy Archer gave his notice today. He's going back to being a traveling RN. We had a long talk. As you might expect, he's very disappointed in his brother and feels the need to move on from Langford. He asked that I let you know. He's very thankful to you that the escort service was discovered but also very sad."

"I understand, MJ. He idolized Theo. I hope he finds peace with it one day."

"I'm at work, and we're busy, so I need to go. Stop by when you can. We miss you but are so glad you passed up that 'really dirty' martini."

Meg's oceanfront home looked warm and inviting as I pulled up. Patrick's patrol car and Meg's Jaguar were the only vehicles in the driveway. The three of us were early. Good. We'd have our chance to talk right away.

"Hello, Maeve," Patrick said, hugging me as soon as he opened the door.

"Hi, Pat, Meg."

"We've been waiting for you. Patrick is going to fill us in on Arianna's status."

I grabbed a raspberry lime seltzer and sat down on one of the high-backed counter stools. Pat had a mug of coffee, and Meg sipped a glass of Chablis.

Patrick raised his glass. "*Sláinte*."

"*Sláinte*," we replied in unison.

"So, once again, my intrepid sisters solved the crime."

"We can't take the credit this time," Meg said, laughing. "The bottles literally fell into our laps."

"Well, Arianna has confessed to killing both Theo and David and waived a trial. She'll go to prison for life." Taking another sip, he continued, "As you know, she found David's computer files and uncovered the escort service. He was a frequent hiker, and she poisoned his water. Because he was on a cliff and fell, no one questioned the death. Arianna knew her husband was extremely regimented and took no water breaks until he reached the summit."

"Good thing he didn't share his water." I shut my eyes and had visions of Arianna mixing our fatal cocktails.

"And then her career was born?" Meg said with a sarcastic leer.

"Yes, Arianna went to a group for people who lost partners. She said she did it to avoid suspicion." Patrick looked solemn.

"But she couldn't have gotten that bit about 'fast-track-mourning' from a typical grief group," Meg said, exasperated. "Where did that come from?"

Patrick grinned. "I knew you would ask. It seems Arianna joined a grief group to help cover her guilt. That's where she unexpectedly discovered a few people who were not too fond of their *loved ones.* They wanted nothing more than to move on. So, Arianna took a seminar with that guru in California, and she was on a mission.

"So, she had this idea, and her career was off and running?" Meg asked.

"More or less," Patrick agreed. "She was a case of right place, right time. A TV producer was one of her first clients. He became a true believer and gave her an opening. The sky was the limit once she was on the morning shows."

"Did she say anything more about why she went on to kill Theo?" I asked.

"It's pretty much what she told you. She was afraid her 'sainted' husband's reputation would be damaged if it ever came to light that David was a silent partner in an escort service. The more success she had, the more paranoid she became about her online presence being attacked if that came to light. After David was handled so easily, it didn't take her long to see poisoning Theo as the logical answer to her worries." Patrick stopped and looked pensive. Then he observed, "She may be the coldest person I've ever come into contact with."

I nodded slowly and said, "I think I see what you mean. She killed David out of disgust for his behavior as a trafficker of young women. But Theo? That was just to make sure nothing happened to her influencer image."

I suddenly felt the need to stop talking about Arianna. "I've been in touch with President Saunders. She's devastated knowing the college had a part in this. Rosemont will offer counseling and funding to all the Spirit scholarship women."

"What about the Cortes Foundation?" Meg asked.

"It was a dummy corporation. Apparently, Theo and David paid various women to meet with the scholarship recipients to ensure the paperwork was signed. We may never be able to identify them."

"What about the men who used the service?" I asked.

"We are searching computer files. Arianna may have deleted them, but we have our internet squad working on it. The Langford Police Department will hold a press conference at 7:00 p.m. I wanted to tell the two of you this news in person. I need to be there for the announcement, but Olivia will be by with the girls for dinner."

"Patrick, I'm ordering dinner for the department," Meg said. "You will not miss a magnificent Chinese feast, and the officers deserve a nice meal, especially after all this."

Pat just shook his head, smiling. He knew better than to try and stop Meg.

After a magnificent repast, Henry set out fortune cookies and bowls of pineapple ice cream. Happy voices filled the room. Family dinners were the best.

Mom sat at the head of the table, decked out in a white sweater with bright green sequins. "I set my TV to record Patrick's press conference," she announced, cracking open a fortune cookie. "We don't need to talk about m-u-r-d-e-r in front of the children. All we need to know is that my M&M's did a great job once again. I'm so proud of the both of you and Patrick."

Mom would live off this adventure for weeks.

"Ha, look at my fortune," Mom said. "*Find the destination to true happiness.* See, I'm definitely going on a trip."

"Oh, Mom, I have a lottery ticket for you. It must have been left in my bag when I bought some for you last week." Meg handed Mom the ticket and a quarter for scratching.

"Oh, it's a Lucky 8 scratcher. I love these. If you get eight number eights, you win a prize!"

Olivia reached for a bowl of ice cream. "I love this flavor. It's so distinctive. I've been experimenting with *mille-feuille* for our next dinner," Olivia said.

Ah, the French lifestyle would stay for a while.

"Zeena," Mom gasped.

We all turned to her. Why was she calling out the fortune teller's name?

"She saw you with babies, Maeve. Okay, babies always surround you. But Meg, Zeena saw you on an airplane. And I told you that you needed a vacation. And me, she saw me with green. Green!" She held up her ticket and started waving it back and forth. "I won the lottery! We're going to Ireland!"

Zeena had been correct on so many issues: crystal flowers, a drinking game, airplanes, money, and green, and who knew…maybe a baby. I was gradually revising my view of her psychic powers.

As I watched Mom celebrate and phone the lobby ladies, I pictured the O'Reilly clan arriving in the homeland.

That sounded like a movie title. I only hoped it wasn't a mystery.

RECIPES

Mike & Tom's Creamy Polenta with Goat Cheese

Serves 4
1 cup yellow cornmeal
1 tsp salt
1 tbsp butter
5 ounces goat cheese
Pepper, to taste

Bring 5 cups of water to a boil.
Add cornmeal and salt and whisk briskly and constantly to avoid lumps.
Reduce to a simmer and cook for 15 minutes.
When done, stir in butter and goat cheese.
Add pepper to taste.

Olivia's Roast Chicken with Tarragon

Serves 4-6

1 4-lb. chicken
1 lemon, quartered
3 cloves garlic
1 bunch fresh tarragon
3 tbsp olive oil, separated
1 tbsp softened butter
3 tbsp chopped fresh tarragon
2 tsp lemon zest
1 yellow onion, sliced in rounds
Salt and pepper to taste

Set oven to 425 degrees F
Clean chicken.
Salt and pepper inside of chicken cavity and stuff with lemon, garlic, and the tarragon bunch.
Mix together 2 tbsp olive oil, butter, chopped tarragon, lemon zest, and salt and pepper and rub on outside of the chicken.
Place onions on bottom of roasting pan and drizzle with remaining olive oil, salt, and pepper.
Put chicken on top of onions and cook for 1 hour and 30 minutes.
A meat thermometer should read 165 degrees F.

Malia's Pumpkin Chocolate Chip Loaf

1¾ cups flour
1 tsp baking soda
2 tsp ground cinnamon
½ tsp ground nutmeg
½ tsp ground cloves
½ tsp ginger
½ tsp salt
2 large eggs
½ cup sugar
¾ cup dark brown sugar
1½ cups canned pumpkin puree
½ cup canola or vegetable oil
¼ cup milk
¾ cup chocolate chips

Preheat oven to 350 degrees F.
Grease a 9-inch-by-5-inch loaf pan.
Combine flour, baking soda, cinnamon, nutmeg, cloves, ginger, and salt in a large bowl. Mix eggs and both sugars until combined. Add pumpkin, oil, and milk to the eggs and sugar. Then combine with flour mixture. Do not overmix. Add in chocolate chips.
Bake 65-70 minutes until cake tester is clean.
Cool completely before removing from pan.

Maeve's Cobb Salad

Serves 4

8 cups iceberg lettuce, finely chopped
2 grilled chicken breasts, chopped
8 slices bacon, crumbled
4 hard-boiled eggs, sliced
3 cups cherry tomatoes, halved
3 cups diced cucumber
3 avocados, sliced
8 ounces Roquefort cheese, crumbled
1 can sliced black olives, drained

Dressing

½ cup olive oil
¼ red wine vinegar
2 tsp honey
2 tsp Dijon mustard
¼ tsp salt
¼ tsp pepper

Place lettuce on a large platter.
Arrange chicken, bacon, eggs, tomatoes, cucumbers, avocados, cheese, and olives in rows over the lettuce.

To make the dressing, whisk together the olive oil, vinegar, honey, mustard, and salt and pepper. Serve with salad.

Will's New England Cornmeal Pudding

Serves 4

4 ½ cups whole milk
½ cup yellow cornmeal
½ cup maple syrup
1/3 cup brown sugar
¼ cup molasses
2 eggs, slightly beaten
2 tbsp butter, melted
1 tsp salt
¾ tsp ground ginger
¼ tsp ground cinnamon
Vanilla ice cream

Preheat oven to 300 degrees F. Grease a 2-quart baking dish.

Pour 4 cups of the milk into the top of a double boiler and place over simmering water. Save ½ cup for later. Heat until the milk is hot but not simmering. Stir cornmeal slowly into milk and cook until thickened, about 20 minutes. Stir as needed.

Whisk maple syrup, brown sugar, molasses, eggs, melted butter, salt, ginger, and cinnamon together in a bowl. Stir this mixture into cooked cornmeal until thoroughly combined. Pour into the prepared baking dish. Pour remaining ½ cup milk over top of pudding.

Bake for about 2 hours. Pudding will be set but will be slightly quivery on top. Allow to stand 30 minutes before serving. Serve warm with vanilla ice cream.

ABOUT THE AUTHOR

Christine Knapp practiced as a nurse-midwife for many years. A writer of texts and journal articles, she is now thrilled to combine her love of midwifery and mysteries as a debut author. Christine currently narrates books for the visually impaired. A dog lover, she lives near Boston.

To learn more about Christine Knapp, visit her online at:
https://www.thoughtfulmidwife.com/

Made in USA - Kendallville, IN
37227_9798303921733
12.30.2024 2017